MURDER AT THE BEACH

"I picked up some scuttlebutt after you left the Sandbar last night," Grody said.

"Yeah?"

"The Candle Beach cops are bringing in the state police to investigate Vinnie's death," he said.

"The state police for a simple drowning? Isn't that unusual?"

Grody paused. "Might not be a simple drowning."

I shivered. "What?"

"A buddy of mine works in the county prosecutor's office. Word through the grapevine is that there's some physical evidence suggesting his death could be more than an accident."

I knew Grody had connections around Ocean County. I figured his information was reliable. "Are you saying…?"

"Yep. Murder."

Books by Suzanne Trauth

SHOW TIME
TIME OUT
RUNNING OUT OF TIME
JUST IN TIME
NO MORE TIME

Published by Kensington Publishing Corporation

No More Time

Suzanne Trauth

LYRICAL UNDERGROUND
Kensington Publishing Corp.
www.kensingtonbooks.com

LYRICAL UNDERGROUND BOOKS are published by

Kensington Publishing Corp.
119 West 40th Street
New York, NY 10018

All Kensington titles, imprints, and distributed lines are available at special quantity discounts for bulk purchases for sales promotion, premiums, fund-raising, educational, or institutional use.

Special book excerpts or customized printings can also be created to fit specific needs. For details, write or phone the office of the Kensington Sales Manager: Kensington Publishing Corp., 119 West 40th Street, New York, NY 10018. Attn. Sales Department. Phone: 1-800-221-2647.

Lyrical Underground and Lyrical Underground logo Reg. US Pat. & TM Off.

First Electronic Edition: July 2019
eISBN-13: 978-1-5161-0723-0
eISBN-10: 1-5161-0723-0

First Print Edition: July 2019
ISBN-13: 978-1-5161-0724-7
ISBN-10: 1-5161-0724-1

Printed in the United States of America

Thanks to everyone who entered the *No More Time* play title contest, especially the winners: Debbie Proud, Glen Holley, and Laura Coccimiglio. You'll find your entries in the pages of this book! Thanks, once again, to the folks at Kensington for their great work, especially John Scognamiglio. I appreciate Dru Ann Love, Lori Caswell, and Leslie Bedewitz for helping to promote *No More Time*. I am grateful to my supportive readers and everyone who offered advice for this latest Dodie O'Dell mystery. I owe you one…

...for those who encouraged my writing adventures from the beginning...
especially Charlene, Grace, Helen, Lori, and Elaine

1

"Here ya go. A gin and tonic and a Creamsicle Crush." The bartender at the Bottom Feeder, a tiki bar next door to the beach, made change from Bill's twenty and sauntered away after pocketing a liberal tip.

"You're in a generous mood," I said, taking my first sip and letting the vodka and OJ land on the back of my throat before swallowing.

"Dodie, a Creamsicle Crush sounds like a kid's drink." Bill elevated an eyebrow, and his quirky grin emerged, one side of his mouth ticking upward.

"Uh…not exactly."

The sun shifted lower in the sky signaling the beginning of early evening. Swaying palm trees danced and dipped to the Polynesian music.

"Don't forget we have an early dinner at the Sandbar. I told Grody we'd be there about seven with appetites. I think he's creating something special."

Bill groaned. "I forgot about dinner. I hoped we could hang out here for a few hours, scarf up some of that cauliflower tempura and spicy shrimp we had the other night, and then collapse at our bungalow, lulled to sleep by the music of the rolling waves and the scent of salt air."

I stared at him. "When did you become so poetic?"

"Must be the heat."

I studied him, my glass at my lips. "That's been your reason for pretty much everything these days."

Bill, aka Etonville, New Jersey, police chief and my current squeeze, was totally enjoying our Jersey Shore vacation. He leaned back into the bar stool. "I haven't had a beach vacation in years. Not since I was nineteen."

"Nineteen? Jersey Shore?"

"No. I was with a bunch of guys, and we spent spring break in Fort Lauderdale." He stirred his drink.

"How traditional of you." I swiveled sideways in my seat to get a better view of the ocean.

"Nothing traditional about the way we hit the town and—"

"Whoa!"

"What?"

I gawked at a table of guys at the other end of the bar who were hooting and drinking and enjoying themselves royally. "I know that man."

"Who?" Bill took a swig of his gin and tonic.

"Him. At the table." I glanced behind me.

"Which him? There's five hims there," Bill said.

A man rose, waved off the offer of money from one of his compatriots, and walked directly toward us. I watched his progress. He approached the bar on Bill's right, retrieving his wallet from a back pocket. "Another round for that rowdy crew."

He grinned amiably at us. "Great weather."

"Uh-huh," Bill agreed.

"Vinnie?" I said. I recognized that confident stroll, cocky grin, and golden tan.

Bill was as amazed as Vinnie Carcherelli. Or Vinnie C as I knew him. "You know each other?"

Vinnie tossed three twenties on the bar's glossy surface, his back to me. "Sorry. But…?"

"It's been a while. Dodie O'Dell? Jackson's…friend?" I said, trying to be helpful.

Vinnie looked at me. A series of reactions flitted across his face: confusion, then astonishment, finally chagrin. He had an aha moment accompanied by his world-class smile. "Of course I remember you. Dodie! How've you been?" He leaned in to kiss my cheek, the spicy, clean scent of his aftershave tickling my nose. A thin silver chain around his neck swung forward and grazed my cheek.

"Fine. I relocated to Etonville up north after Hurricane Sandy. This is Bill Thompson. My…" Did "boyfriend" sound too casual?

Before I could finish my sentence, Vinnie had his arm extended, pumping the life out of Bill's hand. "Nice to meet you."

"Are you still in the boat business?" I asked. Vinnie had the polished façade of someone who had been doing well for himself—a crisp white shirt that set off his tan, beige cargo pants, and a TAG Heuer watch with a gold bracelet band. Had to have cost a bundle. Sunglasses were perched atop his lightly graying hair. He reeked of affluence. This was not the Vinnie who had spent his days on a charter fishing boat with Jackson in a tattered T-shirt and bathing trunks ferrying tourists up and down the shoreline, in and out of bays and inlets.

"Yeah," he said vaguely. "Took a while to rebuild things after Sandy."

"Have you heard from Jackson since he left town?" I asked politely.

"Hey, we're getting thirsty!" A heavyset man at Vinnie's table raised his voice and waggled his arm as if flagging down a cab.

"Gotta go. Maybe we can catch up some time. Really great to see you"— he glanced at Bill.—"and meet you." Vinnie grabbed a tray of drinks and headed to the table whose occupants let out a cheer when he reached them.

Bill observed Vinnie, then picked up his gin and tonic. "That was...?"

"Jackson's old charter boat partner," I said.

"Jackson. Your former...?"

"Yep. Boyfriend."

"Uh-huh. You said Jackson wasn't all that successful as a businessman," Bill said.

"He wasn't. Never seemed to have more than a few bucks in his pocket when we were dating years ago. And the two of them were hopeless at managing the books. I offered more than once to help out. They were always in debt." I finished my Creamsicle Crush. "They named their boat the *JV*..."

"...for Jackson and Vinnie. Not too original."

"The way they carried on, it also stood for juvenile."

"Vinnie must have turned the company around."

"I guess. The price tag on his watch has got to be five thousand plus," I said.

"No kidding?"

"I saw an ad for them in a magazine," I said noncommittally. I had researched men's watches as a potential Christmas present for Bill last December. TAG Heuer was definitely not in my ballpark. My attention was riveted on Vinnie, as if he were a magnet drawing me back to the past. A light wind wafted through the open-air bar. I shivered.

* * * *

"Try this." Grody delivered two plates of gourmet seafood risotto—one of the Sandbar specials—to our table. "You'll like it." He sat and waited, arms akimbo, until Bill and I each took forkfuls, nodding with enthusiasm. "Am I right? Super delicious?" He grinned at his own success and tossed a bar towel over his shoulder. "We crushed it tonight."

"Grody, this is wonderful!" I said.

"It's the black truffle and leeks combo. Shhh. Don't let the word get out," Grody mock-whispered.

"I'd love the recipe to take home," Bill mock-whispered back.

Grody let out a huge belly laugh, one of his trademarks from way back, and ran one hand over his damp, bald head. "Because you're here with Irish, I'll make an exception."

"Irish" was one of his nicknames for me. It had something to do with my auburn hair and green eyes. Grody Van Houten, aka Surfer G, and I went back a decade when he hired me to manage his first restaurant here in Candle Beach, the Jersey Shore town near where I grew up. It was called Bigelow's. Destroyed during the hurricane like almost everything else on the boardwalk at that time. Grody and I had transitioned from employer/employee to big brother/little sister, and when the storm wrecked his livelihood, we parted ways. He moved to North Carolina to regroup; I moved north to Etonville to manage the Windjammer restaurant. We'd kept in touch via email and texts during the past couple of years, but I was thrilled to see him back in Candle Beach. The scene of so many shared culinary escapades. He'd recently opened the Sandbar, and from all appearances business was booming.

A waiter cruised by, whisked away our appetizer plates—we'd already stuffed ourselves with fried shrimp and calamari—and left a longneck beer for Grody. "I love what you've done with the place. Simple, no fuss. Like Bigelow's." The restaurant featured indoor seating under a thatched roof with the bar surrounding an open kitchen. Outdoor seating had tables and chairs sunk into the sand and a fabulous view of the ocean and jetty.

"I wasn't sure I could reopen another one." Grody tugged on his pirate's earring. "I was so burnt out and depressed after Sandy." He stared at the water. "But then a year ago I started to feel the old itch. I woke up in the middle of the night and researched recipes, went to seafood markets, experimented with sauces and spices." He raised his hands helplessly. "Once an old cook…"

"An old beach bum, you mean," I teased.

Grody tugged on a strand of my hair. "Hey, knock it off, Red."

Another of Grody's pet names for me.

"I think you made the right choice," Bill said. "If tonight is any indication, so do the folks down here." The Sandbar was full. Every table taken, with some patrons waiting at the bar for seating.

"People have been real receptive."

Grody was too modest. "You're a pillar of the Candle Beach community. A different story from those early days when you surfed all morning, cooked the rest of the day, and then hit the waves again at dawn."

"I'm too old for that kind of carrying-on. Like you said, I'm an over-the-hill beach bum."

We laughed and I gave him a hug.

"Speaking of the community, the New Jersey Community Theater Festival is holding its contest down here. Part of the Labor Day weekend celebration," Grody added.

"I saw a poster about it on the boardwalk." Lola Tripper, the current artistic director of the Etonville Little Theatre and my BFF, informed me that they had entered the competition but ended up on the runner-up list. Lola was philosophical about it, claiming that now she had a low-key end to her summer instead of an ELT crazy-busy one. I agreed.

"...so I kind of got roped into catering the opening night reception." Grody grunted. "Henry tells me you have theater theme nights at the Windjammer. You can give me some advice."

My mind wandered. I'd lost the thread of the conversation, but apparently Grody was providing food for the community theater event. And his cousin, my boss Henry, chef/owner of the Windjammer restaurant, had described my various theme food experiments. "As long as I can give the advice from my beach towel."

"Sure."

"In exchange for a colorful drink with a miniature umbrella."

Grody chuckled. "You got it, Irish."

The night was warm and sensuous...every muscle in my body was limp, my skin was tingling from the heat of sunbathing, my mind was dull and woozy. This was my kind of vacation, spending a holiday at the shore, basking in the sun, indulging my passion for seafood, not a care in the world, no responsibilities to assume. Away from the Windjammer restaurant that I'd managed since my arrival in Etonville. Away from the on- and off-stage melodrama of the Etonville Little Theatre. And, even though I loved them all, away from my BFFs, Lola and Carol, and friends in my small but gossipy town.

We chatted a bit more. I filled Grody in on the status of the Windjammer and Henry's culinary competition with his cross-town nemesis, La Famiglia. He regaled Bill and me with stories about getting restarted at the shore. Henry and Grody were first cousins with the restaurant connection and their bald heads common ground. Personality and temperament? Distant relatives.

"So the area has pretty much come back from the storm?" Bill asked.

"Yes and no. There are plenty of businesses and people who've been able to rebuild with FEMA, insurance, and state aid. But there are lots of horror stories of residents who got ripped off. Houses deserted and left sitting in their post-hurricane state because their money was stolen before work was completed." Grody shook his head. "I'd like to get some of those con artist contractors and strangle 'em," he said vehemently.

We all sat in silence for a moment. I had a vision of Surfer G with his hands around the neck of a cheating contractor. *Sheesh!*

"Hey, do you remember Vinnie C? He was Jackson's partner in the charter boat."

Grody frowned. "Vinnie...?" Then he lit up. "You mean Vincent Carcherelli."

"Vinnie's moving up in the world. Bill and I ran into him at the Bottom Feeder during happy hour. He reeked of money."

"I heard he's in a high-end situation. No rusty tub for him anymore." Grody took a pull on his beer. "Ever hear from Jackson?" He slid his eyes in Bill's direction, who was scraping the last bit of risotto off his dinner plate, ignoring Grody and me.

"Only two or three emails the year after he moved to Iowa," I said. "Facebook once."

"Iowa?" Grody frowned, then snapped his fingers. "Now I remember. He went to work for his brother, right? Selling...what was it?"

"Farm equipment," I said with a straight face.

"I don't mind you talking about Jackson. As long as I don't have to meet him," Bill said as we ambled down the boardwalk.

"No chance of that. Some dinner, right? Grody's recipes could rival La Famiglia. Earn him four stars." Henry was peeved that the Windjammer had only garnered three and a half stars from the local rag, the *Etonville Standard*, to La Famiglia's four.

"Beautiful." Bill tilted his head and studied the night sky. "I love the dark expanse over the ocean. There's Aquila and Lyra."

"Huh?"

"Constellations. See? There." Bill pointed skyward to the mass of stars. I had no idea what he was seeing.

"Wow. You're into astronomy. I can't even find the Big Dipper."

"Part of Ursa Major," he said. "I spent a lot of time at the planetarium in Philly."

Where he was a deputy chief of police before his Etonville gig. "Impressive."

"Well...I like stars." He grinned.

"Hmmm."

"What?" he asked.

"It's all so peaceful. I can't believe I have another week of this."

"Don't think about it ending. Just be in the moment," he said.

"In the moment? Has Suki gotten to you?" Suki Shung was Bill's deputy chief, a martial arts specialist, and a Buddhist. Even in the midst of harrowing law enforcement episodes, she managed to maintain her equilibrium.

"Suki? No. It's the—"

"Heat!" My cell buzzed signaling a text coming in.

Bill took my hand and squeezed. "Ignore it."

He was right. I was on vacation. Anyone who needed to communicate with me could wait until tomorrow. Besides, Bill seemed to be getting a little frisky, and I knew where that could lead. I laid my head against his shoulder. "Good idea."

We crossed Ocean Avenue, entered Atlantic Street, which ran perpendicular to the boardwalk. I could see our cozy bungalow, only a block from the ocean, up ahead. A living room, kitchen, two bedrooms, a lovely patio, and a large screened-in porch. Perfect for outdoor sleeping in this weather.

"Are you thinking what I'm thinking?" he asked, one side of his mouth curving upward.

We arrived at our rental. "You bet," I murmured sexily and climbed the front steps, Bill grasping my hand close behind. "Why don't we pop the cork on that champagne we've been chilling?" I opened the screen door, and my foot scraped a large object. That moved. I jumped. "Eek!"

"What's going on?" Bill yelled, catching me as I fell backward.

A voice in the dark hollered, "Dudette!"

My heart banged in my chest. I knew only one person who referred to me as dudette. "J-Jackson?" I said, unbelieving.

"It's me. In the flesh." He cackled.

"Jackson?" Bill ushered me onto the porch and flicked on the light.

"What are you doing here?" I gasped.

"It's a long story." He caught sight of Bill. "Hey, what's happening, man?" He did a kind of bro handshake, his brown curls bouncing off his forehead and around his neck as he tried out variations on gripping the hand of the police chief of Etonville, New Jersey. "Hope you don't mind I kind of made myself at home on your porch."

In the dim light I could see a sleeping bag and an open backpack with clothes spilling out of it. "What are you doing here?" I asked again. My mind not putting it all together. "Why aren't you in Iowa?"

"I had to split that scene. Missed the ocean. I kinda got fed up with tractors, combines, balers—"

"Jackson!" I practically screamed.

"Yo! You're killing my eardrums." He plopped on the ground and leaned back against the chaise lounge. "So what've you been up to?" He got a glimpse of Bill and grinned lazily.

"Excuse me." Bill, tight-lipped, went into our house.

I counted to ten to calm down. "Okay…I'm happy to see you. We can get together for a drink and talk old times. Good night." I opened the screen door for Jackson to leave.

"That's a problem. I got a negative cash flow. No place to stay. Hey, I could crash out here."

"Here?" My voice skidded up an octave.

"For tonight. For old times' sake." I remembered that young, boyish grin that usually got him whatever he wanted. Including me. "Puleeeease?" he whined. "I'll make breakfast in the morning. I rock the kitchen."

A light went on inside our bedroom. *Yikes.* Poor Bill. "For one night," I said emphatically.

He nodded. "Nighty night. Sleep tight."

I slammed the door into the house. It was supposed to be a romantic end to our day, Bill and me under the stars, monitoring a constellation or two…my cell pinged. Once, then twice. Who was so insistent? Might as well check it. The night couldn't get any worse.

It was Lola: *ELT chosen for NJ CTF!!! Cranford had to bow out. Food poisoning! We're coming down the shore. Can't wait to see u!*

Geez.

2

A clanging yanked me from the throes of a dream—I was on the beach buried in sand up to my neck being force-fed seafood risotto. My eyes fluttered open. I rolled to my side, slapped the top of the alarm, yanking the bedsheet with me. Seven thirty. Bill was asleep, snoring beside me, utterly unaware of the racket. Had he set the alarm?

His chest rose and fell, the spikes of his brush cut pointing every which way, and sandy-colored stubble covered his face. He'd been a real trouper about Jackson last night after I'd joined him in bed. Claiming that he wasn't upset that my former boyfriend had shown up unannounced on our doorstep, making himself at home on our porch, and had ruined our romantic evening. As long as Jackson's visit ended this morning. I insisted that our guest would be gone after breakfast and Bill was satisfied. I wasn't.

I watched a fly zoom around the room, banging into the window screen before it gave up and flew into the bathroom. What had brought Jackson back to the shore this summer? Was it really his boredom with farm equipment? What had taken him so long to return? It had been four years since Hurricane Sandy, and Jackson had a short attention span.

"Hey. Did the alarm go off?" Bill yawned and kissed my cheek.

"Yep."

"What time is it?" He leaned over my torso and squinted at the clock. "I have to get going or I'll be late. Captain Cook waits for no passengers." He stumbled out of bed and headed to the bathroom.

"Captain Cook?"

"Deep-sea fishing? Remember?" Bill asked and stepped into the shower.

Right. Bill had made these plans weeks ago. A day out on a boat trying his luck with a rod, reel, and tackle. He'd been so excited, like a kid in the proverbial candy store. I didn't see what all the fuss was about. Even when I lived down here, I avoided any activity that included raw bait, a pitching sea, and the possibility of throwing up a recent meal. My one experience deep-sea fishing had left me hanging over the side of the boat willing it to sink. Not caring that my parents and brother were aboard.

"What are you doing today?" Bill toweled off and dressed speedily.

"A bit of sun, happy hour, maybe a visit with Grody."

"Sounds like fun."

"By the way, I got a text from Lola and guess who's coming to town? You remember that theater festival Grody mentioned? Apparently, something happened with the group from Cranford. Food poisoning. Anyway, they're out and the ELT is in."

"Soup's on!" yelled a voice from down the hall. It was Jackson.

"What's that mean?" Bill asked, wary.

"No idea. But I'll find out." I threw on a robe and strode out the bedroom door, whipping the ties around my midsection.

"Yo, Dodie. Whoa!" Jackson snickered at my morning ensemble. He whisked his brown strands into a man bun with an elastic band.

"Very funny." I stopped and sniffed. "Is that French toast? And bacon?"

"Totally. And my special homemade syrup."

The table was set for three. I was flabbergasted. I'd never seen Jackson lift a finger in the cooking department.

"Hope you don't mind I kind of dumpster-dived into your refrigerator." He flipped the French toast expertly. "Have a seat."

I smelled Bill's minty clean aftershave before I saw him. "What's this?" he asked, standing behind my chair.

"Jackson's cooking," I said politely.

"Yeah?" Bill nodded. "Oh."

"Breakfast, bud?" Jackson asked.

I'm not sure anyone had ever referred to Bill as "bud." I sneaked a peek—he was peaceful, his smile gracious. Deep-sea fishing can be a narcotic for some people.

"Sorry. I have a date with a boat." Bill swung a backpack onto his shoulder.

"Been there, done that," Jackson said. "Spent the best years of my life on the sea."

"The best years? Aren't you exaggerating a bit? Anyway, the sea was only inlets and bays." I doused a piece of French toast with syrup and bit into the golden-brown bread. It was to die for.

Jackson opened cabinets, searching for something.

"What are you doing?" I asked.

"Got it." He found a takeaway mug and filled it with coffee. "Hey, dude. Here you go."

Bill reached for the mug carefully as if it might explode. "Uh, thanks."

"Have fun. YOLO," Jackson said and saluted.

"YOLO...?" Bill was confused.

"You Only Live Once. Catch the big one, Moby Dick." Jackson fist-bumped Bill, who gave me a pleading look and ran out the door.

"Serious dude." Jackson popped a strip of bacon into his mouth.

* * * *

At ten o'clock, after stuffing myself with Jackson's feast, I was ready to go back to bed. We'd spent the last hour rehashing our recent pasts and catching up. "Now I know why I don't eat like this every morning. I feel like a blimp," I said.

Jackson cleared dishes, refilled my coffee cup, and studied me critically. "I'd say looking excellent."

"Thanks." Jackson had always been ready with a sweet compliment back in the day. One of the things I appreciated about him.

"I didn't expect to see you again. Ever," he said.

Ditto for me. "Well...here I am. And here you are too. Speaking of which, I'm sorry, but you need to—"

Jackson raised a hand to cut me off. "Got it. My bags are packed."

I peered out the screen door. His belongings were still strewn around the porch.

"Figuratively speaking," he said. "But not to worry. By the end of the day, no more cash flow issues." He crossed his arms confidently.

"That's...great." I emptied the last dregs of my coffee. "Hey, guess who I bumped into yesterday? Vinnie C. Looking very spiffy."

"He's around." Jackson wiped down the kitchen table.

"You don't sound surprised."

Jackson shrugged. "We've, like, been in communicado."

"I assumed he left town after Sandy. Got out of the charter business, like you. From what I heard he's doing well."

"Mmm." Jackson scrubbed a skillet, loaded the dishwasher, and draped a wet towel over the dish rack.

What was he not telling me? "Are you going to hook up? I know there was some...tension when you split up."

"Heh. Sounds like we were married," he said.

"If I remember correctly, you spent more time with him when we were together than you did with me," I chided Jackson gently.

"It's water over the bridge."

"Under the bridge," I corrected him.

"That too." Jackson stuffed his hands in his pockets and scrunched up his face like a kid. "Mind if I use the outdoor shower?"

The cold shower most beach houses employed to remove sand from sunbathers instead of having the stuff tracked into the house. "You can use the indoor plumbing. Towels are on the bathroom shelf."

I followed Jackson to the porch and watched as he dug through his possessions and withdrew a clean pair of shorts and a shirt. "By the way, you never told me how you found out where I was staying."

He strolled past me on his way to the bathroom. "I got my connections."

"Jackson!"

"Uh...Grody. But don't tell him I told you."

* * * *

"Sorry, kiddo. He made me promise not to tell you. Said he wanted to surprise you." Grody lifted his hands in surrender. "I wasn't sure how you two left things, so...I assumed he wanted to clear the air."

"He camped out on our porch last night."

Grody stifled a grin. "You dodged a bullet with Jackson."

I sipped a strawberry margarita, savoring the chill of the crushed ice, the sweetness of the fruit, and the tang of the tequila. I rarely drank this early in the day, but I was on vacation and, as my great-aunt Maureen believed, *It's happy hour somewhere in the world.*

"But hey, I like Bill. You done good there, Red."

"I agree. He's been understanding. So far." With Jackson out of the way, tonight could be a reboot: chilled champagne, the summer breeze, Bill enamored of the constellations...and me.

"...suggestions, I'd like to hear them," Grody said.

I'd gotten lost on my screened-in porch. My old boss had inquired about theater theme food advice for the New Jersey Community Theater Festival. "I've had some hot ideas, like a seafood buffet for *Dames at Sea*, Italian night for *Romeo and Juliet*, a 1940s food festival for *Arsenic and Old Lace—*"

"I like that one." Grody scribbled on an inventory sheet.

"Slight hiccup there. The director died, and I was left with fifty pounds of hot dogs and a case of black-and-white cookies."

"Too bad." Grody frowned.

"Then there was the early American food for *Eton Town*. But due to the show being postponed, the Swamp Yankee Applesauce Cake was mostly eaten by the cast and crew."

"Postponed?" he asked.

"Another hiccup."

Grody studied me. "So, Henry was right about you investigating murders."

"Yep. But hey, the last show had a food contest that went over well. People loved it. And nobody got murdered inside the Windjammer or the theater." I giggled. Grody joined in, his belly shaking as the laughs bubbled up and burst out of him.

Happy hour at noon was an excellent invention.

A waiter appeared with a plate and a setup. Lobster rolls and chips.

"Yummy," I said. "Where's your lunch?"

Grody dismissed my question. "I don't eat during the day, remember? I'll catch up tonight. At some point this afternoon, I need to talk with Sam Baldwin."

"Who's that?" I bit into my sandwich. The succulent lobster meat melted in my mouth.

"He's the sponsor of the theater festival. A local guy. Baldwin General Contractors did a lot of Hurricane Sandy reconstruction. Kind of Candle Beach's town father. I want to find out what he has in mind for the reception."

The margarita made me loose…and generous. "I could run interference for you. Stop by the theater and check things out. Where is the theater anyway?"

Grody snatched a cocktail napkin and drew a map. "Down the boardwalk until it ends. Right on Cummings Street by the Surf Shack. Go three blocks to the town park. You'll see a gazebo. The theater is behind it. An old converted barn. Hey, thanks, Irish! I owe you one." Grody grabbed my bill. "Lunch is on the house." He hurried off before I could change my mind.

Fortified by lobster and alcohol, I sauntered out of the Sandbar and headed down the boardwalk. The squawking of the wheeling seagulls, the surge and crash of the surf, and the slap of my flip-flops on the faux wooden boards were familiar, comfortable sounds. I passed the Candy Kitchen, where I popped in for half a pound of taffy, the souvenir shops with hats and shirts and beachwear for sale, the arcade where kids badgered their parents for money to play games, and the Candle Diner. Where Bill and I had already sampled the breakfast specials.

I chewed taffy and followed Grody's map, hanging a right on Cummings Street. In a matter of minutes, I reached the old barn, where prominent signage indicated the New Jersey Community Theater Festival was set to open in a few days. I approached the main entrance and entered the lobby. Even from out here, the odors of paint thinner and sawdust assaulted my nose. In the theater a crew of carpenters was installing a backdrop on the stage while two electricians had mounted ladders and were hanging instruments on lowered battens. As a result of my familiarity with the Etonville Little Theatre, it was a scene that I knew well. As a matter of fact, I felt right at home in the theater, having sewn a costume or two and done my share of ascending ladders to assist with the hanging of curtains—

"The theater is closed to outsiders," a cranky voice said.

If I closed my eyes, I could swear it was Penny Ossining, the Etonville Little Theatre stage manager barking at me. Instead it was a tall women in overalls, hair in pigtails, clipboard in hand. "Hi. I'm looking for Sam Baldwin? I was told he might be here?"

"Who wants to know?" she asked, full of herself.

I tilted my head back to meet her gaze. "I'm here for Grody Van Houten. The Sandbar is catering the opening night reception, and I need some information from Sam."

Apparently nothing I said held much sway with the woman. She scanned me from head to toe. "Wait here and don't go wandering around. Otherwise you'll get in the way." She stomped off.

Talk about a bedside manner. Could be Penny all right.

"Ignore Maddy. She gets off on intimidation. She's really harmless."

I whipped around and saw a smiling, older gentleman in a beige linen suit who leaned on a cane. I extended my hand. "I'm Dodie O'Dell. Helping out with catering for the reception."

"John Bannister. I'm the unofficial official welcoming committee for the NJCTF." He took my hand. "Glad to meet you."

What a sweetheart. "Same here. Is Sam Baldwin around? I'm supposed to get the lay of the land for Grody Van Houten at the Sandbar."

"Come on. Sam's out back wrestling with the load-in schedule. Several of the community theaters have arrived in town early and want to get onstage to rehearse. This is a very competitive event." John arched an eyebrow and pursed his lips, laughing.

Friendly and funny. "Lead on," I said.

I followed John down the center aisle of the theater, up a small stair unit, across the stage—careful to avoid stepping on cables and shop tools—and out a rear exit. A parking lot was filling with vans and cars and milling theater folks. No wonder Maddy was a bit crabby. In the midst of the chaos was a short, stocky fellow with a deep tan, a fringe of gray hair, sunglasses, and a tropical shirt stretched around a bulging belly. He had a cigar in one hand, a piece of paper in the other.

"That's Sam," John said.

"Busy guy." Sam flapped the sheet of paper in Maddy's face. A tall, thin brunette in a tight wraparound skirt and stiletto heels snatched the sheet, gestured for the stage manager to step aside. "Who's that?"

"Mrs. Sam. Arlene Baldwin. She directs plays in Candle Beach now and then. Brings in musical groups in the summer," he said.

"She seems to be in charge. Should I speak with her?" I asked.

"No. Sam's your guy." John approached Sam, said something in his ear, and gestured at me.

Sam marched past and motioned for me to come along. John waved good-bye. I wished I was dealing with him. Back through the chaos onstage and into the house we trekked. Sam stopped when we reached the last row of seats.

"We can talk here."

"Kind of hectic," I said sympathetically.

"I was nuts to take this on. These theater people are crazy. Everybody wants to get on the stage yesterday to rehearse. They don't like the dressing rooms, the lighting's too dark or too bright, they need more tickets, they want to warm up in the lobby." He shrugged.

The lobby was a small strip of space, separated from the seating by curtained barriers. Not made for the kind of warm-ups Walter Zeitzman— former artistic director of the ELT—usually undertook with *his* casts.

"Grody says you're like Candle Beach's 'town father.' This sort of thing comes with the territory, I guess."

Sam focused on me intently. "Who are you?"

"A friend of Grody's. I offered to check things out for him. I've had experience doing theme food for a community theater. Pairing the plays with concessions or dinners or—"

"Yeah. Yeah. Tell Grody anything he wants to do is fine."

"Maybe we can coordinate food choices with the shows? For example, I did an Italian night for *Romeo and Juliet* and—"

"Yeah, yeah."

"Do you know what plays are being presented?" I asked.

"Of course I do," he said abruptly.

I waited a beat for him to continue.

"See Maddy. She has a list," Sam said.

"All right. And setting up tables?"

"Anywhere outside is fine." He fluttered his arm in the direction of the front door.

"And if it rains?" I had experience with outdoor theater. The ELT's production of *Bye, Bye, Birdie* last spring had to contend with bad weather.

"We'll cross that bridge later." He peered at the stage. "Maddy? Get back here!" Sam shouted.

"Producing a theater festival is nothing compared to Hurricane Sandy reconstruction," I said lightly.

Sam Baldwin shifted in his seat and faced me square-on.

"Grody mentioned that you did quite a bit of it," I added.

"What of it?" he growled.

I blinked. I must have pushed a button. Perhaps Sam Baldwin was so over the hurricane that even the mention of it triggered a defensive reaction and—

"What's up, chief?" Maddy had run to the back of the house and was standing in the aisle.

Sam pointed at me. "Get her a list of the shows in the festival."

"Okay, chief." The aggressive, intimidating stage manager had become a pussycat in her boss's presence. She fanned through pages on her clipboard. "Here." She shoved a page at me, her voice threatening. Talk about split personalities.

"Thanks. Grody will get back to you after he's finalized the menu." I smiled graciously. No use creating tension and, anyway, the reception was Grody's responsibility.

A crash onstage caused all three of us to jump. A piece of glittery plywood with the letters NJCTF scrawled on it had fallen from the top of the proscenium, hit the floor, and bounced into the first row of seats.

"What are you doing up there?" Sam shouted.

"What are you doing up there?" Maddy repeated in an equally belligerent manner.

Two crew guys shrugged. One shuffled into the house to recover the damaged sign; the other gawked upward as if the answer to the mishap was written on the ceiling.

"Get it fixed. Now! I got these theaters bugging me to get in here," Sam huffed.

"Get it fixed. We got these theaters bugging us to get in here." Maddy again.

She certainly was a loyal lapdog. They reminded me of Walter and Penny...*sheesh*...two sets of them to deal with this week?

Sam heaved himself out of his seat as I scanned the sheet. "There's a group missing here," I said. "The Etonville Little Theatre. They're a late entry, replacing the Cranford theater."

Sam and Maddy stared at me as if I had two heads.

"That's not possible," Maddy grunted. "I wrote that list myself."

"Well, maybe the change of theaters happened after the list was written up?" I suggested helpfully.

Maddy's expression skittered from mocking to skeptical to anxious. Her eyes darted sideways at Sam, and she tugged on a pigtail. "I...uh...give me that." She grabbed the sheet of paper and slammed it onto her clipboard.

"Straighten this out, Maddy. I don't want any surprises come tomorrow night. We got to get this thing up without any hitches." He trounced off, a real theater lover.

"Okay chief." Maddy shot me an if-it-wasn't-for-you-I-wouldn't-be-in-hot-water expression and followed him.

That went well. I had to avoid the stage manager this week—she would be gunning for me.

I left the old barn, glad to be out in the sunshine, away from the chaos that I had learned was a staple of community theater. I got a vision of Maddy's sheet: *Harvey, Mousetrap, Noises Off, The Sound of Music, King Lear, Cinderella,* and *Death of a Salesman.* I knew all of the titles, mostly because I was privy to ELT season selection discussions. Also because Lola shared her thoughts on various plays. What did they have in common? What kind of theme could we create from that group? A princess and mean stepsisters, a murder mystery, backstage hijinks, the destruction of the American dream... Of course, one of them was out and the ELT was in. Sam and Maddy were touchy about changes in plans.

My cell pinged. Lola: *can't believe we're doing this. Arsenic again... argument with Walter...he wanted Eton Town but Arsenic only thing we could get up this quick. actors ok but couldn't get original ingénue. am I too old to play the role?? ugh!*

I laughed out loud. Poor Lola. She had her hands full with the Etonville theater. Once she was only its reigning diva, playing starring roles in everything from comedies to musicals; after Walter was caught playing fast and loose with the box office till Lola was persuaded to assume his artistic director position. A humiliating defeat for Walter. Now he was simply an actor/producer/director/playwright. I'd seen him wear all four hats; some fit better than others.

I passed the gazebo, surrounded by beds of hibiscus, peonies, and sunflowers. A beautiful venue. Grody could set up the food inside...my mind played with reception possibilities as I hiked the three blocks to the boardwalk. According to my watch it was beach time.

Digging my toes back into the sand and slathering on the suntan lotion made me think about Bill covering every square inch of his torso because he was paranoid about burning. All week his upper body had been swathed in a sun-resistant white shirt, his face streaked with sunscreen that boasted 100 SPF, his spiky hair covered in a Buffalo Bills ball cap. He burned easily and required a steady application of lotion to all visible body parts. Being Etonville, New Jersey's police chief kept him tied to a desk most days, and his ruddy complexion usually only deepened when he was freaked out…sometimes at me. After a week at the shore, his face was permanently flushed an intense shade of pink. I wondered how the deep-sea fishing was going and if he'd provide dinner as he promised.

I rounded the corner at Cummings Street and on a whim decided to pop into the Surf Shack. Bill needed more sunscreen. I was browsing through the various brands and weighing which version of 100 SPF he used when I glanced out the door. A family of four sauntered down the boardwalk, two kids in swimsuits and floaters on their upper arms skipping eagerly. I laughed. So many memories from summers down here when I was their age…

This end of the boardwalk was empty now except for a bench facing the ocean occupied by two men who were seated side by side. I squinted. Was that…? I stepped to the entrance of the Surf Shack. Those brown curls were unmistakable. The guy twisted sideways, his profile now visible—it *was* Jackson. He gestured vehemently, angrily shaking his head, pulling away from the other man's attempt to calm him down by clapping him on the shoulder. The other guy stood. It was Vinnie C. Jackson pointed a warning finger in his buddy's face. What was going on? Instinct told me to stay put, and I eased behind a rack of postcards. This scene was so unlike my former chill boyfriend. Then, also uncharacteristically, Jackson shoved Vinnie, who repaid the favor. They might well have kept at it if an old angler coming up the dock hadn't inserted himself between them. He put his hands on Jackson's arms long enough for Vinnie to move away and escape down the pier. Then Jackson shrugged the man off him and followed Vinnie.

The little hairs on the back of my neck danced. My radar system that alerted me whenever something was dodgy.

3

Music from the tiki bar wafted down the beach, accompanying the pounding of the surf as the tide rolled in. I flipped onto my stomach and buried my head in my arms, my skin absorbing the late-day heat. Good thing I was on my own this afternoon. Bill would have dragged me off the sand an hour ago. I idly watched the young lifeguards as they wrapped up their shift, collecting equipment, toppling the stand to prevent kids from climbing aboard. Their chiseled, athletic bodies reminded me of Jackson seven or eight years ago, before a beer belly aged him. The only remnant remaining of those long-ago summers was his brown, curly mane.

What had Jackson and Vinnie been arguing about earlier? Never mind; it wasn't my concern.

I drifted off…images from back in time surfacing unbidden. Jackson and I partying on his charter boat when he should have been working. Double dating with Vinnie C and a series of girlfriends. Grody teaching Jackson the basics of surfing. Bill and Jackson were about the same age but worlds apart. Responsible Bill with a professional career and a ton of law enforcement proficiency versus Jackson, apparently jobless and broke, the irresponsible beach bum who'd crashed with an old girlfriend. His unreliability was part of the reason we split up. Bill was pretty predictable. But that was fine by me. I had had enough excitement in my life these last years, and I appreciated the fact that he was steady and reliable. Of course, breakfast this morning was a surprising change of pace for Jackson.

Thinking of food made my stomach growl. The sun was slipping lower in the sky, and windy gusts had kicked up. I debated dropping in to the Bottom Feeder for a Creamsicle Crush and some fried shrimp balls, but then I had an image of Bill strolling in the door with a string of fish. Tired, hungry, and wanting a little TLC.

I needed to get home.

* * * *

Nothing like a cool shower after a day of sunbathing. I relished the feel of the water cascading off my shoulders and back, soothing my warm skin and relaxing my muscles. I shampooed my hair, removing the stickiness of sand and suntan oil. I switched off the shower, stepped onto a fuzzy bath mat and into a fluffy towel. I could hear activity in the kitchen. Bill! No doubt beginning the preparations for tonight's seafood dinner. My mouth was already watering...

I ran a comb through my tangled tresses, wrapped my towel sexily around my body, and opened the bathroom door, inviting a gush of cooler air. "How's my fisherman? Something sure smells delicious out there," I called out and moved into the hallway posing by the doorjamb. "Honey..."

"Thanks, babe!" Jackson poked his head out of the kitchen.

"Arggh! What are you doing here?" I screamed. I tore back into the bathroom, retrieved my robe, and yanked it around me. "Jackson!"

"Now don't go all crazy on me. I'm doin' happy hour. 'Cuz you're a great host."

Also an unwilling one. I peeked out of the bathroom. Jackson was wrapped in a chef's apron, spatula in hand.

"What are you making?" I asked darkly.

"Fried oysters wrapped in bacon and lobster wontons," he said proudly. "Didn't think I had it in me, didja?"

Sheesh. "Jackson, you do understand you're not living here, right? You said you'd be gone today. That you'd have your financial...situation worked out. Cash flow, remember?"

"About that..."

Uh-oh.

"Fisherman's home," sang out Bill as he opened the screen door. "Not exactly what I intended to cook tonight, but you won't be disappointed."

"Yo, my man," said Jackson from the kitchen.

Bill, a bag of groceries in hand, removed his Buffalo Bills ball cap, his eyes bulging. "Jackson? Dodie?" Then, "What's that smell?"

"Lobster wontons." I surrendered. "Jackson's doing happy hour."

* * * *

"I have to admit, these are delicious." Bill speared another wonton. Once he'd gotten over the shock of seeing Jackson where he'd left him this morning—in our kitchen—and fortified by a couple of strong gin and tonics, Bill was a gracious host. He amused us with anecdotes from the day's ocean voyage, including his inability to catch anything, and joked about a trip to the fish market to supply dinner since his fishing trip proved futile. This was a very loose Bill, not upset by his failure on the boat or my failure to dislodge Jackson from our bungalow.

"What was biting?" asked Jackson and took a swig of beer.

"Mostly mackerel and fluke. Some bluefish. Some sea bass." Bill shook his head. "Not my day."

"Whadidya use?"

"Swedish pimples and deadly dicks. Some of the guys were using diamond jigs," Bill answered.

Whoa. An X-rated outing? "What are we talking about?" I asked carefully.

Bill and Jackson grinned in unison. "Fishing lures," they said.

The sun had gone down half an hour ago, the air on the porch cooling pleasantly. I reached for the chardonnay bottle on the outdoor coffee table. "Time to get dinner going?" I said. Hopefully Jackson would take the "going" part of my hint.

"I'm on it." Bill drained his glass and headed into the house.

"What're you cooking?" Jackson trailed him like an eager puppy dog.

"Flounder," said Bill.

"Jackson? Can I talk with you?" I asked pointedly.

"Sure, just as soon as Bill and I have a little discussion. Flounder is one of my specialties."

"Specialties? You don't *have* specialties." I lowered my voice. "So you cooked a lovely breakfast. And the appetizers were delicious—"

"Told you you'd be surprised," he said.

"But now it's dinnertime." I let the implication hang in the air.

"And I'm going to make Bill's day. I've got the best flounder recipe," he said.

"Jackson?" I gave up and settled into the chaise lounge. It was going to take more than implications to extricate Jackson from our lives. Their voices floated outside.

"Usually I do a simple recipe. Parmesan cheese, lemon juice, green onions, butter. Nothing fancy," said Bill.

"Uh-huh. That's okay, dude."

Bill took the bait. No fishing pun intended. "What do you do with it?"

"Sometimes I bake it with panko and Parmesan..."

"Me too."

"But my specialty..."

There he went again.

"...is dill and horseradish sauce," Jackson said triumphantly.

In the kitchen both cooks were silent. Bill must have been absorbing this latest bit of culinary confidence. "Now, that would be interesting. Let's try it."

OMG. The two of them cooking partners? This could be an act of daring without a safety net. I emptied the bottle into my glass.

* * * *

"See what I mean?" Jackson said as he scraped the last morsel of flounder off his plate.

"Got it, bro." Was Bill being sarcastic or had he yielded to Jackson's worldview?

"Since you two 'dudes' cooked, I'll clean up." I collected plates and silverware and loaded the dishwasher.

"Awesome cooking with you, Bill. Think I'll hit the sack. Later," Jackson said and flashed a peace sign.

Not yet. Not if I had anything to say about it. "Jackson, give me a hand in the kitchen first."

"Sure."

Bill yawned and stretched. "I'm going to watch the Yankees in the bedroom." Our bungalow was well-equipped with televisions in both bedrooms as well as the living room. "Fishing takes it out of you."

I smiled sweetly. "I'll be there shortly." As soon as the bedroom door closed, I turned to Jackson. "You can't stay here."

"It's okay with Bill. I'm liking that dude—"

"Well, it's not okay with me." I paused. "How do you know it's okay with Bill?"

"I asked him. When we were cooking."

"When he was vulnerable. Jackson, I'm sorry things are tight for you right now, but we broke up years ago and this is...awkward."

"Not for me. Not for Bill." He rocked back on his flip-flops. "You need to get over your past."

"*Our* past. And I am over it. It's your living in my summer rental that's the problem," I huffed.

"Really upset, are we?" he mocked.

"What happened at that meeting you supposedly had? Why haven't you solved your cash flow problem?"

"I'm working on it. We're negotiating a deal. Everything's cool."

"It didn't look cool today when you stuck your finger in Vinnie's face. It looked pretty threatening." I slammed the dishwasher shut.

Jackson did a double-take. "You stalking me?"

"No, I was at the theater, and on the way back to the beach I stopped in the Surf Shack and happened to see you two. On the boardwalk. Arguing." *Accompanied by a shoving match.* Confronting Jackson with what I witnessed might nudge the cash flow conversation forward.

If Jackson was miffed about my accusation, I didn't see it. "We were talking over old times. Two bros who haven't seen each other in a while." He tugged on an earlobe.

I knew it. Jackson was lying. Years ago, whenever he was playing fast and loose with the truth, his go-to comfort gesture was that earlobe tug. So there was more to that confrontation on the beach than he was willing to admit. "You two did more than talking. You pushed him and then Vinnie pushed you back. Jackson, if you've got a problem and need to talk it out, I'd be willing—"

He threw up his hands in self-defense. "Not to worry, babe. Vinnie and I went down the dock and had a beer on *The Bounty.* That's his new boat. Said he got the idea for the name after watching an old movie."

"*Mutiny on the Bounty.*" I hoped the name hadn't brought Vinnie bad luck.

"Helloooo! Dodie?"

A body materialized at the screen door. "Lola? The ELT's not due here until tomorrow." I opened the door and hugged her. "Come on in."

"They're not. I decided to come tonight and beat the morning traffic. Besides, I was antsy at home and wanted to see you so we could spend the morning on the beach—"

Jackson popped out of the kitchen.

"Oh...hello," Lola said, cocking her head and swishing her blond ponytail.

"Lola, this is Jackson. He's *visiting,*" I said.

"Hey there. Wassup?" he said by way of greeting.

Lola peeked sideways at me. "*The* Jackson...?"

"The one and only. In the flesh." He gripped Lola's hand, holding it a bit longer than necessary.

"Oh. And where's Bill?" she asked brightly.

"In bed," I said.

"Dodie, I'm sorry it's so late. I'll register at the hotel and come back tomorrow. I didn't realize you'd have company."

"Neither did I. Did you eat?" I asked.

"I stopped on the Parkway and ate a sandwich, but I could use a nip of something." She beamed at me, then Jackson.

"I'll get it." He bounced away.

"The bottom shelf," I called after him.

Lola pulled me into the living room and whispered, "What is going on?"

"You won't believe it. I'll fill you in tomorrow. But tonight, why don't you stay here? We have a guest bedroom," I said.

"What about Jackson?"

"He's happy on the porch."

Jackson appeared with three glasses, wine, and a plate of cheese and crackers. He winked at Lola. "At your service."

* * * *

By midnight I was ready to pass out. Lola had kicked off her shoes, gotten comfy on the sofa, and accepted my offer of the spare bedroom. I sipped on half a glass of wine while she and Jackson consumed the rest and made quick work of the cheese plate. Jackson was completely mesmerized by Lola's tales of the ELT, just as he'd been rapt by Bill's stories of his fishing escapade. When had he become a skillful listener? For that matter, when had he become a skillful cook? This rehabilitated Jackson was giving me a case of whiplash.

"So you're doing *Arsenic and Old Lace* at the festival this weekend?" he asked politely.

Lola ran a hand through her hair, which by now had come free of its moorings. Her white knitted top and shorts were set off by a rosy glow that spread from ear to ear. It was either the wine or Jackson's attention. Lola had been a widow for over a decade, and as long as I had known her, she'd been pursuing the dating scene. Online, at two theaters, even abroad during a European vacation. She hadn't had much luck.

"Yes. The actress who played the ingénue for the Etonville production wasn't available, and nobody else could fit the costume and learn the lines quickly." She paused to consider Jackson over the rim of her wineglass. "I hope I don't strike everyone as too old for the part."

"What're you...thirty?"

She tittered like a schoolgirl. Jackson was only sixteen years off. Lola was a young forty-six-year-old with a daughter in college.

"Don't worry. You'll crush the part." He downed his wine. I'd had enough. "Can't keep my eyes open. Sorry. The bed's made up and there's towels in the bathroom." I kissed Lola good night. "See you in the morning."

Lola nodded. "Thanks."

"Sleep tight." Jackson waved and grinned.

I crawled into bed quietly to avoid waking Bill. He must have been exhausted and didn't move a muscle as I climbed under the sheet. I was asleep in minutes.

* * * *

"That bikini looks hot on you," I said to Lola as I smeared lotion on my legs.

"I did a shred emergency," she said.

"Huh?"

"Lost five pounds in the last two weeks. Low carbs, low protein, low fat."

"What did you eat?" I asked.

"Salads and chardonnay."

"It worked."

"Thanks. By the way, you're glowing too. Must be the sun...or Bill," Lola teased.

I frowned. "It's been a rocky start to our vacation. First my parents were here, which was fun, but we didn't have much private time, and then as they left Jackson showed up and, well, you can imagine that scene."

"He's kind of cute..."

"Lola!"

"I'm browsing," she said quickly.

Jackson *was* cute. Another thing I'd liked about him.

"For an ex-boyfriend." Lola opened a water bottle. "Not like my exes... one dead and one in jail."

Lola was the victim of a patchy love life: One old flame turned out to be a jewel thief and another was guilty of fraud.

"I've got to stop dating criminals," she said. "Speaking of which, I'm sorry I missed Bill this morning."

"He got a call at six a.m. that he was needed at a hearing for a court case in Creston." Etonville's larger, next-door neighbor. "He'll be back tomorrow. By then I am determined to be done with Jackson."

"Hmmm."

"What's that mean?" I asked.

"He seems awfully interested in staying with you."

"Awfully interested in mooching off me, you mean. He claimed he had a meeting yesterday that would take care of his money problem," I said.

"And?"

I filled Lola in on my spying episode, Jackson's history with Vinnie C, and the change in his old partner. "Things didn't end amiably with the two of them. When Jackson went to Iowa after Hurricane Sandy, they dissolved the business. Maybe there were some loose financial ends. At any rate, it didn't look as though the two of them were happy to see each other. With the shoving match and all."

"Some kind of falling-out, I guess."

Lola dozed and the sun rose higher in the sky. I opened the latest Cindy Collins's mystery that had occupied my attention in recent days. *Murder Most Cordial*. I was addicted to murder mysteries and thrillers, and Cindy Collins's novels were among my favorites. I stared at the cover page. A sassy redhead with a million-dollar grin plastered on her mouth. In my experience—and unfortunately there had been a significant amount of it since I'd arrived in Etonville—murder was never cordial. Gruesome, scary, shocking, violent…but never friendly. I'd begun to garner a bit of a reputation as a freelance sleuth investigating a series of deaths in Etonville and its environs. Bill's initial misgivings about my detection had segued into a grudging acceptance of my skills tempered by a dash of caution.

By noon we were both hot and famished. I suggested a break from the sun at the tiki bar and we gathered our beach gear and trudged through the sand to the Polynesian music. We were halfway through our bucket of steamed clams when an elderly twosome at a table next to ours gasped in shock. We couldn't help noticing.

"Is everything okay?" I asked gently.

The woman's head bobbled, and her wide-brimmed sun hat swung from side to side. She picked up the newspaper she'd been reading, the *Candle Beach Courier*, a local rag, and shoved the front page at us. "He was such a nice boy. We knew his parents years ago."

I smiled sympathetically and scanned the sheet. Then *I* gasped.

"Dodie, what's the matter?" Lola said.

"Were you acquainted with him too?" the woman asked.

I nodded numbly. Was I ever. The headline read "LOCAL MAN DEAD." Underneath was a photo of the victim: It was Vinnie C. I rotated the paper so Lola could see the front page. "It's him," I said hoarsely.

Lola blinked. "Vincent Carcherelli," she read.

I scanned the story. Apparently his body had washed up on the beach sometime overnight and was discovered by a jogger early today in time to make the mid-morning edition. The police were calling it a drowning and speculating that he'd fallen off his boat, *The Bounty*, which had drifted half a mile off the shoreline. No foul play suspected at the moment, but the investigation was ongoing.

I offered to return the newspaper, but the couple refused to accept it, saying the story was too upsetting. They picked up their bill and left.

"Wow. What a coincidence. We were talking about how Jackson saw him yesterday..." Lola stopped. A light bulb went on. "The police will want to speak with Jackson. He might have been one of the last people to see Vinnie alive."

It was Lola's last word that brought me up short: alive. Jackson had been steamed during that meeting on the boardwalk. Did he know anything about Vinnie's last hours? If Bill was here, he'd tell me to mind my own business, let Jackson alone, let the police determine the actual cause of death. Bill was right, of course. But something about the whole event didn't sit right with me. Why did Jackson lie about what happened when he met Vinnie?

"Hate to be selfish, but I hope this doesn't put a damper on the theater festival. Local guy dying and all." She sucked on her Creamsicle straw, slurping up the last remains of the drink. Her cell pinged. "The party's over. The ELT is at the theater trying to load-in. Walter and Penny creating havoc, no doubt."

"I think they'll meet their match with Sam and Maddy," I said.

"Who?"

* * * *

Lola and I finished our lunch. She left to check in to her hotel, the Windward, and connect with the rest of the ELT gang: Walter, Penny, Abby, Edna, and Romeo. I went back to my bungalow to shower and to find Jackson and get the truth out of him. On the way I would call Grody. I'd gotten so distracted yesterday that I'd neglected to update him on the NJCTF reception that he was catering.

It was a workable plan until I exited the boardwalk and entered my street. Ahead a Candle Beach police cruiser was parked in front of my rental property. So soon? Had they found out about Vinnie and Jackson already? I wished Bill was here.

I tapped Grody's number in my contacts. His cell rang twice, then he picked up.

"Sandbar."

"Grody, it's me. I wanted to fill you in." I relayed Sam Baldwin's message that Grody was free to choose the menu and set up anywhere he wanted in the town park.

"A free hand, huh?"

"Yep."

"Hey, any suggestions on the theme thing? 'Cause I only have a few days to get this catered."

"I saw the play list. Everything from old chestnuts to Shakespeare to *The Sound of Music* and *Cinderella*. I'll give it a think today and stop in tomorrow."

"Thanks, Red. Talk later."

"Grody, wait a minute. Did you see the paper?" I asked.

"About Vinnie? Yeah. Rotten luck. He probably had one too many and fell overboard. Poor guy," Grody said.

I was skeptical. "You think? Vinnie was a seasoned sailor."

"If he was three sheets to the wind, it wouldn't have mattered how skilled he was."

Huh. "So...you have reason to think Vinnie might have been intoxicated?"

Grody's voice lowered as though he had cupped the phone in his palm. "Listen, don't quote me, but word around town is that Vinnie has been on an extended toot for the last month or so."

Was Jackson aware of this? I told Grody I'd be in touch and clicked off.

I reached my bungalow and slowly ascended the steps. The door from the porch to the interior of the house was open, and beyond the entrance I could see two uniformed officers. Jackson was out of sight. I walked into the house. "Hello?"

"Hey, Dodie." Jackson sat on the living room couch. He was a mess. Hair tousled, T-shirt dirty, Hawaiian shorts frayed on the edges. Where the hell had he been? "These dudes are Candle Beach cops." He grinned as though they were simply two more bros he'd picked up on the beach. The cops did not reciprocate.

"Hi," I said patiently. In case Jackson had neglected to mention it, I added, "This is my rental."

"So we hear. Were you also an acquaintance of Vincent Carcherelli?" asked the older of the two officers. Unsmiling, tall, and whippet-thin, edgy, bouncing on his feet.

"I knew him a number of years ago. Before Hurricane Sandy." Why was I being hesitant?

"See him lately?"

"Two days ago in the tiki bar. The Bottom Feeder."

"Did you speak with him?" asked the younger cop. He was the opposite of his partner: undersized, pudgy, and sympathetic.

"Very briefly. I don't think he remembered me. I had to tell him who I was," I said. "We only talked for a minute or two."

The older cop glanced at me, writing something down. Then he closed a notepad and stuffed it in his pocket. He shifted his focus to Jackson. "Thanks for your cooperation. If we need to speak to you again, we can find you here?"

Before I could scream "No!" Jackson nodded. "Sure thing." Then he shook their hands and escorted them out as if they were houseguests.

I counted to ten to compose myself, then gave up, grabbed a sofa pillow, and threw it at Jackson. It caught him off guard.

"Hey! Wassup?"

I grabbed another pillow and whacked his midsection.

He ducked his head. "Ouch!"

I couldn't remember when I'd last been this angry. "What is the matter with you? These cops are not some surfer dudes. They are not your bros. They are investigating a death that may be suspicious, and you are most likely one of the last people to see Vinnie alive. And you had a fight with him hours before his body was found!" Out of breath, I collapsed on an easy chair.

"Didn't know you cared." Jackson sprawled on the sofa.

"Jackson...you look like crap. Where have you been?"

He shrugged. "Here and there. On the beach."

I was almost afraid to ask. "What did the police have to say?"

"They're groovy guys looking into Vinnie's death. He fell overboard." Jackson shook his head sadly.

"How did they find you here?"

"Vin had my number in his cell phone. I left him a message that I was camping out on your porch," he said.

"What about your argument with him yesterday? That got so physical someone had to get between you two? Did you tell the police about that?" I asked.

"I told you. It was an old issue. Some bookkeeping stuff." He stopped. "Vinnie owed me some money."

Aha. The cash flow problem. "Jackson?"

He yawned. "I said I'd seen him around noon and we discussed our former working relationship."

I hoped I wasn't boring him. "You may need a lawyer," I said, suddenly uneasy.

"What for? I didn't do anything illegal. Anyway, hiring a lawyer's not in my financial game plan."

Neither was a hotel room, apparently. My cell buzzed. Lola: *Walter panicking...need to rehearse tonight...but theater off-limits...any way we could use your place??* I sighed. Rehearsing scenes for the NJCTF was not how I imagined I'd spend this night. But neither did I think I'd have to babysit Jackson. I texted okay. Then added: *did J go to sleep on porch when you went to bed?* Lola replied: *THANKS! not sure...went to bed first about 12:30. Oh... what does that mean??*

What *did* it mean? Demanding answers from Jackson now was pointless. He was snoring on the sofa. I jumped in the shower and took out my frustration with my loofah! My skin did not thank me...

4

"Hey, O'Dell, mind if we rearrange the furniture?" Penny Ossining, the ELT stage manager, in flowered capri pants and an oversized T-shirt sporting the masks of comedy and tragedy, beat a pencil on her ever-present clipboard and fiddled with her whistle. Which I fervently hoped she'd forego tooting for the sake of the neighbors. It was her favorite way to round up the members of the Etonville Little Theatre.

"No problem." I'd been playing host for the past hour, serving drinks and setting out chips and nibbles. Jackson—after a nap, a shower, and slipping into clean clothes—was very presentable, brown curls neatly combed into his man bun. He was super friendly with Lola, which irritated her ex-love Walter, who was directing the scenes from *Arsenic and Old Lace*. "Glad to see everyone made it down here."

Penny smirked. "O'Dell, you should know by now that somebody has to keep the trains from running into each other. On time. *Moi.*"

"Yes, Penny, I do realize you are the reason the trains usually derail," I said, all innocent.

"You got that right." She waddled away to organize the shifting of the coffee table and chairs.

Walter pointed here and there, and Penny followed his direction. "Lola, dear, could you speak with me?" Walter got whiny whenever he was feeling insecure—usually when Lola had the attention of another male.

Lola was a dutiful artistic director and maneuvered herself away from Jackson, who took it upon himself to be social director and engage two of the actors in conversation: Abby, manager of the Valley View Shooting Range in Etonville, and Romeo, who played the former lover of Juliet in *Romeo and Juliet*. The name stuck. As irritated as I was with Jackson, I had to admit that getting those two to chitchat was a minor miracle. They could compete for first place in a moody/surly contest.

"Dodie, I read in the paper that Candle Beach had a 10-32 today," Edna said confidentially and raised an eyebrow. She was the dispatcher for the Etonville Police Department and loved her police codes. I could only assume a 10-32 was a drowning.

"Yes. Really unfortunate. The police think he might have fallen overboard."

Edna whispered knowingly. "That's what they all say until they end up with a 10-55."

What?

"Coroner case," she added.

"I hope not." I meant it.

"Copy that." She shoved a pencil into the bun atop her gray-brown head and swept up a handful of baby carrots.

Jackson sidled up to me. "These theater people are crazy, man." He bit into a piece of celery. "I coulda been an actor."

Given his encounter with the Candle Beach police today, he already was.

"We're not done talking, Jackson. I want some answers," I said.

He smiled ingratiatingly. "Yes, Mother."

I gritted my teeth.

Walter started the rehearsal with a warm-up, which I knew was his *modus operandi* for most rehearsals. Some of them were outlandish and involved blindfolds, twirling like balloons, and flying into one another. Luckily, tonight the cast was only required to sit silently and focus on their scene. There was a mixed response: Abby and Edna, playing the elderly Brewster sisters, central characters of *Arsenic and Old Lace*, obeyed Walter's request, though Abby was less enthusiastic about it. Lola, out of unwavering loyalty, joined in, and Romeo, her younger romantic partner in the scenes, sneered his way through the exercise. *He was still playing Conrad Birdie from the spring musical.*

Jackson sat cross-legged on the floor and closed his eyes. Who knew what *he* was focused on.

After fifteen minutes, Walter called the rehearsal to order, and the actors ran the scenes entered in the festival.

I intended to decamp to the bedroom, where I had fifty pages of my thriller *Murder Most Cordial* left to read. Jackson cleaned up some plates and glasses and I intercepted him in the kitchen. "Hang around here tonight. Keep a low profile."

Jackson inclined his head as if to get a better angle on me. "You're worried about me," he said solemnly. Then burst out laughing.

"Shhh! They're trying to work out there," I rasped.

Penny stuck her head in the kitchen and plastered a finger crossways on her lips.

Jackson murmured, "Don't wait up for me." He lifted a strand of curly hair and placed it behind my ear. "Mom!"

Jackson was maddening. Had he always been this frustrating?

* * * *

By nine thirty the ELT had run through its scenes five times, Walter had delivered his to-be-expected lecture on festival performance and its many pitfalls—biased audience members, competition with various theaters, placement in the evening's schedule—and the actors were yawning. Also planning trips to the beach tomorrow.

"Don't forget. Call is five o'clock tomorrow afternoon. Sharp. At the theater. You're going to wear makeup and costumes, so no sunburn," Penny announced as the cast put my living room back in order.

"As if," Romeo said under his breath.

As the actors trooped out the door, Penny yelled, "We go on after *The Sound of Music* and before *King Lear.*"

The ELT was sandwiched between singing kids and nuns and the Shakespearean ranting of an old man facing the end of his life. Which play had been cut?

"*Harvey*'s out," Penny said.

I jumped. "What?" I had almost gotten used to Penny reading my mind. She cackled. "Who needs a play about an invisible rabbit?"

"Right. Better to have one about two old ladies poisoning poor old gentlemen with elderberry wine," I said.

Penny eyed me. "O'Dell, you crack me up."

"Dodie, thanks for letting us use your house. We needed this tonight," Lola said. "Do I look too old?"

"Not a bit."

She brushed her hair off one shoulder and looked around. "Where's Jackson?"

"Who knows? I hope he stays out of trouble."

I closed the screen door on the last of the ELT and agreed to meet Lola for breakfast at the Candle Diner. I did a final clean-up in the kitchen and settled into a thickly padded rocking chair on the porch. The night was balmy, with only a trace of the humidity that had made the day sticky and hot, and the sky was overcast. No trace of those constellations Bill was so excited about. What was he up to...doing paperwork in the office, hanging out at home, sleeping... I felt restless and not yet ready to hit the sack. I plucked a lightweight jacket from a hook near the door and locked up, leaving the porch open in case Jackson planned to spend the night here, which I was sure he did.

Atlantic Street was peaceful, the houses dimly lit. But a block away the boardwalk was bright as day and full of life with music resounding up and down the shoreline and people of all ages strolling in and out of shops and restaurants. The ambience was pleasant and inviting. I ambled past the tiki bar, Grody's Sandbar, the shop dispensing frozen yogurt, and the mini-golf course. The tide was coming in, and half a dozen hardy souls who were willing to brave the cold water at night dove in and out of the waves. I sat on a bench adjacent to the beach. Why was I so fidgety? I missed Bill, but it was more than that. Jackson had me on edge. Though I wanted to believe that he knew nothing about Vinnie's death, in my heart of hearts I knew better. Something was fishy. I could not get the image of Vinnie and Jackson's fight out of my mind.

On a whim I jumped to my feet and race-walked to the south end of the boardwalk until, slightly out of breath, I stopped opposite the marina where Vinnie's boat was moored. This end of the boardwalk was deserted. The Surf Shack was closed for the day. The police must have had *The Bounty* towed in. Out of curiosity I stepped off the boardwalk and slowly headed down the dock. I passed three boats—*Miss Betty, Three G's,* and *Sea Witch*—that bobbed gently in the wash resulting from the incoming tide. Given the time, it made sense that all interior lights were off in the boats. But when I approached *The Bounty*, a dim glow emanated from the cabin below the deck. A bell on one of the boats clanged. The slap of the water striking the hulls accompanied creaking as the boats pulled on their tie lines like impatient kids trying to break away from diligent parents. I inhaled the odors of pine tar and diesel fuel.

With Vinnie gone, who or what created the glimmer of light that leaked from the cabin? I leaned against a piling, ten yards from *The Bounty*, and observed the silhouette of a figure as it shifted back and forth behind a curtained window on the lower deck.

A large shadow rushed to my left stopping inches from me. My heart lurched in my chest.

"Whadya doin' here?" The male voice was unfamiliar, harsh, and hostile. He towered over me and stood close enough that I got a whiff of cigarette smoke and sour breath. He wore a beat-up nautical captain's cap.
"I-I'm going for a walk."
He trained a utility flashlight on me, so bright my hand immediately shot up to shield my eyes. I couldn't see his face. "This area's off-limits."
"I didn't realize—"
"Walk somewhere else," he grunted.
"Sure. Sorry." I backed up, tripping over a loose board on the dock.
"Keep moving. Go on." He flicked the light off and vanished in the dark.
What was that about? As I edged away, the light in *The Bounty* went off, leaving Vinnie's boat completely in the dark. I jogged up the dock and didn't stop moving until I set foot on the boardwalk. When I turned around, all I could see were the outlines of the watercraft peacefully rolling and dipping. No signs remained of the frightening incident.
I darted down the boardwalk to the well-lit areas by the bars and restaurants. I needed a friend.

* * * *

Grody plunked down on a bar stool next to me, patting my back. "Calm down yet, Irish?"
"It's like I imagined the whole thing," I said and guzzled my seltzer.
"Did you?"
"No!"
"Vinnie's death has spooked lots of Candle Beach regulars. The guy could have been a fisherman protecting his territory." Grody had one eye on our conversation and the other on the dining room. He shifted in his seat and gestured to a waiter to check on a table across the restaurant. I appreciated his taking a moment to listen to my tale, given that the Sandbar was full this evening.
"Sorry to distract you. I can see how busy you are."
"No problem. Hey, friends, right?" He hugged me like a big brother.
Grody was right…about both friendship and the possibility that someone was acting territorial on the dock. Yet, why was there a light on in Vinnie's boat when its captain was out of the picture?
"I wish Jackson was more open about his and Vinnie's relationship. He claims there's nothing to tell me, but I swear I know different."
"Why're you suspicious? Maybe he's telling you the truth."
"I can read Jackson like a book." In the past anyway.

"It could be he's changed. Everybody should have the chance to change their life, kiddo," Grody said softly.

I'd changed enough since I split with Jackson: Etonville, Bill, the Windjammer, helping solve murders. "True. I should trust him." Grody burst out laughing. "I didn't say trust him. Just allow for the possibility that this Jackson is different from the one you knew years ago." He bounced off his bar stool. "Sorry. Got to take care of a customer."

"Go. You have a restaurant to run."

I drained my seltzer, said so long to Grody with the promise of a theater theme first thing in the morning. I tramped back to my rental property, aware of the dark once I left the boardwalk for the street. I didn't need any more threatening run-ins. The moon passed behind cloud cover; rain tomorrow. I hurried into the house and locked the door behind me. No sign of Jackson on the porch. I had no desire to press him for information he resisted sharing. Grody was correct. I had to give Jackson the benefit of the doubt where Vinnie and his death were concerned. Maybe he had changed…

* * * *

A wave curled over my head, and I dove into the green foam, the crash of water on the sandy beach familiar music to my ears. I floated, buoyant in the ocean, swept along by the incoming tide. I was in heaven. Next thing I knew, I was up to my neck in seafood—shrimp, scallops, calamari, lobsters—I opened my mouth to scream, and a giant prawn floated in, choking me. I awoke with a start, gurgling, panting. Some nightmare.

My last thought as I fell asleep was Grody's menu for the theater reception. I'd run through possible theme food ideas with no success. And this was how my subconscious reacted? Different types of seafood attacking me? When I closed my eyes again, the giant prawn latched on to my head. Was it trying to tell me something? Seven plays, I mused… different seafood…hmmm…I had it! I bounded out of bed and snatched my cell phone out of its charger. It was eight o'clock. Not too soon to text Grody: *problem solved re. theme food. call me.*

I had no sooner finished the text than my phone rang. I checked the caller ID and tapped on Answer. "Hey there, handsome. Miss me?"

"What do you think?" Bill yawned in my ear.

"You just wake up?" I asked.

"Nah. Been at work for an hour. Trying to tie up this court case."

"Too bad it had to interfere with your vacation," I said in my sexy voice.

"That's what I told the judge. So what's happening on the Jackson front?" he asked. "Am I still sharing my vacation rental?"

I hesitated. How much to disclose? "He's working on his cash flow problem."

"That means he's still occupying the front porch?"

"I'm sorry, Bill. I can't believe he showed up in Candle Beach needing a place to stay," I said ruefully.

"It's not your fault. I'm thinking of offering to pay for a motel room for the next couple of nights. Maybe he'll get the hint and skip town." Bill chuckled.

Jackson was *not* going to be skipping town any time soon. "When are you coming back?"

"What time is happy hour this afternoon?" he asked.

"Whenever you get here...dude."

Bill clicked off with the promise to see me suck down a Creamsicle Crush at the tiki bar by four o'clock. I had to have a down-and-dirty talk with Jackson by then. My cell rang.

"So what's the solution to the food theme?" Grody asked.

"Did my text wake you?"

"Uh-huh."

"Sorry. Listen to this." I related my dream with the seafood, which Grody considered too bizarre for words, and explained my solution. Seven plays, seven types of hors d'oeuvres, each one named for an entry, like *Cinderella* crabmeat canapés, *King Lear* scallops in bacon, *Mousetrap* spring rolls, *The Sound of Music* calamari... Grody got the drift. It wasn't my most creative brainstorm—and Grody wasn't a hundred percent convinced—but the food was all in his wheelhouse, easy enough to prepare in the days remaining before the festival opening.

"I'll have the kitchen get on it today."

"You'd better let Sam Baldwin review the menu, although he didn't seem to care what you did one way or the other."

"I'll give him a call. Thanks, Red," Grody said.

"See you later. We'll drop in for dinner. The crew from Etonville has hit Candle Beach and I'm not sure what their rehearsal schedule is, but—" My cell buzzed. "Sorry. I have a call coming in."

"Hey, I picked up some scuttlebutt after you left the Sandbar last night," Grody said.

"Yeah?"

"The Candle Beach cops are bringing in the state police to investigate Vinnie's death," he said.

"The state police for a simple drowning? Isn't that unusual?"
Grody paused. "Might not be a simple drowning."
I shivered. "What?"
"A buddy of mine works in the county prosecutor's office. Word through the grapevine is that there's some physical evidence suggesting his death could be more than an accident."
I knew Grody had connections around Ocean County. I figured his information was reliable. "Are you saying...?"
"Yep. Murder."
I clicked off and accepted the new call. "Yo, Dodie. What took you so long?" Jackson asked, irritated.
"Jackson? I heard some unsettling news—"
"I need a ride."
I had a bad feeling. "Where are you?"
"I'm in the CBPD," he said and barked a laugh.
"The what...?" Then I got it. "The police station? Are you being arrested?"
"What they're calling a 'person of interest.' They're interested in me." He chuckled.
"I know what a person of interest is. Have they interrogated you?" I asked, alarmed.
"Nah. They're cool. We're shooting the breeze."
His attitude was giving me a headache. "These cops are not shooting the breeze. They are—"
"Anyway, can you pick me up?"
"Where's your car?"
"Had a run-in with a fire plug. Gonna be out of commission for a while."
Would it never end with Jackson? I agreed to pick him up and deliver him to my place to shower and change. Then I had to get together with Lola at the Candle Diner.
Forty-five minutes later I cruised through the town of Candle Beach on my way to Varick Street, where the police station was located. I pulled into a parking lot that fronted a single-story, neatly landscaped, light brick building with "Candle Beach Police Department" signage prominently displayed. I left the engine of my red MINI Cooper running as I rapped on the steering wheel impatiently. The front door to the building opened, and I sat up alertly. A young woman exited, crying, clearly distraught. Next, an elderly duo, arm in arm, got out of a car and entered the station. Where was he? I was about to call Jackson's cell number when he strolled

out the door as if he were completely stress-free. I was beginning to think something was drastically wrong with him.

"Yo, Dodie," he said and climbed into the passenger seat. "Groovy ride. What happened to the Metro?"

My Chevy Metro that had been my constant companion for over a hundred thousand miles had died a catastrophic death months ago. But that was another story... My used MC wasn't my Metro, it hadn't become a cherished friend yet, but it was comfortable. In a nod to my departed automotive companion, I'd bought another red car.

I glared at Jackson. "You're a mess. Where did you spend the night? Not on my front porch." I put the MC in Reverse and backed out of my space.

"I crashed at a friend's pad."

"Where?" I asked, suspicious. *Why didn't you crash there the past few nights instead of sleeping on my porch?*

"He's from years ago."

"From your days with Vinnie on the charter?" I veered down Ocean Avenue, gliding to the curb. I shifted into Park.

"Yep."

"I think there are some things I didn't know about that time. About you and Vinnie," I said.

Jackson peered at me. "Why d'ya say that?" He tugged on his earlobe.

"A hunch. The way you've been acting, Vinnie's death, your grilling by police."

Jackson smiled his hundred-watt grin and put a hand on my shoulder. "Babe, you don't need to stew about me."

I shrugged his hand off me. "Somebody has to, because you're not taking all of this seriously enough. The police think Vinnie might have been murdered." I was shrieking.

"What're ya talking about? Vinnie drowned because he probably had a few too many and fell off *The Bounty*. Anyway, who'd want to murder him?" Jackson asked.

Who, indeed. I shoved the MINI Cooper into Drive and eased back into traffic. Candle Beach was awake, and a steady line of cars made their way toward the parking lots by the boardwalk. Which reminded me. I had to hurry if I was going to meet Lola on time. I drove to Atlantic Street and parked in the driveway.

"Hey, where's my man? No BMW," Jackson observed.

Bill's gold luxury car was one of his prized possessions. "Up north. Lucky for you, because he's getting a little tired of you overstaying your welcome," I huffed.

"No way. We're buds."

I unlocked the front door, then requested that Jackson leave the bathroom presentable and stay out of trouble. I had no idea where Jackson would spend his day or what Bill would say if he ran into Jackson in the house without me there.

* * * *

When I opened the door of the Candle Diner, Lola beckoned from a booth in the back of the restaurant. I scooted onto the bench. "Like Coffee Heaven, right?" Coffee Heaven was Etonville's old-fashioned Jersey diner that featured typical dishes plus updated coffee choices such as caramel macchiato, my obsession.

"But without Jocelyn and a ton of eavesdropping customers," Lola said and sipped her coffee. Coffee Heaven was also one Etonville location where folks, including waitress Jocelyn, met to chatter and gossip. "Upset?"

"Jackson," I admitted.

"What's he done now?"

I filled Lola in on his latest antics, and we ordered breakfast. I missed my Coffee Heaven caramel macchiato and cinnamon bun, but the diner's omelets and homemade pastries were superb.

Lola swallowed a forkful of her spinach and goat cheese omelet. "You think Jackson had something to do with Vinnie's death?"

"I don't know, and that's what scares me. He's so nonchalant, like he's in surfer-dude mode, that he's got to be guilty of something. Besides, he's been tugging on his ear a lot lately." I had to explain Jackson's nervous tic that always gave him away. "Do you think I'm being too judgy? Maybe I should leave him alone."

"Dodie, you might have to do some snooping around down here. It's not Etonville, but you're a terrific investigator—"

"Oh no! Not me. I'm keeping my distance from Jackson's problems. Sure, I'm concerned because he's not *and* we have a history from years back *and* even if he hired a lawyer, which he can't afford, he'll need someone else on his side. Of course, this could be a moot point if he doesn't become a suspect, but I can't imagine Bill's reaction if I said I was digging into a murder case in Candle Beach that involved Jackson." I took a breath.

"You sound awfully involved already." Lola wiped her mouth.

I hadn't intended to get involved.

"Hi, Dodie! Lola said you'd be here." Carol Palmieri, my other BFF from Etonville, the hair and makeup specialist of the Etonville Little Theatre and the owner of Snippets salon, Etonville's primary rumor central, arrived. "Isn't this exciting? The ELT a finalist in the NJCTF." She giggled. I shoved over and she plopped down, then squeezed me. "Only by default. If it hadn't been for the Cranford theater's food poisoning epidemic, we'd be in Etonville. The company had a picnic at their town park last weekend and everyone ended up sick. They thought it was the potato salad," Lola said. "Still, it's a compliment to be included." "I'll say. It's an honor," I added. "It means the ELT is among the best community theaters in the state," Carol said proudly. "Along with Westfield, Cape May, Hackettstown...I heard that Cranford is steaming over having to withdraw."

Lola glanced at her watch. "Speaking of which, I have a meeting with Walter and Penny at the theater. We have a tech rehearsal this afternoon, and Walter wants to 'commune with the space.' I told him we could do it during the tech but he was insistent." She moaned. "Some things never change."

Meaning Walter's demands on Lola's attention. She was a good sport where her former paramour was concerned. *Was I the same with Jackson? Patient, understanding...not really.* "I'll go with you. A stroll on the boardwalk will wear off a few calories." Besides, I felt antsy once again and needed to take my mind off Jackson. His behavior was mystifying... and frightening.

5

Lola opened the door to the theater, and we were met with a blast of commotion. Some crew members put the final touches on the false proscenium announcing the New Jersey Community Theater Festival while others sprang up and down ladders adjusting lights on battens and poles, calling back and forth to one another. Super stage manager Maddy yelled at clusters of actors gathered in the house to "keep it down." Sam Baldwin stood, arms akimbo, center stage facing outward as if surveying his kingdom. I'd spent enough time viewing the ELT crews during technical rehearsals that I recognized this last-minute mayhem. Sam's wife, Arlene, sat in the first row, her head bent over papers in her lap.

"I see some people from the Westfield Drama Club. I'll be back." Lola scooted down a side aisle and joined a group in a heated discussion. They greeted Lola warmly.

"Hey, O'Dell." Penny stood beside me in the aisle, slapped her own clipboard against her leg, and pushed her glasses a notch up her nose.

"Hi, Penny."

She jerked her thumb over her shoulder. "Can you believe her?" Penny pointed at Maddy.

"She's certainly in control."

Maddy threw her clipboard to the floor and charged some wandering visitors who emerged from the back of the stage, apparently lost.

Penny observed me warily. "Kind of goes overboard, don't you think?"

I swallowed a chuckle. Had Penny ever seen *herself* in action? "As you always say, production manager means managing the production."

"O'Dell, you yanking my chain?"

"Me?" I asked simply.

"It's not even performance conditions," Penny griped. "Can't wait till tech this afternoon."

"Are you all set?"

Penny pulled herself up to a ramrod-straight five-foot-two. "Of course the ELT is ready. We're pros, O'Dell."

Well, actually, they weren't, being a community theater.

"Even if we are a community theater," she said.

Penny's habit of reading my mind was alarming most of the time. Today it didn't bother me.

"The competition could be rough," Penny muttered.

"Lola said the ELT's happy just being one of the finalists."

"Finalist shminalist. We're in it to win it. But some of the big guns have been here before. *Harvey* was the odds-on favorite, but since they got deep-sixed by food poisoning, word is that *Mousetrap* and *Death of a Salesman* are the ones to beat." Penny was pleased with herself. "I did my homework." She narrowed her eyes. "Spoiler alert. *Cinderella* could be a dark horse. People love that fairy-tale crap."

"What about *King Lear*? It has gravitas. Shakespeare?" When the ELT did *Romeo and Juliet*, the word "gravitas" was tossed around like a freshly made salad.

Penny hooted. "Not a chance. Anyway, who wants to see scenes about an old guy blinding himself and then marrying one of his three daughters."

Penny's mash-up of *King Lear* and *Oedipus Rex* was obvious even to me, and I hadn't been an English lit or drama major in college. "I think you've got your kings mixed up."

"Whatever. The ELT's got to pull up its bootstraps. Later, O'Dell."

Penny sauntered off. Across the theater, Walter chewed his nails and gestured to Lola, whose attention was focused on an attractive, gray-haired man from the Westfield company. I glanced at the stage. Sam Baldwin paced back and forth and talked on a cell phone. Was Grody on the other end of the call telling Sam about my theme food suggestion? Sam didn't look overjoyed at whatever he was hearing. My hors d'oeuvres weren't such a hot idea? Ultimately, it wasn't my responsibility. Grody and Sam could work it out.

I waved to Lola, who now stood, patient, as Walter spoke urgently in her ear. I headed out into the sunshine. After all, this was my vacation, and the surf and sand were calling. I strolled down the boardwalk and over a block to my rental, feeling more relaxed. The shore had a way of doing that to me. I even felt calmer about Jackson. I should trust him and let him work out his own issues as far as Vinnie's death was concerned. And encourage him to find a motel before Bill's arrival.

I was happy about my decisions and bounded up the steps to the bungalow. "Jackson? I'd like to talk to you."

No answer. I stuck my head in the living room, knocked on the guest bedroom door, even peered into the master bedroom, though I couldn't imagine why Jackson would wander in there. As if. I was irrationally irritated. Jackson had every right to be out and about in Candle Beach, but I had made up my mind to clear the air. Now I would have to postpone our truce.

Never mind. The beach was calling me to get some rays for the next couple of hours. I changed into a blue-striped bathing suit, stuffed a towel, suntan lotion, and my book into my beach bag, and popped on my sunglasses. I locked the door—Jackson would have to fend for himself if he came back before I did—and turned to go. My eye caught his belongings strewn about at the end of the porch, draped over the rocking chair, and partially tucked under an open sleeping bag. Jackson's sloppiness was one trait from his past that remained. His trail of debris everywhere he went used to drive me crazy.

I dropped my beach bag, scooped up several T-shirts and two pairs of shorts, and placed them into a duffel. I straightened out the sleeping bag and folded a jacket he'd tossed on the chair. My hand grazed the inside pocket and felt a lumpy object. My curiosity was always on high alert, but even more so now that Jackson had been designated a "person of interest."

I instinctively glanced down the street—no one walking by at the moment. I knew I was trespassing, but someone had to figure out what Jackson was up to. I withdrew the object—an envelope containing folded bills. I flipped through them. This was a lot of money. A scribbled IOU for nine thousand dollars signed by Vinnie and dated the day before Vinnie's body was found washed up on the beach was also in the envelope. My heart clunked. What was this about? Why was Jackson sleeping on my porch with this kind of dough in his possession? Did the money and IOU have anything to do with Vinnie's death? I jammed the envelope back into the jacket pocket.

* * * *

"Yoo-hoo! Dodie! We're over here!" The Banger sisters flapped their aged arms and gestured for me to join them.

Yikes! I had planned on a solo sunbathing afternoon, soaking up enough rays to chill out before Bill's arrival. That ship obviously had sailed. I waved back and gamely trudged through the hot sand to a spot halfway down the beach, where citizens of Etonville, including actors, had staked out a decent-sized chunk of the Jersey Shore. They were settling in for the duration despite Penny's warning about sunburn and makeup and the tech rehearsal later this afternoon. Actors Romeo, Abby, and Edna were ramming beach umbrellas into the sand while townsfolk Mildred, her husband Vernon, and the elderly Banger sisters smoothed blankets. Carol and her teenage son Pauli, my personal tech guru when it came to digital forensics, unpacked a cooler.

"Hey," Pauli said as I approached.

"Hey yourself." I gave him a hug and he blushed. "Nice to see you here."

"Janice had to go visit her relatives in Boston so…" He shrugged. Pauli had met Janice, his new, probably first serious squeeze, during an ELT co-production of *Bye, Bye, Birdie* with the Creston Players earlier this summer. She was a senior at Creston High. As far as Pauli was concerned, a trip to the shore with his mother was better than staying home. "I'm taking shots of the ELT rehearsing today. For their website." In addition to his extensive knowledge of all things Internet-based, Pauli had been designated the theater's photographer. He was a young man of many talents.

"Dodie, this is our first time on a beach in years, don'tcha know," said one of the Banger sisters.

"We're going to get wonderful tans," said the other.

"You'd better slather on that sunscreen or it will be a wonderful sunburn," I warned with a smile.

They nodded in unison, their permed gray hair bobbing around their delighted faces.

"Dodie, how were things at the theater?" Carol asked. "Ready for the tech later? I think Lola's a little nervous, what with the ELT's becoming a finalist so late."

I had an image of Maddy throwing her clipboard around and Penny's intel on which theaters were the ones to watch. "All good."

Carol doled out sandwiches. "Because I heard that the groups from Cape May and Hackettstown—"

"—*Sound of Music* and *Noises Off*—" Abby interjected and accepted a tuna salad on rye.

"…were the ones to beat."

Could Penny be that wrong? "I heard *The Mousetrap* and *Death of a Salesman* had the inside track."

Mildred, director of the church choir at St. Andrews in Etonville, opened a bag of potato chips and held it out to her husband, Vernon, who was lying on his back with earphones plugged into his ears. "I wouldn't believe any of it. The Etonville Little Theatre has as good a chance as any of those other theaters," she said emphatically. "Vernon! Chips?" she shouted.

"I'd say *Arsenic*'s a 10-45A," said Edna proudly.

"Translate, please," begged Mildred.

Edna chuckled. "The patient's in excellent condition."

I popped the top off a can of seltzer. Carol rubbed lotion on her arms and legs and passed the bottle to Pauli. The Banger sisters, taking my warning seriously, covered themselves with oversized beach towels. Romeo, oblivious to the sun's dangers, refused Edna's offer to share her suntan lotion and stood, stretching and scanning the beach. Flexing muscles, he slipped on his sunglasses.

Carol ogled the actor and murmured, "Could those swim trunks get any tinier?"

I opened one eye. "What swim trunks?" We giggled like schoolgirls. Romeo modeled his bikini beachwear until two teenagers traipsed by, giving him a second glance. He followed them to the water.

Geez.

"Where's Bill today?" Carol asked.

"He had a last-minute court appearance. Couldn't be postponed," I said.

"That's too bad. And during his vacation." Mildred tsked.

Edna sat up. "The wheels of justice never stop turning." She bit into a potato chip. "The chief has to deal with that."

"It's still too bad," said Carol.

"How's Jackson doing?" Edna asked.

"Who's Jackson?" asked one of the Bangers.

Did Edna have to bring him up? "He's...an old friend," I said.

"An old *boyfriend*, I hear," Carol teased.

"Lah-dee-dah," said the other Banger.

"He's been sleeping on Dodie's front porch," Carol murmured.

Heads swiveled to see my reaction. How did Carol find out this quickly? Had to be from Lola. No place was safe from Etonville gossip...not even the Jersey Shore.

"He happened to be in town and needed a place to stay," I said lamely.

"He was nice." Edna.

"Kinda cute. I liked his man bun." Abby.

"Of course, he's not Bill." Carol.

Right. A gull swooped in squawking, then dove onto some food half-buried in the sand. Saved by a bird! Pauli wandered down to the water, and soon he and Romeo were splashing and diving and swimming through the waves. The Banger sisters tiptoed hand in hand to the waterline, making footprints in the wet sand, retreating up the beach when the ocean swells rolled in. Carol fell asleep, and Edna, Mildred, and Vernon played a game of gin rummy. I settled into the warm sand and pictured the money I'd found in Jackson's possession.

The sun ascended.

* * * *

My cell buzzed, and I opened one eye. It was three o'clock. Had I been sleeping for an hour? Bill texted that he was sitting in Parkway traffic due to an accident and not to count on him for happy hour. More like dinner. I texted that it was fine and to meet me at the Sandbar whenever he arrived. I'd kill time jawing with Grody. Then Lola texted: *Stop by the rehearsal if you're bored! Haha!*

The ELT crew packed up their beach paraphernalia and headed to the Windward to shower before the tech rehearsal. I planned to do the same. Even if I stopped by Grody's before dinner, I had a couple of hours to kill. A good opportunity to give Lola some moral support.

I said good-bye to Mildred, Vernon, and the Banger sisters, who opted to give the sun another half hour, and ambled back to the bungalow. The porch was empty, Jackson's belongings exactly where I'd left them. I sprang into the shower and scrubbed the afternoon's oil and sweat off my skin. Then pulled on white three-quarter pants and a pale blue tank top that flaunted my tan and muscled upper arms. No harm in letting Bill see what he'd missed the past twenty-four hours…

The boardwalk was filling up with strolling sunbathers, kids running in and out of the arcade, and tourists heading to happy hour. I power walked its length until I reached the end, glancing at the line of luxury boats moored at the pier and shivering at the memory of being unceremoniously kicked off the premises. Vinnie's boat was exactly where I'd seen it last night.

Unlike my previous two visits to the theater, milling groups swarmed around the entrance and spilled into the gazebo, many in costume. Actors in modified Elizabethan dress lounged next to a handful of nuns and young children in lederhosen. The cast of *Arsenic and Old Lace*, sporting 1940s gear, stood under a cluster of palm trees. Romeo's face and arms were red. Penny wore her you-should-have-gotten-off-the-beach-sooner expression. Pauli fiddled with his camera, snapping casual, unposed shots.

Lola spotted me. "We're running behind schedule. We should be going on in fifteen minutes but it's anybody's guess." Lola twisted a section of her blond hair. It was a nervous gesture.

Penny had schooled me well: There was real time, theater time, and tech time… "Things always run slowly at a first tech, right? And with seven different shows to account for, moving scenery must take extra time." I was my supportive BFF self.

Lola squeezed my hand. "I could do with some chardonnay," she said.

"Later," I muttered.

Maddy thrust her body out the door of the theater and, to my utter amazement, blew on a whistle around her neck. She out-tooted Penny! Every conversation came to a standstill with the shriek. Maddy examined her clipboard. "I need *Sound of Music* on deck and *Arsenic and Old Lace* in the house. Pronto."

Penny rolled her eyes—she had finally met her match—and the two companies followed Maddy into the theater. *The Sound of Music* stood in the wings ready for their tech while the ELT sat in the first row of the house, as per Maddy's instruction. I hunkered down in the last row to keep out of Maddy's line of vision. I had no desire for a second run-in with her. The stage was empty save for a stack of two-foot-square black boxes. Where was the set for *Death of a Salesman*? The actors from that show moved from one spot to another as the light crew tinkered with instruments, adjusting focus, and Maddy yelled "Go!" and "Hold!"

Penny, apparently bored, wandered to the back of the house as the crew set up for *The Sound of Music* and the ELT actors headed backstage. She sat down next to me.

"Where's the scenery?" I asked sotto voce.

Penny assumed her world-weary expression. "On the stage."

"Those cubes are the set? For every show? They're so…black." I said.

"O'Dell, this is a black box theater. Those are the black box sets. Duh." She toyed with her whistle. No doubt wishing she could use it.

"I get it. But they're a little…plain…for a theater festival," I murmured.

"The set's not the point. It's the acting, the directing, the costumes. There's no time to get sets on and off the stage with seven shows. Anyway, black boxes save money." Penny shifted her focus to the stage, where the cast of *The Sound of Music* was singing about the hills being alive. "See that actor on the end? She thinks she's Julie Andrews. I caught her warming up an hour ago in the ladies' room. She tried to carry a tune in a bucket. No dice," Penny cackled.

Maddy shot a glare into the house, and Penny and I scrunched down in our seats like bad kids avoiding the principal's reprimand. I'd been there, done that in grade school. And on the tech went, the Austrian kids with

Maria, their nanny, singing "Do-Re-Mi" and "My Favorite Things." Maddy
hussled them along from light cue to light cue.

My cell vibrated. Grody sent a text wanting to know if I was at the
theater and if I'd seen Sam Baldwin. He'd left a message for Sam but
hadn't been able to speak in person. Would I mind speaking with Sam if
he was around and obtain his approval of the theme food hors d'oeuvres?
Of course, I texted back.

Maddy yelled "Places," for *Arsenic and Old Lace*. Penny hauled herself
out of her seat. "Showtime," she said grimly.

Walter maneuvered his cast for the first beats of a scene between Edna
and Abby as the Brewster sisters. It was approaching the dinner hour
and Bill would be here soon. Lola would understand if I snuck out. Sam
Baldwin had not made an entrance this afternoon, so Grody could follow
up with him later.

I signaled my departure to Pauli, who was discreetly taking photos
of the ELT actors, and exited the theater, appreciating the late afternoon
breeze after sitting inside. I sauntered past the gazebo and stopped when
I heard a voice. It was Sam on his cell. He wasn't visible, but his side of
the conversation was audible. I hesitated. I could wait a few seconds to see
if his call ended, but then it would seem as though I was eavesdropping.

"I said 'no.' We're done with that guy," he growled. "Cut him loose.
We'll find other transport."

*This wasn't the voice of a patron of a theater festival. It belonged to a
mob boss. Like from* The Sopranos.

Grody could handle this himself. I turned away.

"You want something?" Sam stood in the center of the gazebo addressing
me, his stare cold and unwelcoming.

"Uh…well…yes. Grody from the Sandbar asked me to speak with you
about the food for the opening night party. The hors d'oeuvres named for
each of the plays?" I added helpfully.

Sam studied me. "Sure. Tell Grody the food's fine." He lit a cigar. "Was
that hors d'oeuvre thing your idea?"

His change of tone caught me off-guard. "As a matter of fact, yes."

"Uh-huh. Smart."

Was he sizing me up? "Thanks. I'll tell Grody the menu's fine." As I
dashed off, I could feel his eyes boring a hole through the back of my skull.
Whoa.

I was happy to reach the boardwalk. Sam Baldwin gave me the creeps.
The descending sun meant it was time to hit the Sandbar and check in
with Grody. My mind wandered about, jumping from thoughts of Sam

and the theme food hors d'oeuvres to the ELT's tech rehearsal to Jackson's predicament to Bill's arrival. I hadn't received any updates on the Garden State Parkway traffic.

The boardwalk was crowded. Families and pairs left the beach for drinks, dinner, arcade games, and rides. Up ahead a small assembly of people had gathered near a bench that looked out on the ocean. One person stood in the center of the group and held out a newspaper. I slowed down, something making my skin crawl. I eased to the edge of the gathering and took in the comments:

"I can't believe it."

"In Candle Beach? What's the shore coming to?"

"Poor guy."

"My cousin knew him. They were fishing buddies."

I peered over the shoulder of a young woman. She turned to me. "Like, murder here? I mean, that's like something in the movies."

"Who was murdered?" I asked, but I already knew the answer.

"Vinnie Carcherelli. At first police said it was a simple drowning. More than that now," said the guy whose cousin fished with Vinnie. "Damn."

* * * *

Palm trees surrounding the perimeter of the Sandbar swayed in the gentle wind while the tiki torches scattered shadows throughout the seating area and onto the sand. I sat at the bar sipping my drink and nibbling on fried clams. The restaurant was full, as it undoubtedly was most nights this summer, and Grody played the role I usually found myself inhabiting— keeping one eye on the open-air kitchen and the other on his customers. Moving from table to table to confirm that everyone was satisfied and pleased with their dinners.

"Crazy-busy night," he said as he paused behind the bar to fill a glass of water.

"Business is rocking. Can't knock that." We clinked glasses.

"You got that right."

"You see the *Candle Beach Courier*? They put out a special afternoon edition."

"Vinnie was well known in Candle Beach. People liked him. Or at least they tolerated him when he'd had one too many. He threw money around like he was drowning in the stuff." Grody took a drink of his water. "Sorry. Bad comparison."

"The article said the medical examiner found evidence that Vinnie had died before he was submerged in water. No water in his lungs," I said.

"Yeah. It's called dry drowning."

"What's that?" I asked.

"Years ago, a surfer from Ocean Port got hit on the head with a board and died." Grody snapped his fingers. "Just like that. When they pulled his body out of the ocean and did an autopsy, his lungs were dry. He died before he inhaled water."

"You're suggesting that something happened to Vinnie and then he was... what? Dumped overboard?"

"And his body washed up on the shore," Grody said.

"Never mind washing up on the shore. Maybe he was only dunked in the water and then dumped on the beach," I said and drained the last of my wine. "To make it appear like a drowning."

Grody regarded me carefully. "Henry told me about the murders in Etonville and how you 'assisted the police,'" he said.

I shrugged. "My instincts were helpful on a couple of occasions," I said modestly.

"Not according to Henry. He says...how did he put it...you were the 'investigative linchpin' more than once."

Wow! "Henry said that?" I didn't realize my boss paid much attention to what I did outside the Windjammer.

Grody leaned over the bar and murmured, "You got any instincts operating now?"

I chuckled. Then got serious. "Only that Jackson is in deep water and has no clue how to get himself out of it. Talk about drowning."

He refilled a bowl of peanuts, nibbled a few.

"The police claim Jackson's a person of interest, being one of the last people to see Vinnie alive and..." I hesitated. Could I share what I'd discovered with Grody? "Between us..."

Grody studied me. "Yeah?"

"I accidentally found a wad of bills in his jacket pocket."

"Accidentally?" Grody grinned despite the gravity of the conversation.

"I was cleaning up his clothes that were thrown around my front porch where I, and Bill, have been letting him sleep out of the kindness of our hearts, and I folded his jacket and I accidentally touched something and had to investigate—"

"—of course."

"—and there it was. Or they were. The money and an IOU signed by Vinnie," I said.

"How much?" he asked.

"I didn't count it, just fanned through it. Hundreds. Could be a thousand."

Grody let out a soft whistle.

"Right."

We were silent for a moment.

"What does Bill think about Jackson? He's a cop, after all," Grody said.

"He's told me more than once that I have an overactive imagination and to keep my nose out of other people's affairs. Including Jackson. He even offered to rent a motel room to get him off our porch."

Grody arched an eyebrow. "Looks like Jackson could pay his own way."

Where was my former ex anyway? "I should tell Bill to forget the motel. Save his bucks for Jackson's bail," I said, only half-joking.

"Hey, settle down. It won't come to that." Grody patted my hand.

"I don't know. Bill's probably right. I should cut Jackson loose and stay out of his life. But…we have history." Grody nodded sympathetically. "My aunt Maureen used to say 'when your past calls, hang up and pretend it's a wrong number.'"

"Great advice. And speaking of Bill…" Grody said quickly.

I was so caught up in Vinnie's murder and Jackson's plight I hadn't noticed the hunky guy standing behind me! I whipped around. "Hey there, stranger." Bill embraced me enthusiastically and planted a big one on my lips. *Yowza!* "Guess you missed me."

"Guess I did," Bill plonked down on a bar stool next to mine. "What's for dinner? I'm starved."

"Crab specials tonight," Grody said and signaled a waiter to bring menus. "Let's get you two a table….or else a room," he said.

We laughed. It was terrific to see Bill unwinding and playful. The circles under his eyes had disappeared, the tension in his body melting away. Ditching Etonville—except for yesterday's court appearance—was healthy for him.

Grody sat us personally at a table on the sand and took our orders. Soft shell crabs for Bill, crab legs for me with sides of roasted Jersey corn and tomatoes. And a pricey bottle of wine compliments of the house. I loved Grody. Almost as much as Bill…

6

"C'mon, it'll be fun," Bill said and tucked my hand into his as we strolled down the boardwalk.

"But I haven't golfed in years," I said and shivered. It had gotten downright chilly during our dinner on the sand. The shore had a way of doing that, the temperature dropping unexpectedly.

Bill put his jacket around me. "That better? Besides, it's not real golf. I don't play either. This is miniature golf."

I knew all about miniature golf. I'd spent hours and hours on the course as a teenager, but I hadn't held an iron in my hands in over a decade. "Okay, but I'm not letting you off easy. I used to be a very respectable player."

Bill studied me. "I don't picture you as the athletic type."

"Oh, so there's only one athlete in the family?" I said, then stopped myself. Is that what we were becoming? Family. It had a comfortable ring to it, and—

"Guess you can take the folks out of Etonville…" He jerked his head in the direction of the golf course up ahead.

Sheesh. Mildred, Vernon, Edna, and Penny stepped out of the payment line, putters and balls in hand. "Do you think they saw us?" I took Bill's arm. "Let's run back to the bungalow and pretend we didn't see them. That way—"

"Hi, Dodie! Hi, Chief!" Edna waved to us.

"Too late," Bill muttered and put his quirky smile on display.

"Candle Beach isn't big enough for all of us." I waved back.

"Might as well be good sports about it."

We approached the miniature golf entrance. "You're in an awfully chipper mood," I said.

"Must be the wine…or the company." He squeezed my hand.

Yowza.

The course was busy with twosomes and families trying their hands at knocking the ball into the cup while bypassing miniature windmills, tunnels, and sand traps. It was slow going with the Etonville crew ahead of us: Mildred giving advice to Vernon, who pretended he didn't hear her and pointed to his ears; Edna painstakingly lining up each shot and insisting that if she banked off the side she'd get the elusive hole in one and win a free game; Penny taking half a dozen strokes for each hole, and then banging her iron on the fake grass in frustration.

"O'Dell," she said. "This is harder than real golf."

"You golf?" I asked.

"Back in the day," she said.

What day was that?

"Driving the golf cart was the best part." Penny whacked the ball. "I'm only three over par on this hole."

"Keep up the great work," I said and lined up my own ball.

"What hole is this?" Bill asked quietly.

I pointed to the flag. It was only the ninth hole and we'd been on the course for an hour. It was like watching paint dry.

He groaned. "Miniature golf was a super idea."

"Next time I'll come up with the post-dinner game," I said suggestively.

"Dodie! Calm down…" he said and knocked his ball into the cup. He wrote down his score. "I'm ahead by two strokes."

"Not for long." The ninth hole featured a sloping fairway and a moving windmill. Back in *my* day, if I timed my stroke perfectly, the ball spun between the rotating blades and plunked into the cup for a hole in one. I gripped the putter and knocked the ball. It spun forward, just managed to scoot between the blades, then spun out the back of the windmill and into the cup. The Etonville crew erupted in applause.

"Yes!" I said triumphantly.

"Dodie, you've got magic with that putter. I'm glad at least one of us has a hole in one," said Edna.

"You can have my free game."

"Say, that guy's death was a 10-55," Edna said.

Bill placed his ball on the tee. "What guy?"

"Vinnie—"

Edna jumped in. "Name's Vincent Carcherelli."

"What's a 10-55?" asked Mildred, picking up her ball after a bunch of strokes and placing it in the cup.

"Coroner case," Edna said.

"Is that the charter boat operator you knew?" Bill lined up his shot.

"O'Dell, you knew the victim? Oops. Not a good sign," said Penny.

"He was an acquaintance from my past. When I lived down here before Hurricane Sandy," I said.

"I'm so sorry you lost a friend," said Mildred sympathetically.

"Thanks. We weren't close. He was a friend of Jackson's," I said before thinking.

"I like Jackson. Really nice last night serving the snacks and all," said Edna.

Bill paused midstroke. "Last night?"

Geez.

"We had a rehearsal at your place. Thanks for the hospitality," she added.

"Don't mention it." Bill's eyebrows inched upward.

I bent over to retrieve my ball. "I'll explain later."

We completed the course by eleven and parted company with the Etonville crowd, who headed to the hotel two blocks from the boardwalk. "Dodie, are you coming by the theater for the dress rehearsal tomorrow night?" asked Edna.

"Maybe. I'll see how the day goes."

Bill and I headed off in the opposite direction. Once we were alone, he faced me. "So what's going on with Jackson? And this Vincent guy?"

"You heard Edna. It was a 10-55," I said. "At first the newspaper said it was a drowning, so according to Grody, people suspected that Vinnie had one too many and fell overboard. His boat was found drifting off the shoreline."

"But...?"

"Today's paper said the investigation revealed evidence that Vinnie was murdered," I finished.

"That's it?" he asked.

"What do you mean?"

"I mean, that's all you know about the death of this Vincent Carcherelli? Partner of your old flame?"

Bill was a little touchy. "Why should I know more?" I asked, pretending innocence.

"Dodie, you tend to get yourself involved in the murder investigations of people you're acquainted with."

"That's back in Etonville. I'm on vacation here." I slipped my hand in his, attempting to change the subject.

"I hope so." Bill put an arm around my shoulder.

The boardwalk was emptier now that it was edging toward midnight. I pulled Bill's jacket tighter around my midsection to ward off the gusts blowing in from the ocean and glanced up at the stars. A jet-black sky was dotted with bits of white. There were no skies like this in North Jersey. Only down the shore. Were Bill's constellations on view tonight?

"...and Jackson?" he asked.

"Sorry. Got distracted by the night sky." I leaned into his body and grasped his right arm. "What did you call that one?" I pointed upward. "Ursa Minor?"

"Ursa Major."

"Last I checked, Jackson's belongings were still on our front porch. Neatly folded, however," I said lightly. "He spent last night with someone else, so I'm hoping he's planning on bunking there tonight."

I neglected to mention Jackson's interviews with the Candle Beach Police Department—in our living room and at the station—as a person of interest because he had a history with his old partner and had seen Vinnie the day before the murder. Making him one of the last people to see Vinnie alive. I also avoided mentioning the fight on the boardwalk and the contents of Jackson's pocket. Bill wouldn't approve of me rifling through clothing, but my intentions were pure. For the most part. I wanted Jackson out of our lives, and the most efficient way to do it was to clear up any suspicious behavior on his part that would entangle him further in the murder investigation of Vinnie C. Revealing all of this to Bill would only complicate my life.

Bill paused on our screened-in porch. No trace of our boarder. "Jackson had been a friend of Vinnie's. The Candle Beach police will want to interview him."

"You think so?" I asked and unlocked the door, flicked on a light, and headed to the kitchen for a glass of water. And to avoid Bill's scrutiny. He had a way of reading me that could be unnerving.

"Are you telling me everything about Jackson?" He stepped up behind me, his arms around my waist. I smelled the musky scent of his aftershave and felt his muscled torso pressing against my back.

Had he guessed that I was holding out? This required a full-frontal attack. "Mmm." I rotated in his arms and kissed him squarely on the mouth. That ended the Jackson discussion...

* * * *

I gazed into the dark of the bedroom with only a thin slice of moonlight that had crept in under the window shade providing illumination. The digital alarm clock read 2 a.m. I'd been awake for an hour, tossing this way and that under the sheet, afraid that I would disturb Bill. No danger there; his breathing was deep and regular. *This was ridiculous.* I eased to the edge of the bed and executed a rollover that barely jiggled the mattress but landed my feet on the floor. I pulled on a T-shirt and shorts and padded noiselessly to the living room, where I switched on a table lamp.

A series of notions jostled one another in my mind, each pushing the other out of the way to grab first in line: What specific evidence did the Candle Beach police have that convinced them Vinnie was murdered? *Had Vinnie been killed somewhere else and dumped on the beach?* And—I gulped—what did Jackson know about the murder? When we talked this morning, he had been a person of interest. What was he now? And for that matter, where was he now?

Sleep was miles off yet, so I opened my laptop. What did I know about Vinnie Carcherelli besides him being Jackson's partner in the charter boat business before the hurricane? Neither he nor Jackson was very capable in the bookkeeping department, their venture continually teetering on the brink of disaster. Vinnie was a happy time Charlie and liked to party; he had no steady girlfriend when I knew him. That was it.

I typed his name in the search bar of my computer. Up popped a handful of links for four different Vincent Carcherellis—an account manager in Florida, a photographer in the Bronx, and two in Italy. A father and a son. Vinnie C's links consisted of newspaper articles on his death, and further back, one from a year ago, about the opening of his new charter enterprise with a shot of a beaming Vinnie standing in the hull of *The Bounty*. The article described how Vinnie had lost his previous boat due to the ravages of Hurricane Sandy—and bad management, if you asked me—and that he and his partner would soon be serving visitors to the Jersey Shore. The writer ended the story wishing the twosome smooth sailing. A puff piece with few details and no mention that the new boat business had a particular wealthy clientele in mind. Who was the other unnamed partner and what was his or her status, and that of the business, now that Vinnie was dead? *Did Jackson have any idea?*

I was wide awake and had no intention of spending the rest of the night flip-flopping in bed, preventing Bill from getting a decent night's sleep. So I cleared Vinnie's name, typed in "dry drowning," and clicked on the first link, a definition and discussion. Though Grody was correct in his description of the condition—no water in the victim's lungs—curiously it was a medically discredited term. In 2002, a World Congress on Drowning established a consensus definition: Drowning was the process of experiencing respiratory impairment from submersion or immersion in liquid and that the end result of hypoxemia (low oxygen in the blood), acidemia (abnormal acidity of the blood), and death was the same regardless of whether water entered the lungs. Experts discouraged the use of the terms "wet drowning" and "dry drowning" to avoid significant confusion and because the terms were not relevant to drowning care. Huh.

However, the term *was* significant if it indicated that someone had murdered Vinnie on a dry dock and dumped him on the beach to give the impression of a drowning. What about Vinnie's blood alcohol level? According to both Jackson and Grody, Vinnie was famous for tippling a bit too much. Drinking could have contributed to his death. No doubt the toxicology report from the autopsy would confirm if that was the case.

I leaned into the sofa cushions and closed my eyes. I waited a moment. Nope, I wasn't ready yet to head to bed. My fingers played over the keyboard of my laptop. I looked at my email, the shore weather for the next five days, and researched new casserole recipes. I'd been encouraging Henry to experiment with some one-dish specials at the Windjammer. Like chili rellenos, cheesy broccoli and quinoa with sausage, a variation on a creamy tuna noodle casserole...

I yawned. On a whim I typed "Sam Baldwin Jersey Shore" into the search bar. The results were surprising. The link describing his Baldwin General Contractors was straightforward, and a website provided an overview of the company. Services included additions, renovations, bathrooms, and kitchens, with a mention of carpentry, masonry, roofing, and siding. A portfolio page boasted photos of completed remodeling projects, and the "About Us" page described the founding of the company in 1990, listed reviews from satisfied customers, and included a picture of Sam and his wife, Arlene, sitting on an outside deck. Presumably one he'd built. Sam's business appeared to be a very successful enterprise. I studied the photo. Both Sam and his wife looked as if they were in their early forties. It had to have been taken a while ago.

I went back to the Internet links. Though I knew he was a benefactor of the New Jersey Community Theater Festival, his philanthropy extended far beyond the arts. Article after article described his donations to various institutions in the area: a hospital wing, a school athletic field, the Candle Beach library, an aquarium... If the articles were to be believed, Sam was a sugar daddy of the Jersey Shore. Not exactly the impression I got from interacting with him.

What startled me were the links illustrating Sam's activities since the destruction of Hurricane Sandy. I'd read newspaper stories and seen a *60 Minutes* segment on construction and insurance fraud after the brutal storm. But in recent years I hadn't paid a ton of attention to the ongoing reconstruction crises. Skimming stories on the storm revealed examples of price gouging, swindling, and theft by shady contractors and scam artists to the tune of millions of dollars. Some residents of the shore area were assaulted twice:

first by the hurricane and then by greedy predators. Without much effort, I am back in 2012. I can hear the roaring of the wind, see branches from the elm tree in my front yard crashing through the roof of my home at the height of Sandy's wrath. I shuddered. It was this devastation that had driven me to North Jersey.

Sam Baldwin was actually one of the good guys. Not only was he an honest contractor—according to testimonials—but he'd made it a point to combat the dishonest members of his profession by holding town hall meetings on how to avoid being a victim of unscrupulous companies and how to navigate the tangle of state and federal red tape that was wrapped around relief programs. There were photos of Sam shaking hands with shore residents, municipal government officials, and the governor. Another link went to an article on Sam hosting a party for children of homeowners victimized by the storm at the Candle Beach amusement park. Kids played in the arcade and enjoyed the rides. I was impressed...my outlook on Sam shifted about three hundred and sixty degrees.

I jumped, startled by a light *thunk* from outside my bungalow. Possibly Jackson returning. Late, or early, depending on one's point of view.

I set my laptop aside, opened the front door, and muttered, "Jackson, where have you been? We need to..." I paused and glanced around. No sign of my errant former boyfriend. His pile of belongings was undisturbed. A creepy sensation freaked me out. Was the noise my imagination? Did it originate from one of the properties next door? The houses on both sides were dark. All on the street was quiet.

I could rouse Bill, but why disrupt his sleep if it was only a nighttime house noise or some non-human critter nosing around the perimeter of the place? Such as a raccoon investigating the trash. I stepped inside and shut the door quickly. I needed to get back into bed, where any wayward noises were drowned out by Bill's—

"Yo."

A tap on my back. "Arrgh!" My heart shot into my mouth.

"Shh! You'll wake the house," Jackson admonished me.

I whacked his arm.

"Ouch. Cut that out." He ducked away from me.

"Why are you sneaking up on me? And how did you get in here?" I pushed him onto the screened-in porch. He collapsed into the comfy rocking chair. An outdoor lamp provided enough illumination to see how guarded and stricken Jackson looked.

"First of all, I wasn't sneaking in the house. The porch door was locked, and then I remembered how you used to leave back doors open in case you forgot a key," he said wearily.

Had I left the back door unlocked subconsciously? "You look worse than you did this morning. What's going on?" I asked, a trifle kinder.

Jackson blew out air from between pursed lips and tugged on his earlobe. Oh no...I could *not* take another round of lies and evasions from him. "I recognize that sign."

He self-consciously put his hands in his lap. "You always could read me, Dod."

"Jackson, have you heard what's happening?" I asked quietly.

"About Vinnie? Yeah. I been thinking about blowing town. Head back to Iowa. Selling farm equipment's not so bad..."

My jaw dropped. "Blowing town? You are a person of interest in a murder investigation. Leaving town is the equivalent of confessing. Are you out of your mind?" I struggled to keep my voice and irritation under control. "Jackson, I want the truth about what went down with you and Vinnie."

He rubbed his eyes. "Not that again. Gimme a break—"

I poked him. "You're not going to sleep until I get the truth out of you."

The creaking of the rocking chair cut into the silence. The planes of Jackson's weary face created scary shadows. This was not the man I split up with years ago. His shoulders sagged, his cocky confidence melted away.

"Vinnie was, like, my man..." Jackson was about to cry. "When the *JV* was running we were, like, best bros. Did everything together." He smirked. "Well...almost everything."

"Right. Got it."

"Anyway, when Sandy hit and the *JV* was destroyed and you and I... well...things were rocky there."

"They were."

"It was time to move on. And my blood bro needed help." Jackson shrugged. "So, Iowa."

"Were you in touch with Vinnie while you were away?" I asked kindly, assuming an ounce of honey would get me more answers than a whole bottle of vinegar.

"Nah. Not for three years. Then he began emailing and texting last year. All about his new boat *The Bounty* and some job opportunities and did I want in. Truth is, I'm a class A salesman."

Didn't I know it. Jackson had sold me a bill of goods on many occasions. "I can sell anything. Almost anything. But tractors, harvesters, cultivators? Not my thing," Jackson said.

"So when Vinnie proposed bringing you onboard, so to speak…"
Jackson grinned innocently. "I hit the road and showed up here."

"With no funds and no place to stay?" I asked.

"I planned to bunk with Vinnie, but that was a no go. Then I heard from Grody about you being here and I thought, what the hell, maybe for old times' sake," he said.

"You and Vinnie met up and…what…talked about his new charter boat business?"

"Something like that," he said evasively.

"Did he give you any details? Like who his clients were?"

"Nope. Hey, where's Bill?" he asked suddenly.

"In bed. Where I should be—"

"Me too. Let's talk in the morning." Jackson headed to his stockpile of clothing. "Did you…fold my stuff?" He was suddenly wary.

"You left things in a mess." Instinct told me to keep my discovery of his money to myself.

"Sorry about that."

I felt vulnerable. "Jackson, you want to sleep in the guest bedroom?"

"Thanks but, like, I'm having fun out here. Kind of like sleeping under the stars." He snickered. "Anyway, need to give you and Bill some privacy."

That particular horse was out of the barn.

* * * *

I lay awake. But this time I mulled over my past with Jackson. What had drawn me to him? I was younger then—nearly ten years younger when we embarked on our relationship. He was cute, funny, always a great time. We laughed a lot and liked the same things: sunbathing, sailing, and seafood. We both spent a lot of hours on our jobs and were fairly loose about demands on each other's time. We took things easy. What had changed? Hurricane Sandy sobered us up. Forced us to confront reality—we weren't meant for each other, and life offered more interesting prospects. I wasn't sure Iowa had been all that productive for Jackson; however, Etonville had brought me Bill, friends, and work that I enjoyed. I loved my life. I didn't think Jackson could say the same.

7

"Dodie!" Bill's strangled cry yanked me from a pleasant dream. I was serving seafood hors d'oeuvres to a large, appreciative theater audience who chewed and smacked their lips.

"Wha—? What?" I sat upright in bed, my pulse racing. Bill held on to the doorjamb for support. Clearly distraught. He must have seen Jackson on the front porch. "I can explain. I was up late and Jackson showed up and he needed a place to sleep and I even offered him the bedroom but he said the porch was fine and—"

"Dodie! Stop!" He raised his hand like a patrol cop. "I don't care about Jackson."

He *was* upset. "What's the matter?" I hopped out of bed and grabbed my robe. It was only seven thirty.

"My car. It's gone." Bill tore at his hair, then opened and closed drawers as he jerked on jeans and a clean T-shirt. "I'll need your car."

My mind was fuzzy, craving caffeine to get it functioning. "What do you mean 'gone'?"

"Gone. As in, I left it parked on the street and now it isn't there."

He did? I couldn't remember. "Bill...what the...are you sure? Maybe you left it by the boardwalk and forgot. I've done that."

We both knew that wasn't Bill's MO; he was a police chief, after all. He had to keep track of where he left things. Like his automobile.

"I need to get to the Candle Beach police and make a report."

"Wait. I'm coming with you." Now it was my turn to tug on a T-shirt and jeans. "What were you doing up so early?"

"I was going to bring you breakfast in bed with donuts from the bakery. I went to the kitchen to put on the coffee and looked out the window. No BMW."

"I'm so sorry."

"Me too. Let's go."

I crossed my fingers that Jackson was asleep and that we didn't need to confront his presence. Too late. As we stepped onto the porch, his head poked out of the sleeping bag, his face covered in stubble, his long mane tousled. "Wassup, bro?"

"Never mind. Go back to sleep." I nudged Bill forward, but he paused in his tracks.

"Did you hear anything early this morning? Like an engine starting or somebody creeping around? My car's missing," Bill said.

"Dude, I am soooo sorry. But nada on the sound thing. 'Course, I sleep like a baby. So something like a car engine might've got by me."

Jackson was going to be no help. "Don't leave the house until I get back if you want to spend another night here," I said more sharply than I intended.

Bill scrutinized me and Jackson saluted. "I'll drive." I brushed past Bill, unlocked my MINI Cooper, and slid behind the wheel.

"A little harsh with him, weren't you?" Bill asked. "I mean, the poor guy's practically penniless."

If he only knew.

* * * *

Bill was so addled by his missing BMW that he didn't question my heavy foot on the accelerator. I raced down Varick Street and pulled into a parking space in front of the station. Bill was already out the door and halfway to the entrance before I could lock the MC. I caught up with him inside the station and looked around. Not completely unlike the Etonville Police Department: a dispatch window, an outer office manned by staff, a hallway that probably led to inner offices. The place was quiet, possibly because it was only 8 a.m. Bill approached the dispatch window. I stood behind him as he explained his problem. Then my eye caught an officer striding down the hall toward the lobby. It was the no-pleasantries, all-business cop who had interviewed Jackson at my rental. If he identified me, I would have to enlighten Bill about Jackson's situation. It was too early to tap-dance around the truth. Besides, he had enough on his mind and didn't need Jackson's dilemma piled on.

"I think I'll wait in the car. Better yet, I'll find us some coffee. Text me when you're finished here. Bye!" I said, ignoring Bill's quizzical expression, and took off.

I steered my MC onto Ocean Avenue, traveling a quarter of a mile until I reached the Candle Diner. I hurried inside, stood at the takeout counter, and waited for my order. I was shocked that Bill's car was missing. I knew that luxury automobiles, like BMWs, were hot-ticket items for thieves, but what truly mystified me was how someone drove the car away from the curb without any of us, especially Jackson, hearing something. Could he have been sleeping that deeply? He was exhausted when we spoke, but—

"It's Dodie, isn't it?" said a male voice.

Behind me stood the lovely gentleman who worked for Sam. "John! Nice to see you. How are things in the community theater world?"

He smiled, a scattering of laugh lines visible around his sparkling eyes, making him appear younger than his probable sixty years. "Coming along. I think Sam will be happy when the festival is over."

"I've seen his website. He must be a busy man."

John removed a straw fedora and dabbed at his forehead. "Are you planning to remodel your home?"

As if I owned a home to remodel. "Me? No way. Just curious about Sam. How does he have the time to babysit the theater event? I imagine his contracting business is booming."

"It is," said John. "But Sam has always been committed to his community."

"I noticed. His philanthropy, his work after Hurricane Sandy... impressive," I said.

"I'll pass on your compliments," John said warmly. "He's even delivering a eulogy for Vincent Carcherelli today."

The memorial service. There had been a mention of it in the *Candle Beach Courier*. "Was he a friend of Vinnie's?"

"A work acquaintance. But that's the way Sam is."

I accepted my coffees and pocketed the change. "Good luck with the festival."

John laughed. "We'll need it."

"Tonight's your dress rehearsal. I'm thinking of stopping by."

"Glad to have you on the premises. We appreciate calm, sensible people, such as yourself," he said.

I got it. Theater folks could be a mite zany as they drew near an opening. I had witnessed the wackiness at the ELT on numerous occasions. "Bye."

John stepped to the counter to place his order. I had no sooner opened the door to exit than my cell buzzed. Bill must be ready for pickup. I juggled the coffees and read the text. It was Lola: *What's up today? I'm free till afternoon. Lunch?* I hesitated. Who knew what was up or if Bill would require some man-handholding. I texted back that I wasn't sure and would call later.

I nosed my car into the beach traffic—sunbathers in Candle Beach emerged early to avoid the worst heat of the day—and drove to the police station. I parked and sipped my coffee; I had no intention of interrupting police business with a text. Bill would get in touch when he was ready. The sun was warm on my face and neck as I leaned out the window, little evidence of the humidity that would almost certainly descend on the town later. Despite the caffeine, I felt drowsy. I'd had only a few hours of sleep last night. My mind flitted like a butterfly from flower to flower...I fluttered from Bill's BMW to Vinnie's murder to Sam Baldwin and the theater festival. Sucking the nectar out of each event, I thought poetically, and visualized the home where Aunt Maureen had lived for many years in Ocean Port, not far from Candle Beach. Her yard was full of hydrangeas, roses, and a swarm of butterflies and bees, always fragrant, sweet, and warm. I missed her...

My eyes popped open. I *did* know what I'd be doing later this morning. I texted Lola and hoped Bill wouldn't be peeved at being deserted, especially on the day he'd lost his wheels. As if he read my mind from a distance, he sent me a one-word message: *Ready.*

* * * *

"Thanks." Bill slammed the passenger side door of my MC and flipped the lid off his container of coffee.

"Sorry it's not hot anymore."

"No problem. As long as it's caffeine." His brow puckered. "Were the police optimistic about getting the BMW back?"

"Not really. Turns out there's been a string of carjackings and thefts in towns along the shore for the last year. They've got some leads, but nothing's resulted in any arrests. Or in many recovered cars. They go after luxury models. Mercedes, Lexus, Maseratis, Porsches, and—"

"BMWs. Since you're a police chief, I'm hoping you'll get some extra attention."

"Dodie, it doesn't work like that. Down here I'm just another tourist."

We drove in silence for a minute. I'd never seen Bill so down. He loved that car as much as I'd loved my old Metro. When I'd had a slight run-in with a tree stump and some hedges while driving his car earlier this summer, Bill was downright miserable until the body work to remove the scratches and dents was completed.

"I don't understand how they got into the BMW and drove it away. Don't you have some high-end security devices in it?" I asked.

"Yeah, but apparently car thieves have high-end electronic devices to override anti-theft measures. They can use relay boxes to jam and transmit signals from a keyless fob in the vicinity of the car."

"You're kidding?"

"Nope. They're so smart they can attach universal key fobs to a car and record a code when the door is locked remotely. Once they're inside the car, all they need to do is press the Start button. Who stands a chance with that kind of high-tech theft?" He paused. "I don't understand how Jackson didn't hear anything."

"Maybe he did and thought it was our neighbor's car." I pulled into the driveway of our bungalow. "Why did you park on the street last night?"

Bill sighed. "I was in a hurry. To join you for dinner."

I switched off the engine. "What's next?" I asked softly.

"I'll drop by the station tomorrow to review my statement, pick up some more intel from the state car theft unit. They're working with local municipalities like Candle Beach," he said.

"Sounds like a plan," I said.

Bill reached for the door handle.

"By the way, did anyone mention Vinnie's murder?" I asked.

"No, why?"

"No reason." I tapped the steering wheel. "Well, actually Jackson is kind of a person of interest—"

"What?" Bill exclaimed.

"—he met with Vinnie the day before the murder and had a past relationship that…might have been rocky. Any chance you picked up some murder intel as well as car theft intel?"

He exhaled loudly. "Dodie, what's going on in that head of yours? No, don't tell me. I don't want to know." Bill opened the car door. "We're on vacation, right?"

"Right."

"I'm sorry about Jackson, but I can't help you out here," he said.

"Even to ask how it's going?"

"No," Bill said firmly.

"I understand how you feel about Jackson—"

"It's got nothing to do with how I feel about Jackson—"

"But he and I have a history and it's hard to walk away and pretend I'm not bothered by his...predicament," I finished lamely.

"Dodie, you and I have a history too," Bill said gently.

Which part of our history was Bill referring to? My participation in murder investigations or our relationship? "You're right. I shouldn't have asked you to nose around."

"I hope we never break up," he joked. "You'll be stalking me forever!"

"Very funny," I said as I got out of the car. Bill hugged my shoulders and kissed my forehead.

The porch door opened. Jackson stuck his head out. "Hey, bro. Any news?"

"Nope," Bill said.

"So breakfast would help. Got a delish Spanish omelet ready to go."

Bill perked up. "I could do with some food. And hot coffee." He went down the hallway to the bathroom.

"Coming right up." Jackson brandished a spatula and headed to the kitchen.

I followed, examining him. Gone were the grungy shorts and frayed T-shirt. Instead he sported khakis and a white button-down shirt. Both were badly wrinkled, but at least clean. His curly hair was neatly contained in his man bun. "What's the deal? You have clothes on," I said and poured Bill and myself cups of coffee, grateful that Jackson had assumed control of the kitchen.

"I do clean up well." He smirked, then leaned in closer, serious. "The dude's got some bad luck." Jackson flipped the omelet.

The dude certainly had. "So why the change in clothes? Got an appointment today?" I asked, hopeful.

"Nah. It's for Vinnie. His memorial service." Jackson glanced at the wall clock. "In an hour."

"Right. I read about it. I think I'll go with you."

Jackson rolled his eyes. "Dodie, I don't need a chaperone."

From bingeing on mysteries and thrillers, I knew that a funeral could be a clever friend to an investigator. Who came, who broke down, who spoke to whom. Bill had said on more than one occasion that funerals were excellent opportunities to gather investigative information. I'd seen him in action—out of uniform, expression neutral. Who would be in attendance at Vinnie's service?

"This isn't about you. It's about Vinnie." Or partly about Vinnie.

"What's about Vinnie?" Bill accepted the mug of coffee. "Something smells super."

"His memorial. It's this morning. I'm going," I said.

Bill considered my comment. "You were that close?"

"No," Jackson said.

I nodded and said, "Yes."

Bill took his cup of coffee and eyed us each in turn. "I'm going to sit on the beach and bake."

"Don't forget the sunscreen. You burn easily."

"That would be twice I'd get burned today." Bill propped his head on a fist.

Poor guy. Jackson garnished the Spanish omelet with green onions and tomatoes and delivered plates to the table. We all dove in. Conversation was sparse and light.

* * * *

After seeing Bill trek to the beach, Jackson and I drove down Ocean Avenue to the end of the boardwalk and the town park. The gazebo was surrounded by folding chairs on three sides. People had gathered, filling most of the seats, and Sam was sitting in the gazebo talking with several people, none of whom I'd seen before. Arlene Baldwin sat in the front row next to an older woman who could have been Vinnie's mother. Jackson insisted on planting himself down front. I refused to join him and found a seat in the last row. A great vantage point from which to scan the assembly and note who was present. I knew practically no one in Candle Beach except for Grody, Jackson, Vinnie—no longer with us—and the ELT bunch, who were probably soaking up rays and flirting with the kind of sunburn that would wreak havoc with their makeup *and* Penny. I chuckled to myself. Still, I was on the alert for suspicious behavior, whatever that might be.

"Scoot over, Dodie," Lola whispered.

"Lola? What are you doing here?" I asked and shifted one seat over.

"When you mentioned where you were going this morning, I thought, oh shoot, I shouldn't let you go to Vinnie's memorial alone." Lola inspected the crowd and smoothed her elegant white lace dress that set off her golden tan and blond hair. She looked spectacular. Lola knew how to rock a funeral. I glanced down at my capris and blouse. No competition. "Is Jackson here?"

Oh no… Was Lola boyfriend hunting? "He's down front. You didn't need to come. Vinnie wasn't that close a friend."

Lola was no fool. Her eyes widened, then narrowed. "You want to study the assembly and see if anybody appears shady."

Sheesh. Was I that obvious? "Keep that to yourself."

Lola had barely mimed zipping her lips when someone tapped my back. "Hi, Dodie."

It was the Banger sisters trailed by Edna, Carol, Mildred, and a clearly unenthusiastic Vernon. They trooped into the row in front of Lola and me. "What are you...?" Never mind. Why ask?

"We like a splendid funeral," said one of the sisters.

I corrected them. "It's not a funeral. Just a memorial service."

"Is there a body?" asked Vernon.

Mildred shushed him. "We're here to support Dodie. The deceased was her friend."

"We're like an 11-52," Edna whispered to Mildred and Vernon. "Funeral detail. Without the corpse."

"Dodie, how are you holding up?" asked Carol.

"Fine." I smiled my appreciation. You had to hand it to Etonville folks. Nothing brought out the spirited inner daffy of the town's citizens like a death.

A murmur went through the throng, then a hush fell over it. Sam stood and walked slowly to the edge of the gazebo and spoke into a microphone. He welcomed everyone, said how pleased Vinnie would have been to see old friends and Candle Beach acquaintances, and reminded the gathering to turn off their cell phones. He paused for a moment, then reviewed the order of the service: an invocation by a minister from a church Vinnie supposedly attended; a eulogy by Sam; remembrances by anyone who wished to speak; and, finally, a reading to close the service. We settled in and everyone bowed their heads for the prayer.

Next, Sam began to speak. He described Vinnie's vitality and love of life—I'd seen that in the past—and his entrepreneurial gifts for business ventures—that I had never seen. Vinnie had changed these last years... what had led to his abrupt shift in organizational skills? Sam continued on, recounting Vinnie's early days at the shore surfing and partying, then his maturation as he segued into the charter boat business—no mention of his partner Jackson. Odd. Sam's voice was soothing as he recalled Vinnie's life and added, regretfully, that his time had come too soon. No mention of the words "drowning" or "murder." Sam Baldwin was a mystery to me. A chameleon. A cigar-chomping, gravelly-voiced dock worker one moment and a comforting, community-minded colleague and philanthropist another. Which was the real Sam?

After about fifteen minutes, he invited anyone in attendance who wished to speak and offer a recollection of Vinnie to come forward. As usual at these services, unless you were in Etonville, individuals took some time to venture forth. A young woman from the front row awkwardly approached the microphone. She introduced herself as Maxine, Vinnie's fiancée. *Aha, now things were beginning to get interesting.* I craned my neck around Vernon. When I knew Vinnie, he was having fun playing the field, but obviously he'd opted to settle down. Maxine was a petite, twenty-something brunette dressed in a stylish black suit and heels. She carried a white handkerchief and dabbed at her eyes as she spoke. She appeared doll-like, fragile.

"Vincent was my soul mate, my best friend, my confidant," she began in a soft, wispy voice.

Hearts broke throughout the crowd as Maxine shared how they met at one of Sam's charity events—hmm—and their plans for the future. I tried to get a glimpse of Jackson to see his reaction, but he'd shifted his attention away from Maxine to study the houses beyond the park. Was this a passive-aggressive response to Vinnie's fiancée? It hadn't occurred to me before, but there was a possibility Jackson was jealous of Vinnie's new life: another boat, money, a future wife. Of course, Jackson had some money now... I wondered what would become of the IOU now that Vinnie could not pay up.

Maxine haltingly read a selection from *Jonathan Livingston Seagull* that she said was appropriate given Vinnie's life at the shore and anyway was one of his favorite books—really? The she broke down. Arlene leapt to her feet and escorted Maxine back to her seat. Other folks told stories, some funny, about their experiences with Vinnie, and the assembly responded appreciatively. Things were winding down and the service was ending when Jackson rushed to the gazebo. Sam, who had been about to bring the minister back to the microphone for the final prayer, paused and moved to the side.

Lola poked me. "Jackson's going to speak."

Oh no.

"So... I'm Jackson and I didn't know Vinnie like some of you. Like more recently." Jackson seemed nervous as he handled the mic. Unusual for him. "We were best buds back when. Before the big storm. Vinnie was my bro." Jackson exhaled noisily. Wow. Vinnie's death must be bothering him more than he'd been letting on. "We were partners. Our boat was the *JV*...for 'Jackson and Vinnie.'" He laughed uneasily and hesitated.

Lola leaned in to me whispering, "Is he done?"

"I hope."

Then Jackson roused himself. "I want to say miss ya, dude. The shore won't be the same without you. Won't be like those years we took the *JV* out...fishing...partying...the two of us...actually sometimes it was the three of us."

I stiffened. I had the sinking sensation I knew what was coming.

"Vinnie and me and Dodie. My girlfriend. Uh...ex-girlfriend. Dodie, you want to say something about Vinnie and those years?" Jackson pointed to me.

What I *wanted* to do was disappear into the ground, but people twisted in their seats to face me, including the row of ELT members, who were smiling with sympathy. I stood carefully.

"I'm Dodie. Jackson was right. He and Vinnie and I spent time on the *JV* in the years before Hurricane Sandy. Life was simpler then. After the hurricane hit, their charter boat business...ended." Mentioning Sandy had a sobering effect on everyone. Heads dipped, faces fell. "I was happy to see that Vinnie had launched a new company. There's not much more to say except..." I got an impulse. I could say *one* more thing. "He'll be missed, and I hope his partner will be able to get along without him." I sat.

People swiveled heads, surveyed the gathering expectantly as if they assumed the partner would materialize. No one moved. Sam stared at me before he took control of the microphone and brought the minister back. Mentioning a partner was a gamble that hadn't paid off; I'd hoped somebody would come forward.

"Dodie, that was beautiful," said Mildred and wiped her eyes.

"For Pete's sake, Mildred, why are you crying? You didn't even know the guy," said Vernon.

"We always cry at funerals," said one of the Bangers.

"And weddings," said the other.

"You were the Three Musketeers back then," said Edna kindly.

I'd never thought of us that way. "You could say that."

After extending their sympathy a last time, Mildred, Vernon, Edna, Carol, and the Banger sisters made a beeline for the refreshment tables, where punch and cookies were being served.

Lola hung back. "Jackson seemed awfully upset."

"Yeah. Surprising." His last meeting with Vinnie didn't hint at the kind of emotion Jackson had displayed this morning.

"Why? They were old friends who shared a lot of life's experiences," Lola said.

"True," I admitted.

"Like us." She put an arm around my waist. "See you tonight?"

"Not sure." I gave her the brief version of Bill's missing car.

"That's awful. Bill must be beside himself. And to think he's a police chief..."

She let the rest of the notion dangle. I knew what she meant.

My attention was drawn to Jackson, who now stood next to Sam's wife, Arlene, bouncing his head and smiling. I'd love to hear that conversation.

"...so you can text me later about the rehearsal," Lola said.

I'd been distracted by Jackson and Arlene. "Sorry?"

"I'm joining Walter for lunch." Lola shifted her gaze to Jackson. "If he's not busy, he should get a kick out of the dress rehearsal. I can say he's a supporting member of the ELT." She tossed her hair off her shoulder.

"Uh...well...I'll see. You have fun with Walter."

Lola rolled her eyes and gave me a quick hug before she went off.

I weaved my way through the swarm of guests that had surrounded the food and drink tables. I intended to buttonhole Jackson and engage him in a continuation of our discussion from early this morning. As I neared the refreshments, I saw someone vaguely familiar in an earnest conversation with Sam. Who was he... I flashed on my encounter with Vinnie at the tiki bar not long before he died. He was buying a round of drinks for a table of raucous guys. One of them yelled for Vinnie to hurry up. He was the man with Sam. The tiki guy inclined his head toward Sam, then clapped him on the back, offering sympathy. Sam and Vinnie might have been closer than I thought.

I felt a splash of something wet on my back.

"I'm so sorry. Someone bumped me from behind," said Maxine, Vinnie's fiancée, and held out a half-empty punch cup. She immediately blotted the remainder of her drink from my blouse with a paper napkin.

"Don't bother. In this heat it will dry quickly." I smiled warmly. "Maxine, yes?"

"Uh-huh. And you're...?"

"Dodie. Jackson's ex-girlfriend."

Maxine studied me, then whispered, "I couldn't believe Vincent's life before the storm. He never talked about it. He never even mentioned that he had another boat business with another partner."

Her eyes were wide, deep brown, and distressed. So innocent.

"Maxine, would you like to talk about Vin...cent's past with me? It could give you some..." Comfort? Insight? Relief that she'd never married him? Because deep down, as much as I enjoyed Vinnie during my previous life in Candle Beach, I knew he was trouble then and I was pretty certain he would have been trouble now.

She lit up like a firecracker. "Yes! I'd love to."

"Where can we meet?" I asked.

She withdrew a pen from a clutch bag and scribbled on the napkin. "Call me tomorrow."

I crumpled the napkin in my fist as an elderly woman drew near. "Maxine, dear, I'd like to go."

"Of course. Mrs. Carcherelli, this is Dodie...?"

"O'Dell," I added.

"She knew Vincent years ago," Maxine said.

Maxine made me sound like I was ancient. "Before Hurricane Sandy," I said.

Mrs. Carcherelli swayed a little. "I was glad that other boat sank. The *JV* was nothing compared to *The Bounty*."

She toddled off, Maxine giving me one last look to confirm our phone call. Had the *JV* actually sunk? No, but it had been smashed up. I stuffed the ball of a napkin in my bag and searched the dwindling assembly for Jackson. If he took off, there'd be hell to pay from me. Ease up, I told myself. He's got to be here somewhere. I moved through the crowd. Sure enough, there he was, speaking to Sam. The tiki man had been replaced by Jackson. From the looks of their body language, it was a profitable conversation, Sam smiling and Jackson shaking his hand. Sam was one popular guy today.

"Ready to go?" I tapped Jackson on the arm.

He straightened. "Yo, Dodie, this is Sam—"

"Baldwin. We've met. About the catering for the opening night reception," I said.

Sam rolled a cigar between a thumb and forefinger, probably anxious to bow out and have a smoke. "I remember." He scrutinized me. "You knew Vinnie from before."

"Yes. When Jackson and I were living down here. And Jackson and Vinnie were partners."

"Uh-huh. Well." He rotated toward Jackson. "I'll get back to you."

"Awesome." He beamed as Sam moved away.

I tugged on Jackson's shirt. "What was that about?"

"Employment. The guy's got a lotta irons in the fire down here," Jackson said. "He could throw something my way."

"You approached him about a job at Vinnie's memorial?"

Jackson shrugged. "He didn't mind. By the way, you crushed it with your life-was-simpler-before-the-storm thing. Nice."

"Thanks. Let's go."

"What's the hurry?" He hung back.

"We need to talk."

"There you go again," Jackson griped.

I had intended to march us directly to my car and, if I had to, lock Jackson inside. I got a better idea instead. "Let's head over to the boardwalk. I'll buy you a beer."

"Now you're talking."

We stopped at a beach bar and bought hot dogs and beers. I led us to a picnic table facing the ocean. We sipped and munched for a minute, taking in the scene: the seagulls swooping onto the sandy beach and, in the distance, waves battering the shore. "So, Vinnie read *Jonathan Livingston Seagull*?"

Jackson stuffed the last of his sandwich into his mouth. "More like *Sports Illustrated*. The swimsuit edition."

We shared a laugh.

"Did Vinnie ever mention his partner to you?"

"What partner?" he asked.

"In his new charter business."

"Nope. I think he was getting ready to make *me* a partner," Jackson said.

"I read an article in the *Candle Beach Courier* online. A PR piece when Vinnie launched his new business. It referred to an unnamed partner," I said.

Jackson shaded his face to follow a swimmer as he paddleboarded out beyond the plunging waves. "He didn't say anything to me about another guy. Vinnie was like that."

"Like what?" I asked.

"I dunno. He liked secrets. Right before the storm, he told me we had a third partner in the *JV*," Jackson said.

"He took someone on without your knowledge?" I asked in disbelief.

"I guess so."

My mouth formed an O. "And you didn't care? No wonder your charter boat business fell apart."

"Who says?" Jackson was suddenly indignant. "The *JV* was doing fine."

"Come on, Jackson," I said softly. "Long before the hurricane, you and Vinnie were under water. I begged you to let me help with the accounting, but you always refused."

"Because Vinnie refused. He said no way. He'd take care of the bills."

Had Vinnie been hiding more than the third partner? I swallowed my beer. "I never knew that."

"Lot of things you didn't know," he said.

"So fill me in. Tell me about the last time you spoke to Vinnie."

Jackson sat up. "I told you. We met up and Vinnie agreed to let me in on the new charter gig," he said evasively.

"What did you say?"

"Told him I'd think about it," Jackson said.

"But you had a fight. You pointed at Vinnie like you were threatening him."

"I wasn't threatening him. He owed me money and was trying to weasel his way out of it. That's why he offered me the job," Jackson confessed.

"Owed you from before the storm?"

Jackson squirmed.

"For what—?"

"Dodie, bug out of my business!" Jackson yelled.

An elderly couple strolling by peeked at us over their shoulders. "You shoved him and he shoved you back," I said calmly. "Some guy had to step between you."

Jackson rested his head on the back of the bench. "I paid off part of a debt he had and Vinnie promised to repay me, but then the hurricane hit, and well, the *JV* was like completely demolished and Vinnie took off. Checked out. I tried to find him but…nada. So I said what the hell and went to Iowa."

Definitely friction between them at the end. I did not know about the money Vinnie owed Jackson. "I'm sorry."

"Whatever. Now can we forget about Vinnie?" Jackson whined.

Easier said than done.

8

"You're burning, mister," I said playfully.

"Mmmm." Bill's head was covered in a beach towel while his torso and the backs of his legs were left to the mercy of the early afternoon sun.

"What happened to that 'I burn easily' mantra?" I asked.

"Mmmm."

I smeared sunscreen on his back. Bill rolled over and I dabbed it on his cheekbones and forehead. Ending with a quick kiss on his lips. I recapped the bottle, sighed luxuriously, and watched the incoming tide send a skim of water creeping up the beach, then rolling back into the ocean. My senses were on overload and I loved it—the aromas of suntan oil and hot dogs, the crashing of the late afternoon waves, the heat on my skin.

My cell phone pinged.

"Anything important?" Bill asked.

"Mom." My parents had spent the last couple of weeks at the shore too. Visiting old neighbors and friends before they returned to Naples, Florida, their new beach home. We'd overlapped three days with them. Plenty of time for my father and Bill to argue the finer points of baseball in the metro area—Yankees versus Mets—and share tidbits on the most effective way to kill crabgrass. They'd hit it off the moment they'd met. My mother wasn't immune to Bill's culinary charisma. "She said hi and reminded me to send her your recipe for Captain Jack's Spaghetti Carbonara." One of Bill's specialties. It was yummy and could pack on the pounds. I should know.

"Tell her hi back. The recipe's on its way."

Bill and my mother had bonded over kitchen tactics and garden manure.

I was glad to see Bill ease up and not let the theft of his BMW ruin his vacation, or at least his afternoon of sunbathing. But *this* guy was way too chill...what had he done with my *other* guy?

The sun shifted lower in the sky. "Hey, sailor...can I interest you in an early happy hour? A pineapple margarita? Piña colada? Time to go in. You've been out here for..." I calculated. "Over three hours."

"Grody," he mumbled.

I tossed the lotion in my beach bag. "What did you say?"

"I was out of the sun for a while. I had lunch with Grody."

"Nice to see two of my favorite guys bonding. I texted him we might stop in for dinner," I said.

"Nope."

"What do you mean? Tonight's special is—"

"Sesame crusted tuna with teriyaki stir fry," Bill said placidly. "Grody told me."

"But you love tuna," I protested

"I do. But I love the thought of the two of us having a quiet night at home even better."

Yahoo!

"So...you're cooking?"

"Yep. First champagne, then grilled shrimp with orange sesame noodles—Grody's recipe—and a chilled chardonnay. Your favorite. Then we'll see where the evening takes us."

I had a place in mind. But what about Jackson? I'd better text him and—

"I texted Jackson and gave him a heads-up. Scram Sam. At least for the night." He smiled slyly.

"But how did you find him? What did he—?" I sputtered.

"Dodie, I'm a police chief. I'm a pretty successful investigator," he said patiently.

Yes, he was. "I'm...overwhelmed." I kissed his sunscreen-covered nose. "You'd better get that body out of the sun."

"I have a phone appointment at three thirty with the State Police Auto Unit. A guy I knew back in Philly has a connection there." Bill's years as a member of the Philadelphia Police Department had created a network of contacts in the Pennsylvania/New Jersey area he regularly called on for assistance. "Hope to get some details about this car theft ring operating down here."

I packed up my towel, book, and water bottle. "Are you sure you're okay? I mean, you did have your BMW swiped."

Bill raised a hand to warn me off. "I'm not focusing on the negative aspects of the theft..."

Were there any other?

"I'm being proactive. Gathering information, dealing with my insurance company...which I also have to call this afternoon. As well as fax some paperwork over to them."

"I appreciate you being brave, but when I lost my Metro I was devastated." I actually went through the five stages of grief. Denial, anger, bargaining—

"I'm going to get my car back," he said firmly. He pulled on a T-shirt, snapped his cap on his head, and picked up his flip-flops.

What? "Bill, I saw this special on chop shops. They dismantle stolen cars within hours and sell the parts to...wherever."

"I know the facts. But I intend to remain upbeat," he said grimly.

Bill's peaceful aura was worse than I imagined.

"After my calls, I'm going shopping for dinner. Can I use your MC?" he asked.

"Sure."

"Can you keep yourself busy for a few hours? We'll make it a late dinner...say eight, eight thirty?"

I'd told Lola I'd try to visit the dress rehearsal at the theater tonight. *Arsenic and Old Lace* was scheduled to take the stage at six o'clock. Even accounting for theater time—always half an hour later than real time, according to Penny—I should be able to see the run-through.

After showers, Bill and I parted ways. He stretched out in the bedroom with his cell phone, and I texted Lola that I would see her at the theater later. Then I headed to the boardwalk for a happy half-hour with Grody. Enough time to get an answer to a question.

* * * *

The music of the steel drums from the tiki bar next door drifted into the Sandbar. I nursed a Creamsicle Crush and waited until Grody had addressed the servers' issues about tonight's specials. The breeze was cool on my bare, tanned shoulders. Despite the tension surrounding Bill's stolen BMW and Vinnie's death, I felt pretty loose myself. Grody uncorked a bottle of red wine and leaned over the bar.

"All set for the reception tomorrow night?" I asked.

"Hey, that hors d'oeuvre idea? Awesome. Not too much fuss. We'll do a setup at five thirty. Get a jump on things before the dinner hour. And speaking of dinner, sorry you're going to miss my tuna tonight," he said, waggling his eyebrows.

"Me too but Bill's cooking."

"So he said…" Grody filled wineglasses and motioned to his bartender. "Romantic evening at home. Things going to get a little hot, Irish?"

Not sure, but I might have blushed. "Changing the subject…"

Grody guffawed.

"Maybe you have some insight into Vinnie C and the charter boat business with Jackson before Hurricane Sandy."

"Me?"

"Something went on between the two of them. According to Jackson, he paid off a debt and Vinnie never repaid him. That's why they argued the day before Vinnie died."

"So…what're you after?" Grody asked and sipped his water.

"You always knew what went down in Candle Beach. Even now you picked up scuttlebutt about Vinnie's death from your contact in the county prosecutor's office. Was there any gossip floating around about Vinnie back then? Something I missed?" I asked.

Grody motioned to a waiter to pick up a customer. "Ask Jackson."

"I have, and he's been tight-lipped. Like he's hiding something. Obviously, I didn't pick up on problems between the two of them back then," I said, chagrined.

Grody walked around the end of the bar and sat down next to me. "Hey, don't beat yourself up. It's been four years, kiddo. Hard to re-create events from that time."

I understood. Some days it was painful for me to remember Sandy. I swung my bag over my shoulder. "Gotta go. I'm stopping by the theater to watch—"

"I do remember one thing." Grody frowned.

"Yeah?"

"A rumor banging around Candle Beach that Vinnie had gotten himself into hot water," Grody said slowly.

"With the charter boat?"

"No. With some people he owed money to. Vinnie liked to hang out in Atlantic City when he wasn't on his boat."

"Vinnie? A gambling debt? Jackson never mentioned that. I assumed the debt was from the business," I said.

Grody gestured to a waiter. "Vinnie was a fun guy, but he could be bad news. It's a shame Jackson never caught on."

Unless he did.

* * * *

I slid into a seat at the back of the theater. Luckily, no one was manning the door to inquire about my presence there. I was ready with an explanation about being an assistant-something-or-other with the ELT, but no explanation was necessary. I slumped down in my seat. I had no intention of showing up late for Bill's dinner and after-party...I knew each theater was allotted thirteen to fifteen minutes, so that would put *Arsenic and Old Lace*, show number six, between six thirty and seven. Perfect.

Onstage, an older man in an ill-fitting suit and a suitcase wandered around, talking to himself. Had to be *Death of a Salesman*.

"Hey, O'Dell," Penny muttered.

"It's warm in here. Is the air conditioning on?" I asked.

"On the blink. The guy in charge claims it'll be fixed by tomorrow night." That would be Sam. "Hope so. How's it going?"

"Behind schedule. Cinderella had a wardrobe malfunction. Somebody left her 'glass slippers'"—Penny formed air quotes with her fingers—"in the theater's van."

"Oooh, that's too bad."

"The actress threw a hissy fit. And her tiara. Then Maddy threatened to cancel their dress rehearsal." Penny cackled. "That one's a real piece of work."

"So when do you think *Arsenic* will go on?"

"O'Dell, you know better than to ask stuff like that," Penny rebuked me. "It's dress rehearsal, and that means—"

"Got it.

"Besides, the light cues for *The Mousetrap* got screwed up and the perp got caught in his own headlights." Penny waggled her head. "Amateurs."

As if the ELT was a professional theater.

"It's almost a professional theater," Penny said.

Yep...she was in my head once more. "So that's the first two shows. What about the next one?"

"*Noises Off*."

Lola had given me a thumbnail-plot summary of each play, so I knew *Noises Off* was a play-within-a-play about backstage escapades during the run of a show. Pretty funny, I thought.

"*Supposed* to be funny..." Penny said. "The big moment is a guy falling down a set of stairs." She indicated the stage with its collection of black cubes, door frames, and bentwood chairs. "See a set of stairs up there?"

"No. So…?"

"The guy trips over a couple of black boxes. Then falls flat on his face."
She chuckled.

Penny definitely had a cold-blooded streak.

"Why didn't they pick another scene?" I asked. "That would make more sense."

Penny turned sideways in her seat. "O'Dell, every theater's got to put their two feet forward, and that means the most exciting scene. Even if it is a hot mess."

Ouch.

"Penny," Walter hissed, appearing from backstage. "Where's Romeo? We're on in fifteen minutes."

"His call was an hour ago. He's backstage," Penny said confidently.

"He is not backstage!" Walter spit out through gritted teeth.

"How can he not be backstage? His call was an hour ago?" she asked.

"Penny!" Walter clutched his graying hair.

Penny winced. "What do you want me to do?"

"Text him, call him, send a carrier pigeon. I don't care. Just get him backstage!" Walter trounced off.

Ooops. Penny's primary assignment was rounding up the ELT actors and getting them onstage on time. With Romeo missing, she had crashed and burned. Walter was frantic, as usual. Times like this usually required one of his chill pills. I hoped he'd remembered to pack them…

"Later, O'Dell." Penny sighed as she headed to the lobby, already punching Romeo's number into her cell phone.

Willy Loman and son Biff were deep into the second act confrontation, which meant that *Sound of Music* was on deck. Which also meant that if Romeo didn't materialize immediately, Lola would be talking to herself in *Arsenic and Old Lace*.

The stage went silent. *Death of a Salesman* was over.

Maddy popped up from her stage manager's table in the house and tore off her headset. "Clap clap clap. *Salesman* actors offstage. *Sound of Music*, wait for the blue light cue, then places. *Arsenic…Arsenic?* Are you back there?" she yelled.

Penny stuck her head out from behind a side curtain. "Missing an actor," she mumbled.

"What?" Maddy shouted. "We need all actors onstage so we can check lighting. You got to get a body up there."

"We're trying to find him," Penny shouted back. She'd had it with Maddy.

"You got fifteen minutes to get a replacement." Maddy wasn't kidding.

The lights shifted, and the Julie Andrews wannabe belted out "My Favorite Things" while the Von Trapp family skipped around the black box setting and the youngest of them—she had to be about seven or eight—skipped to the lip of the stage. A collective gasp as the kid caught herself in time and skittered backward into the rest of the Von Trapps.

This dress rehearsal was beginning to go off the rails.

"Yo, Dodie." Jackson hunkered down in the seat next to me.

"What are you doing here?" I asked.

"Supposed to hook up with Sam to talk about job prospects."

"Now?"

Jackson squinted at the stage. "Is that *The Sound of Music*?"

"Sam's not here. At least I haven't seen him for the past half hour," I said.

"Not to worry. I'll hang around." He gave me a knowing glance. "I'll need to hang around someplace later too."

Jackson had gotten Bill's text that he and I planned to spend the evening alone. I had no intention of discussing my love life with my ex-boyfriend. "What kind of position is Sam offering you? He has a construction company. What experience do you have in construction?"

"I pick things up fast. Looks like I could end up on another charter boat," he said coolly.

The hairs on my neck were like Mexican jumping beans. Something felt off about Jackson hooking up with Sam Baldwin. "You should think twice before you get involved with him—"

"Is she waving to you?" Jackson asked and jerked his head toward the stage.

Penny and Lola had eased out from behind the wings and were, indeed, waving to me. Penny sneaked offstage—Maddy's head was down, buried in her promptbook—and hurried up a side aisle to reach me.

"O'Dell, get up here," she said. "We need you onstage." She held out a script.

"Me? What are you talking about?"

"We need someone to replace Romeo and sit on those blocks. Just read the lines with the actors. The light crew needs to see if the focus is off."

"But—" I sputtered.

"I'll do it." Jackson grasped the script from Penny's hand and trailed her to the stage.

"Wait a minute!" I called out.

Maddy's head jerked up. "Quiet in the house," she growled.

The Von Trapp family sang their last note, did a group bow, and trotted off the stage, confident in their performance. The stage went dark, then blue light rose as the crew scuffled about, rearranging the black boxes and chairs. Actors entered rapidly and lurched onto the set, lights rising on Abby and Edna, the two daffy old ladies of *Arsenic and Old Lace*, and Jackson, grinning from ear to ear. Abby was shell-shocked as she and Edna began the scene by explaining to Jackson's character, their nephew Mortimer, that they felt sorry for lonely old bachelors and to put them out of their misery, served them elderberry wine spiked with arsenic and a pinch of cyanide. Mortimer was supposed to be stunned at this news, but Jackson read his lines as though he could easily understand their drive to kill. Edna prodded him to sit, stand, and move when required. Abby, disgruntled, stared daggers at both of them.

What had made him volunteer to do the scene? Of course, better Jackson than me... I heard a handful of guffaws in the house, but the lights hit the actors where expected and the scene plodded along.

"Hey." It was Pauli, gasping as though he'd run here from somewhere. "What's going on up there? Like, where's Romeo?"

"Nobody knows and they needed a body to fill in. Pretty nutty, right?"

Pauli shrugged. "The play's pretty nutty." He craned his neck to locate Maddy before furtively withdrawing his camera from his backpack and holding it up to his eye. "The stage manager banned cameras from the dress rehearsal."

"Why?" I asked.

"Dunno. Something about cameras sucking the spirit out of the actors before the play opens."

I hooted softly. "You gotta love these theater people."

"Walter's exercises are goofy, but compared to this..."

We snickered.

"Shh!" Maddy said.

Onstage, Abby yanked Jackson's shirt and pulled his face to within inches of hers to deliver a speech. She meant business. Jackson played along, apparently amused by her intensity. When Abby finished and pushed him backward, he obligingly gave into momentum—having no clue what he was supposed to do—and landed in a chair that toppled over. More guffaws in the audience. *Abby was fit to be tied*, to quote one of my aunt's favorite expressions.

Luckily it was the end of the scene and the actors segued into Lola's entrance. As Mortimer's love interest, she had better luck controlling Jackson by pointing and nudging. Feeding him cues on a silver platter and, at the crucial moment, landing a big whopper on his lips. Which Jackson enjoyed thoroughly. Unlike the rest of the ELT, Lola *was* an actual pro, having spent time Off Off Broadway in New York before committing to the Etonville Little Theatre.

Pauli beamed. "Epic."

"Not sure kissing Jackson like that is in the script," I murmured.

"It's method acting," Pauli said earnestly.

The scene ended, the lights came up briefly for a curtain call—Edna smiling broadly, Abby grinding her teeth, Lola playing the sophisticated diva, and Jackson bouncing on his sneakers beaming. I could imagine the ELT somewhat embarrassed and grateful that their fifteen minutes of onstage terror were over. The crew scrambled to clear the stage for *King Lear*.

Maddy ran through the house and stopped by an emergency exit to talk with someone. It was Arlene Baldwin, dressed as she'd been this morning at the memorial service. She was an enigma…

Pauli capped his lens and repacked his camera.

"Can you do me a favor?"

"Uh-huh. Wassup?" Pauli asked.

"It's about the people running this festival. See what you can find on them?" I knew Pauli's years of online digital forensics classes had provided him with databases and search engine information unavailable to the average civilian. I had personal knowledge of his email hacking skill and facial recognition software.

"Easy peasy." Then he grew quiet. "Is this like about that guy who got murdered?"

Maybe, maybe not. Sam, and by extension Arlene, was simply a scratch that needed itching. "I'm curious about them."

"Got it," he said enthusiastically.

Nothing revved Pauli's engine like digital forensics. Except Janice.

"Should I search on the victim?" he asked slyly.

"Vinnie?" That wasn't a bad idea. If Grody's gossip was correct, something about Vinnie's gambling career might show up. I patted his shoulder. "Go for it."

"Gotta bounce. Going to the beach." Pauli sauntered off.

I checked my watch. I had to beat it back to our bungalow. I texted Lola that things hadn't gone too badly…considering Jackson had assumed Romeo's role. She responded: *"I NEED A DRINK!"* I could sympathize.

I sped from the theater, through the town park to the boardwalk. I had twenty minutes to make it back or Bill would be cracking that bottle of champagne by himself. I laughed thinking about the dress rehearsal. I felt bad for Lola and company, but Jackson on that stage trying to keep up with the dialogue and avoid Abby's verbal browbeating had transformed a comedy into a farce. I passed the Surf Shack, still open, and got a glimpse of the boats moored at the marina opposite. My pulse shot up. Standing by a yacht halfway down the dock was a tall, rough-looking man in a captain's cap. I'd seen him somewhere before. I stooped down to pretend to adjust my sandal strap. The man shifted his position and another person became visible: Sam Baldwin. My mind was like the Indy 500. Thoughts racing in circles, driving each other out of the way. How were the two connected? The big guy…was he the man who had threatened me on the pier a few nights ago? Was it Sam in *The Bounty*'s lower deck whose shadow moved behind the curtained windows? To quote Jackson, Sam did seem to have a "lotta irons in the fire." The two men headed away from me toward the end of the harbor.

Totally flummoxed, I sat down on the boardwalk.

"Are you okay?" said a concerned voice.

I looked up at the young cop who'd interviewed Jackson at my rental. The short, pudgy, sympathetic one with the baby face.

"Aren't you the woman in the house on Atlantic Street?" He extended a hand.

"Yes." I took up his offer, and he pulled me to my feet. "Thanks. My… uh…sandal strap…" I didn't need to bother with any justification. He regarded me carefully.

"Dodie O'Dell."

I was truly stunned. "You remembered my name?"

"I'm terrific with names. And faces. And putting the two of them together," the kid said proudly.

He was out of uniform in neatly pressed shorts and a golf shirt. His light brown hair was gelled up, not unlike Bill's on a night out. "That's a terrific skill to have as a police officer." I judged him to be early twenties. "You were very professional that day. You must have to handle a lot of serious crimes down here in the summer," I said innocently.

He shuffled his feet. "I'm only out of the police academy six months. This is my first assignment."

"Congratulations."

"My first murder investigation too," he said with satisfaction.

Bingo.

"Really? I'd never have known that," I said.

"It's hard handling a major case…lot of offices to coordinate with. The medical examiner, the State Police lab, departments in nearby towns," the young cop said.

"Plus interviewing witnesses and suspects," I added.

"I've only been in on two interviews so far." He was disappointed. Oops. "I read in the *Courier* that there was physical evidence the victim was murdered. And, of course, no water in his lungs."

"He didn't need water in his lungs. He had a puncture wound in his chest that went straight into his heart," the kid divulged.

"Like he was killed someplace and then left on the beach," I said helpfully.

The young man stuffed his hands in his pockets and abruptly retreated. He knew he'd said too much. "Well…have a pleasant night." He did a semi-salute and darted off.

I double-timed it down the boardwalk and raced the block to my place. It had been a profitable conversation with the newbie cop. I'd learned that there were no new suspects, which kept Jackson front and center as a person of interest, and that Vinnie was murdered by a wound in his chest. Which meant it could have happened anywhere—Vinnie's boat, a house in town, even on the beach.

9

"So Jackson ended up on the stage," Bill said and topped off our wine.
"It was either him or me. I'd like to be a fly on the wall when Walter
meets up with Romeo."

"Where do you think he was?"

I sipped my chardonnay and flashed on the actor flexing his pecs on
the beach to impress women passing by. "My guess is either he fell asleep
on the sand or has second-degree burns from the sun and can't get his
clothes on." I scooped up the last of my grilled shrimp with orange sesame
noodles. "This meal was fantastic."

"Thanks. Or rather we should thank Grody. It's his recipe. I couldn't
find the tamari..."

"What's that?" I asked and wiped my mouth.

"Dark soy sauce. I had to settle for the lighter version."

"The fresh orange juice and ginger give it some zip," I said. As a result
of Bill's influence, I was becoming something of a foodie. Managing the
Windjammer certainly kept me attuned to recipes and menus. But Bill's
cooking was of the gourmet variety. He loved to experiment.

The sun had set. The outdoor table in the backyard of our house was lit
with candles. Tiki torches surrounded the patio and threw shadows into
the night. We polished off the very expensive wine and I extended my legs
in front of me. Bill lifted them up and placed them in his lap. It didn't get
much better than this. Relaxing with my guy on a warm summer night...
my cell phone pinged.

"Ignore it." Bill scooted his chair closer to mine. "For one night, we're
going to forget about Jackson..."

He kissed me sweetly on one cheek.

"Vinnie…" He grazed the other with his lips.

"The theater festival…" He pecked my nose.

"And my BMW." He made a beeline for my lips.

I came up for air. "What's left?"

Bill opened the patio door and held it ajar. "Come on in and see."

Yowza.

* * * *

I heard a thump and opened my eyes. Was I dreaming or did something go bump in the night? My digital alarm said 1 a.m. Next to me Bill was conked out, totally oblivious. I debated: get up and investigate or stay put, snuggled up with Bill. It could wait until morning, unless I heard a repeat noise. The house was a cocoon of silence disturbed only by the whirring of the room air conditioner. I tugged the sheet up to my chin and tried to go back to sleep.

Another thump, louder this time. Was it Jackson sneaking in the unlocked back door again? Ready to scare the pants off me? Bill slept on, but I had to satisfy my curiosity. I got out of bed as quietly as I could and picked up my robe and cell phone. The house was dark, save for a night-light in the hallway, a lamp in the living room, and the porch light. I grasped the handle of the front door and hesitated. I should have awakened Bill… I slowly opened the door an inch, then several more inches. I exhaled, realizing I'd been holding my breath. Jackson was tucked into his sleeping bag, the porch chairs rearranged to give him more room. Was that what I'd heard? If so, he'd passed out quickly. It had only been minutes since the second thump. No sense in waking him. At least he'd stayed away most of the night.

I closed the front door, glancing at my cell. It was a bad habit of mine, checking my messages at all hours. I was wide awake now, so no harm in seeing who was trying to reach me during dinner. Lola: *are u up for breakfast tmr?* It depended on Bill's plans. I knew she'd be anxious about the opening night performance and might require some support. Pauli: *found some stuff.* Interesting. Grody: *tuna was a smash success. remembered something else.* Very interesting. Too late to respond to any of them, but first thing in the morning…

I slept on and off until seven o'clock, then gave up and padded softly to the kitchen. I put on the coffee. I set out three mugs, trying to be hospitable and include Jackson. I'd give my textees another hour and then reply. I poured my coffee and carefully opened the front door. I felt sorry for Jackson, caught in the middle of Vinnie's murder, and decided last night before dropping off to sleep that he and I could go to the police station and confront the "person of interest" issue. He could tell them the story that he'd told me about Vinnie's debt and lack of repayment—the truth would set him free.

I peeked at the west end of the porch where Jackson had set up camp. It was empty. He was gone this early? Had I been dreaming last night?

"Morning, sunshine." Bill draped his arms around my middle and kissed my ear. Then abruptly moved to the kitchen to retrieve his coffee.

"Did you hear anything last night? Around one a.m.?" I asked.

"Anything? Like what? You snoring?" he taunted me.

"I don't snore," I said.

"Well…hate to inform you, but…"

"Not my snoring. More like a thump," I said.

Bill scratched his head. "No. Why?"

"I did and it woke me up. I looked out here and found Jackson asleep."

Bill joined me on the porch. "Where is he?"

"Beats me. If he got in late, he didn't get much sleep," I said.

Bill gazed at me over the rim of his coffee cup. "Are you keeping tabs on his snoozing? Time to let go, Dodie," he said gently.

I agreed.

Bill fixed breakfast for himself—he had to revisit the Candle Beach Police Department to sign a statement—and then proceed to rent a car for the coming week. We agreed to meet up for lunch. I texted Lola that I would join her in an hour; texted Pauli to join me at 11 a.m. at the tiki bar; and left a message for Grody that I would see him at noon, with Bill in tow, for lunch. I figured that whatever he had remembered about Vinnie could be shared with Bill, right?

I'd left myself a window of time to connect with Vinnie's fiancée, Maxine, and texted to see if I could stop by this morning. She agreed and gave me her address, at the other end of Candle Beach. Hiking there would be energizing, so I offered Bill the keys to my MINI Cooper. One thing I loved about this town: Most everything was in walking distance. Bill declined the use of my MC, deciding to go by foot to the CBPD to get some exercise, and said he'd get a lift to the rental lot from there. We parted.

I ran through my plan of attack with Maxine. I wasn't sure what I expected, or even wanted, her to say. I had a sense that if I introduced the topic of Vinnie's and Jackson's days aboard the *JV*, maybe she would open up about Vinnie from the past year. And inadvertently offer material that might help solve the mystery of Jackson's former partner. I sailed down the boardwalk to the Candle Diner and arrived early in time to scan today's

Courier for updated news on the murder investigation. Nothing. Either the police were stymied or were playing their cards close to the chest. Except for one young cop.

I flipped through page after page and read articles on the city council voting on new parking regulations and a bunch of letters to the editor complaining about noise on the boardwalk at night and traffic clogging the streets. Small town life. It reminded me of Etonville.

"Whew. Getting warm out there." Lola slid onto the bench of the booth.

"You're looking pretty cool," I said admiring Lola's crisp cotton blouse and matching pale green shorts. "The weather app says we'll hit ninety today."

"Ugh."

We ordered breakfast—scrambled eggs and toast for Lola, pancakes and a hot cinnamon roll for me.

"I hope it cools off by tonight. Grody's serving hors d'oeuvres outside for the reception," I said.

"I hope we don't embarrass ourselves any worse than we did yesterday," Lola moaned.

"It was…a challenging situation without Romeo," I said delicately.

"It was a train wreck!"

"Having Jackson up there didn't help."

Lola softened. "It wasn't his fault. He was trying to help out. We needed a body."

I experienced a flicker of guilt. I could have volunteered. Our meal arrived. Lola picked at her eggs; I dove into my short stack. I'd learned from my mother that hot weather—contrary to received wisdom—gave one a voracious appetite. Yep! "Where was Romeo, anyway?" I asked.

Lola grimaced. "He claims he had a touch of sunstroke from the day before. Nausea, dizziness, and he slept through the dress rehearsal. But Abby spotted him last night at the tiki bar, and he was red as a beet. It was a case of *sunburn* not *sunstroke*."

"Walter throw a tantrum?"

"He was surprisingly unruffled. Must have been the Xanax," Lola said. Walter's chill pill of choice.

"Sorry I had to run out. Chef Bill prepared one of Grody's recipes, and we had an intimate dinner for two," I said.

"Ooh la la!" Lola chuckled.

"A lovely night…"

Lola arched an eyebrow. "Vacation's good for you two. And speaking of twosomes…Jackson and I went out for drinks after the dress rehearsal." Lola peeked at my expression.

OMG! Lola *was* boyfriend hunting. "Oh…well…that's…nice." Now I knew where he was for part of the night—

"You don't mind, do you? Him being an old flame of yours," Lola said.

"Absolutely not." I smiled my fake smile that I saved for those occasions when I was in over my head or at a loss for words. It was the latter this time.

"Because we discovered we have a lot in common." Lola flipped her hair. The sophisticated, beautifully dressed diva of the Etonville Little Theatre and the former surfer dude in torn tees and ragged shorts. Their vocabularies alone set them worlds apart. But I was hooked. "Like what?" I asked honestly.

"Italian white wines, water sports, theater." Lola drained her coffee.

I bought the wine and water part, but theater? Jackson hadn't seen a play in all the time we spent together. Truth be told, I hadn't seen much theater either until I moved to Etonville. We left the Candle Diner; I gave Lola a hug and encouraged her to hit the beach and chill out until tonight. Then I exited the boardwalk and headed toward Maxine's address. Within twenty minutes I was at Land's End facing a house that sat on a spit of property fronting the ocean.

Candle Beach boasted a wide variety of homes—shore cottages no bigger than an efficiency apartment; bungalows like the one Bill and I rented with a handful of rooms and a pleasant deck or patio; two-story family homes that were year-round residences and could have belonged in any Jersey town. And then there were the luxury homes that reeked of shore money. Maxine's belonged in that category. Hers was a bright yellow Victorian with pristine white trim, a lovely front porch with rocking chairs, a second-floor wraparound balcony, and a third-floor widow's walk. It sat on a generous plot of land that was landscaped with dune grasses, palm trees, and sandy patches. The view from the front porch was magnificent, the property so new I assumed it had been rehabbed after Hurricane Sandy.

I knocked on the screen door. Footsteps slapped on tile and Maxine came into view, dressed vastly different than yesterday: She was barefoot, in shorts, a tank top, and an off-the-shoulder beach cover-up. Her hair was gathered simply at the nape of her neck. She appeared even more youthful and delicate than she had yesterday.

"Hi. Thanks for coming," she whispered, then hesitated. "We can talk out here… Vincent and I loved to sit in these rockers. Like an old married couple." She teared up.

"Fine. Unless it's too upsetting?"

She swiped at her eyes. "Would you like something? Coffee, tea, soda?"

She smiled. "I'm having a Bloody Mary."

Actually, a Bloody Mary sounded like a fantastic suggestion, but I needed to stay sober and alert. "Ice water would be great."

Maxine withdrew into the house and I sat, gazing at the ocean. This end of Candle Beach was somewhat unknown to me. I had questions for Maxine but I barely knew where to begin. I needn't have fretted. She reappeared with our drinks and plunged into the conversation.

"Vincent was crazy about this view," she said.

"I can see why. It's fantastic. Have you lived here long?"

"Since 2014. It was completely demolished by the storm so the owners rebuilt it. My father bought it as a summer home, but I live here year-round." She rocked silently. Then as if she needed to explain their whereabouts, "My father lives in New York. My mother's in Florida."

"My parents are in Florida too. Naples."

"My mother's in Naples."

We smiled at the coincidence.

"Were they at the memorial service?" I asked cautiously.

Maxine sipped her Bloody Mary, her voice dropping to a murmur. "They hated Vincent. My father threatened to disown me if I went through with the wedding. They thought I was too young...he was too old for me." Her chin trembled. "Nothing to worry about now."

I felt for her, so young and vulnerable to be handling Vinnie's death alone.

"Vincent never talked about the *JV* and his partnership with Jackson?" I asked tentatively, swinging the conversation into new, less emotional territory. I hoped.

"Never. I thought *The Bounty* was the first boat he owned. He was crazy about it. This spring and summer Vincent was busy all week and I rarely saw him, but on the weekends if he didn't have a charter we'd pack up a picnic and take off. Sometimes we'd go crabbing in the bay. Or fishing in the inlet. At least Vincent fished. I hung out on the deck with a mai tai." She smiled sadly.

Odd, I thought. Vinnie was busier during the week than on weekends? With a charter boat?

"Sometimes we cruised down to Atlantic City," she said.

"You like to gamble?"

"Not me but Vincent could shoot craps twenty-four hours a day." She laughed gently.

So Grody was right.

"Your days on *The Bounty* remind me of some days on the *JV*."

Maxine leaned forward eagerly. "Yeah?"

"Of course, Jackson, Vincent, and I were all younger then. And less serious. The *JV* had summers when business was thriving and summers when they had to scrimp to get by."

Maxine bit into a piece of celery. "So last year was nothing new, I guess." My interest quickened. "Meaning...?"

"I had to lend Vincent money when he bought the boat. He was so cute"—she smiled at the memory—"so afraid to ask for help. As if I wouldn't give him however much he wanted." Maxine stopped rocking, sat up straighter. "I never told my father. It came out of my trust fund," she asserted defensively, as if I would question her judgment.

Aha. Vinnie had a source of funds in Maxine. Not to be too cynical, but I wouldn't have been surprised if that had been one of her main attractions.

"But then things must have picked up." She shrugged. "After about six months he had all the financing he needed. I offered to lend him more, but he refused. Said he came into money he inherited from a distant relative."

Huh. "Maxine, I know this must be painful, but do you have any inkling why anyone would want to kill Vinnie?"

She swallowed hard and shook her head vehemently. "The police asked me the same thing. Vincent had no enemies."

I took a chance. I had no idea what the police had communicated to Maxine, but I had to ask. "I understand that he didn't die on the beach. That his body was...put there later."

Maxine shrunk into herself, dwarfed by the wicker rocker. "Is that true?" she whispered. "I knew about no water in his lungs so he didn't exactly drown in the ocean. But what you're saying...nobody told me."

The young cop was divulging information that hadn't been made public. Even to Maxine. "I'm sure the police department will sort it all out," I said in a rush. "It's been nice speaking with you. Maybe we can do it again." I set my water on an end table.

"I'd like that. Maybe Jackson can come too."

Jackson? Not sure that was a good idea. I stood. "Well..."

"Everybody liked Vincent," Maxine said quickly, defending him. *Not everybody.*

"I mean, like, sometimes he drank too much and got into arguments, but they were never anything serious. Nothing worth killing him over. Sure, one time Tiny almost threw him overboard for cheating during a card game—"

"Tiny?"

"He's a big guy but everyone calls him Tiny. Go figure. He works for Sam sometimes."

Foreboding rippled down the back of my skull. "Sam Baldwin?"

"Sure. Sam's been so sweet to me. Coming over to visit, seeing if he could do anything..."

"I understand he's 'Mr. Candle Beach.' The town godfather," I said.

"I suppose so," Maxine admitted.

"He does a lot of thoughtful things for people down here. Including you," I said.

Maxine regarded me quizzically. "Why wouldn't he? He was Vincent's partner."

* * * *

My mind was in a jumble as I retraced my trek from Maxine's house to the boardwalk and the tiki bar where I had an appointment with Pauli. On the way I texted Jackson: *Where are you? We need to talk. Urgent.* What to make of Vinnie's partnership with Sam? It made sense in a way. Sam was an entrepreneur with many interests in the shore area, and Vinnie's charter boat could have been one of his "irons" in the Candle Beach "fire." Also logical if Sam was the figure I saw on the lower deck of *The Bounty* that night. He had every right to be on the boat if he owned part of it. But why keep it a secret? Why not acknowledge the relationship at the memorial? Was there something Sam was hiding? Had he revealed his partnership with Vinnie to Jackson? I intended to find out today.

I had worked up a sweat by the time I plopped onto a bar stool at the Bottom Feeder. The tiki music wafted onto the beach, the palms swaying gently in a light breeze. Hopefully, the humidity that had left my skin damp and clammy would plummet by tonight, and the theater's air conditioning would be working to eliminate the possibility that perspiration would impact both costumes and makeup, as well as the audience. I ordered a lemonade for me, Coke for Pauli, and a glass of ice water, rolling the latter back and forth across my forehead to cool off.

"Hey." Pauli claimed a seat at the bar, his thumbs at work on his cell phone. He looked up. "Janice."

"How's she doing?" I asked.

"Like, having a miserable time in Boston. It's cold and rainy and she's stuck inside." He grinned.

"That's good news?"

"She misses me even more." He stabbed a straw into his drink and bobbed his head. *"That's* the good news."

Nothing made the heart grow fonder than boredom. "So you did a bit of digging around?"

"I searched for the New Jersey business registration for Vincent Carcherelli. If he had a New Jersey license it had to be registered with the State Department of the Treasury. His charter boat is an LLC and was registered in April 2015."

"Little more than a year ago," I said.

"Co-owners—"

"—Sam Baldwin—" I added.

"—and Arlene Baldwin."

His wife? There were three owners...

"I did a search on Baldwin General Contractors, while I was in the business directory."

"Way to be proactive."

Pauli dipped his head. He wasn't completely comfortable with compliments. "Owner also Arlene Baldwin."

So "Mrs. Sam" was sharing the pants in the family. And keeping a low profile. "Great work, Pauli."

"Uh...that's not all," he said and took a swig of his soda. "Baldwin General Contractors filed for bankruptcy in 2009. It reorganized a year later."

"That year, 2009, was three years before the storm hit. If they were having money problems at that time, the hurricane provided a boost to their company," I mused aloud.

"You think they got something to do with the murder?" Pauli asked, excited.

"Sh." I took a swift glimpse around. The bar was only half full. No one was paying us any attention. The bartender was waiting on customers at the other end. "This is on the Q.T."

"Got it. But in case you think they do...I cross-checked Sam Baldwin and Vincent Carcherelli."

"I love how you're taking the initiative. If you keep this up, I'm going to have to put you on the payroll," I said teasingly.

"Yeah." He smirked.

"Anything come up?"

"Recent stuff like the memorial service." Pauli lifted his head from the laptop. "Sorry I couldn't come. He was a friend of yours, right?"

"In a way. A friend from my past. I didn't expect any Etonville folks to come."

Pauli nodded. "They love funerals. Anyway, on a police database, I found a DUI for Vincent in a car owned by Sam."

"Probably partying too much. They were partners. When was this? Sometime in the past year?" I asked.

"Nope. In 2012."

2012. "So they were acquaintances back then." When Vinnie and Jackson were working on the *JV*. But Jackson didn't have a connection to Sam Baldwin at that time. At least no connection he shared with me. "Let me see that."

Pauli obliged by rotating his laptop to face me. The report included a brief account of Vinnie's arrest, an eyewitness statement, and mention of the automobile owned by Sam Baldwin, who also bailed him out. Sam was noted as "Vincent Carcherelli's business partner." I slumped into the back of my stool. Jackson knew Vinnie had taken on a silent, third partner without telling him who it was. Had he any suspicion the silent partner was Sam? So, Vinnie and Sam were partners on two different charter boat ventures. Did it have any bearing on Vinnie's death?

"Like, okay stuff?" asked Pauli and swallowed the last of his Coke.

I'd say. "Confusing stuff. If you find anything else…"

"Easy peasy." He packed up his laptop. "See you tonight."

I knew I didn't need to remind him, but… "And Pauli?"

"I know. Confidentiality," he said and winked.

Right. The first rule of digital forensics.

10

Grody flew from the dining room to the kitchen. The Sandbar was having one of those days, he said. A large group showed up for lunch without a reservation, a server was out sick, and the kitchen ran out of clam chowder because someone muffed the inventory order. I could sympathize.

I sat at the bar and nursed a glass of seltzer waiting for Bill, who was late and hadn't texted. Unusual for him, normally. I doodled on a napkin, usual for me: *Sam and Vinnie partners twice; Jackson in the dark; Sam bankrupt in 2009; Maxine lent money to Vinnie; Vinnie inheritance for the rest; big guy named Tiny almost throws Vinnie overboard; possibly the guy who chased me off the dock.* I checked my cell. Still no word from Bill. While I was in Messages, I texted Jackson again. I hadn't heard from him, either.

"Hey, Red, if I have another day like this, just shoot me," Grody grunted and collapsed on a bar stool.

"Been there, done that."

"Want a table? Something should open up soon." He scanned the dining room.

"I'm comfortable here 'til Bill comes."

"How's he handling the missing BMW?" Grody asked.

I'd filled Grody in on the details of the auto theft. "Surprisingly well. He's very calm about it all. That wouldn't be me."

"Me neither. I got a scratch on my SUV last year and went ballistic. Couldn't help it." He laughed at himself, his belly shaking at the memory.

"I hear ya. The hors d'oeuvres coming along?"

"We'll be ready," Grody said grimly. "Wasn't counting on a day like this."

"I can help you set up," I said.

"Thanks. I imagined catering was a productive PR decision, get in tight with Candle Beach, make a friend of Sam, etc., etc."

Speaking of Sam… "Hey, you said you remembered something else about Vinnie?"

Grody eyed a table that attempted to flag down a server. "Where's my waiter? Hold on." He took off to appease customers.

Been there too.

I tapped my pen on the bar and debated. Should I wait for Bill? He was almost an hour late. I hoped he wasn't having a hassle renting a car…

Grody grabbed an iPad and scanned the reservation list. "This place is going to be nuts tonight. We're already overbooked. I'm taking you up on your offer to set up for the reception."

"No problem."

"Can you be at the park by five o'clock? The tables and linens will be there by then. The food by five thirty." Grody sat beside me. "I'll send over a few servers and stop by before the show goes up at seven thirty."

"Fine. What about Vinnie?"

Grody stared at me blankly. "Huh?"

"Your text?"

"Oh, that." He frowned. "Yeah. It was the night Sandy hit. Remember?"

Who could forget?

"We closed up early…" he said.

"I closed out and you battened down the hatches. For all the good it did us," I said.

"You got that right," Grody said ruefully.

"Then we went home. I spent the next ten hours listening to the storm wail, the wind really fierce. Terrifying, no power. Then the elm tree crashed through my roof." I trembled involuntarily.

Grody put an arm around my shoulder. "Hey, Irish, at least we lived through it."

We had. Grody's restaurant hadn't.

"Where was Jackson that night?" he asked suddenly.

"Jackson?" As the storm was strengthening, Jackson had left me a message that he and Vinnie intended to moor the *JV* in the next town over, where the marina was more sheltered. I recalled being petrified, then angry that he'd waited so long to dock the boat and left me to weather the hurricane alone. "He and Vinnie took the *JV* to Ocean Port. Better protection there. The boat was wrecked anyway." I paused. "Jackson never made it home that night."

"Well…the week after Sandy, everyone was really crazed, remember? The destruction, the insurance, FEMA, people losing everything."

"Yes."

Grody hesitated. "There was some buzz that Vinnie…and not sure, but might have included Jackson…"

My little hairs stood on end. "What?"

"…they scuttled the *JV* for the insurance money."

My heart sank. I knew Jackson could be irresponsible, but I couldn't believe he'd be a part of something so blatantly illegal. At a time when so many others were scrambling to get insurance help legitimately. I must have turned pale, because Grody poured me a white wine.

"You could use this," he said kindly. "This business with Vinnie…it's triggering a lot of memories. Some not so positive."

"I know what you mean." I downed the wine in three gulps. "I'm going to bail on lunch. I'll text Bill and be at the park to set up at five."

Out on the boardwalk, I messaged Bill that I'd left the Sandbar and would catch up with him at the show tonight. Then I stashed my cell in my bag and marched. I had no destination in mind; I simply needed to let off steam and convince myself that Grody had it wrong. That the rumors were unfounded. That Jackson wasn't involved in Vinnie's scheme.

I power walked to the end of the boardwalk, caught my breath, and treated myself to a double scoop of chocolate fudge ice cream. Sugar had a way of soothing my nerves. I tried to process all I'd learned today about Vinnie, Jackson, and Sam Baldwin. Some of it was predictable enough, some of it downright disturbing. Seagulls swung overhead, diving occasionally onto the boardwalk, which was rapidly filling with beachgoers, then soaring into the sky. Since the warm sand looked inviting, I elected to head back to the bungalow to change. I was so preoccupied that I failed to spot the couple who'd stopped abruptly in front of me.

"Oof," I cried as I banged into a tall, thin man's back.

"Sorry," he said. "Couldn't help it."

Beyond him, a collection of people obstructed the right-of-way on the boardwalk. In the middle of them was a young boy breakdancing to hip-hop music pouring out of a boom box. Some of the shore towns had banned saggy pants, smoking, and bathing suits on the boardwalk. Candle Beach was laissez-faire about what it allowed on its walkway, including boom boxes and breakdancing. As the crowd swelled, blocking more of the pathway, I tried to maneuver around the group in front of me. In the throng on the opposite side of the circle, a blotch of red stood out. There he was. "Jackson!" I yelled.

People close by turned and stared at me. I didn't care. I flapped my arm to get his attention, but the music was too loud and Jackson was clearly absorbed by the performance, enjoying himself, bobbing his head and, along with other onlookers, clapping to the beat of the music. I gently elbowed my way to the outer edge of the audience. Jackson was no more than thirty feet away when he spun away from the entertainment, melting into the mob behind him. I increased my pace and determination and pushed through the crush of bodies until I was free of the mob of people. I searched frantically up and down the boardwalk. Which way to go?

I jogged in the direction of the Bottom Feeder and the Sandbar. I prayed he would duck into one of those places. Suddenly an unruly mane of brown hair atop a bright red T-shirt appeared up ahead. I ran toward him. Jackson ducked into an arcade. The game center mostly attracted young children and families. Years ago, we'd sometimes wander in to play skeeball. I shadowed him as he zigged and zagged through the swarm of video gamers, pinball players, and air hockey competitors. A mass of kids hovered around the bank of crane games and vied for stuffed animals. He cut through a line of youngsters waiting to redeem strips of tickets for trinkets.

"Hey, watch what you're doing!" a young father said.

Jackson signaled an apology and kept moving. He made a right and headed for the skeeball machines along the back wall of the arcade. I was confused. We were rapidly running out of real estate. Where could he be going? Never mind. I was within spitting distance, and this time I would not let him out of sight even if I had to—

A man stepped in front of me. "Don't I know you?" I recognized the gruff voice that had growled at me on the pier. It was the brute from the dock. This had to be Tiny.

"Wh-what?" I tried to squeeze around him, but he towered over me, blocking my way. I craned my neck to see where Jackson had gone—a flash of red departed out a back door of the game center.

Tiny squinted at me. "You're the lady who got curious on the dock the other night."

Yikes! Even in the busy arcade, this guy was frightening.

I took a step away from him. "Sorry, but I have to meet someone—"

"Lemme give you some advice. Bein' alone on the dock at night can be dangerous." His lips smiled, but his eyes delivered a warning.

"Thanks. Now I have to—"

Tiny stooped and retrieved a dollar bill. "Did you drop this?"

"Me? No."

Tiny waved the bill in my face. "Take it anyway." He handed me the five. "You have a nice day," he said and sauntered away as though we were two friends who'd accidentally bumped into each other.

What was that about?

Frustrated and distressed, I retraced my steps through the arcade, stopping by the entrance to offer Tiny's five-dollar bill to a couple of kids trying to outwit the crane and grab a prize. They were ecstatic to receive the money.

I'd lost my quarry. Jackson was long gone. A twinge of unease made me pause. Could Tiny have been deliberately preventing me from tracking Jackson?

* * * *

The Candle Beach park was a lovely setting for the opening night reception. In the gazebo, white linen tablecloths covered serving tables that held platters of food. Café tables and chairs dotted the grounds. A jazz combo played under a banner that advertised the New Jersey Community Theater Festival, while spectators wandered about, sampling Grody's hors d'oeuvres, a different one for each play. He'd used my ideas for some of them—the *Cinderella* crabmeat canapés, the *King Lear* scallops in bacon, and the *Mousetrap* spring rolls—but had supplemented them with *The Sound of Music* shrimp cocktail, the *Noises Off* prosciutto crostini, the *Death of a Salesman* smoked salmon and cream cheese rolls, and, last but not least, the *Arsenic and Old Lace* spicy beef empanadas, plus an assortment of cheeses and crackers.

I'd arrived in time to help Grody's crew arrange the food and set up the beverage counter. All refreshments were compliments of Sam Baldwin, patron of the festival. *He was shelling out the bucks big-time.* I guessed he could afford it. Or at least he wanted to give the appearance that he could afford it. I was thinking about his bankruptcy, which Pauli had unearthed.

"I like this ham on toast," Vernon said and plunked two of them onto a napkin.

"They're prosciutto crostini," Mildred corrected him.

"Don't care what you call them. Or which play it is, I'm hungry." He ambled off.

"I'll bet this was your idea, Dodie. Very clever." Mildred chased after him.

"We loved *The Sound of Music*, didn't we?" one Banger sister asked the other, who bounced her head in agreement. "But I don't think they served shrimp cocktail in the movie."

"I don't either." I smiled. "The hors d'oeuvres are simply fun ways to acknowledge each play in the show tonight," I explained.

"We should eat one of each. That way we're not being partial to any one theater." They wanted confirmation.

"Makes sense to me." Little of what they said ever made sense to me.

Sam made an entrance, Arlene on his arm, both of them in dashing, white linen ensembles. They did a royal promenade around the park, shaking hands, smiling, accepting accolades. Sam definitely was the king of Candle Beach. Which would make Arlene the queen. On the other side of the gazebo, John Bannister, in casual slacks and shirt, was in earnest conversation with a group of theatergoers. He leaned on his cane, his expression attentive. As though he felt me staring, he glanced up and waved.

"They shoulda called it *Cinderella*'s *crabby* meat canopies," Penny chuckled and scooped up three beef empanadas off a tray.

"Canapés. It's French," I said.

"Whatever."

"The fairy princess is acting up?"

Penny chewed thoughtfully. "It's the glass slippers. They don't fit right and they're making her grouchy. But you know what Walter always says…"

I could imagine.

"You gotta suffer for your art. That's the only way to keep your finger on the prize and see failure as success and vice versa."

Huh? "Walter says all that?"

"Most of it."

"How's Romeo doing?"

Penny smirked. "He had to put on two layers of makeup to cover the sunburn. Not in the best of moods."

"Ouch. He *is* suffering for his art."

"You slay me, O'Dell. Later." She took one last empanada before she sashayed to the bar.

Despite my anxiety over losing Jackson and running into Tiny in the arcade, the reception was a soothing tonic. The weather was perfect: sunny, breezy, in the low eighties. People were chatting and enjoying themselves, and the hors d'oeuvres were a big hit. I popped a salmon roll into my mouth, then sipped my white wine.

I had convinced myself that the sooner I spoke with Jackson and got answers to my questions—about the insurance scheme, Sam Baldwin, and the money I found in his jacket—the sooner I could wash my hands of our shared past and get back to my vacation with Bill. Who had sent me a cryptic text agreeing to join me here. Where had he been all day? The problem with my plan was finding Jackson. Did he realize Tiny had run interference for him? There had to be a way to get us in the same location.

"Hi." Lola sneaked up behind me.

"What are you doing out here? The reception's off-limits for actors as per Maddy's orders," I said.

"I didn't have time to eat this afternoon, and I'm starved." She scanned the crowd cautiously. "You haven't seen her, have you?"

"Nope. Coast is clear."

"These scallops look yummy. I'll take two or three. And some of these spring rolls. Is that smoked salmon?" Lola speedily made a plate of appetizers. "Have you seen Jackson this afternoon? Think he'll make an appearance tonight?"

"Funny you should ask." I shared my arcade escapade—leaving out Tiny—and Lola was appropriately perplexed.

"What's behind the arcade?" she asked, her mouth full of salmon and cream cheese.

"An entrance to the rides. The Ferris wheel, the carousel—"

"I'd better scram. If Maddy takes attendance, I'm in deep doodoo." She snatched a napkin from the table.

"Break a leg." I had an impulse. "Could you do me a favor?"

"Sure," Lola said and washed down her food with a swallow of my wine.

* * * *

The sun tumbled beneath the horizon, the hors d'oeuvres platters nearly empty, and folks filtered into the house to get seated. It was showtime.

"Sorry I'm late. Couldn't get away from the dinner service until now." Grody huffed and puffed.

"Did you run here?" I asked.

"Just about. Emergencies at the Sandbar. A waiter dropped a tray of glasses and my bartender cut himself trying to clean up and then a customer slipped on some liquid on the floor and threw out his back. We had to call the EMTs."

Yikes! "No problem. We were fine here. Sam was pleased."

"Did you talk with him?" Grody inspected the remains of the hors d'oeuvres.

"No, but he seemed generally happy," I said.

"Wonderful, because he's going to get a whopper of an invoice. Hey, where's Bill?"

Where, indeed? "He said he'd meet me here... must have gotten waylaid with the state police. Or at the car rental." Neither of those missions should have taken him all day.

"Why don't you go in? I'll take over here." Grody motioned to one of his servers to clean up. "I owe you one, kiddo."

"If you see Bill, tell him I'm sitting in the back of the house on the left aisle."

"Got it."

Lights dimmed as I crept in and parked myself in the second to last row. True to his promise, Sam had the air conditioning repaired and running full steam. The house was almost sold out; nice to have that kind of attendance for an opening, though the festival was scheduled to run two more nights. After each performance, audience members would vote for their favorite scenes, and the winning theater would be honored on the final night. I had high hopes for *Arsenic and Old Lace*, but it would need some *oomph* to recover from the chaotic dress rehearsal with Jackson standing in for Romeo.

A spotlight hit the center of the curtained stage, and Arlene Baldwin moved boldly into her light. She smiled graciously, welcomed the audience, congratulated the finalist theaters, and introduced the president of the New Jersey Community Theater Association, the genial, attractive man from Westfield whom Lola had engaged in conversation two days ago. His name was Graham, and he welcomed everyone a second time and provided a brief history of the community theater association—its expanded membership now one hundred fourteen strong—which information earned applause from the spectators.

"The festival was on hiatus after Hurricane Sandy," Graham said. "This is the first year we are back. We dedicate this week's performances to the people of the Jersey Shore. Resilient and irrepressible."

A soft hum from spectators and sustained applause demonstrated their appreciation.

Then Graham announced the plan for the evening: the performance of the scenes followed by viewers expressing their preferences on feedback cards. He was a handsome devil. Easy to see why Lola glommed on to him... Thinking of handsome men reminded me that Bill was still AWOL. I'd switched off my cell so even if he tried to text me I wouldn't get the message.

Graham wrapped up his speech, wishing every theater best of luck, and escorted Arlene off the stage. They descended the set of stairs into the house, where Graham left Arlene seated between Sam and John. I never did ask John what his mission with the Baldwin enterprises was...other than serving as the "welcoming committee" for the NJCTF.

"Sorry I'm late." Bill slid into his seat as the house went dark and silence descended over the audience.

"Where were you?" I hissed.

"It's a long story—"

"It had better be a good one. I was worried all day—"

A woman in front of us twisted in her seat and politely smiled. The universal gesture for "pipe down."

I stuffed my hands in my pockets, avoiding Bill's hand, which crept from the arm of his seat into my lap. Now that I knew he was safe, I could afford to be a little chippy. At least until intermission. I focused on the stage. *Cinderella* was a great opening...everyone loved the singing and dancing, Prince Charming, the mean stepsisters, and the transformation of the cinder wench into the princess by way of onstage sleight-of-hand and carefully placed screens. Even the glass slippers behaved. If applause meant anything, *Cinderella* had the prize in the bag. *The Mousetrap* was decently acted but ho hum. I, as well as the audience, had seen too many Agatha Christie stories on DVDs and in the movies. I'd pass on it.

Penny was correct about *Noises Off*. It was a funny spoof on backstage bedlam with characters running on and off the "stage." Unfortunately, the crucial moment was the pratfall down some stairs. Difficult to produce giggles with the black boxes instead of actual stairs. Still, the actor gamely hopped and leapt over the stacked cubes. The first act ended with *Death of a Salesman*. Not an upbeat way to close out the half, witnessing Willy Loman and his two sons slog through their battle with family dysfunction. But the cast was talented and, to my amazement, sucked me into the collage of scenes about deception and the American Dream. By the time the curtain came down, I was dabbing at my damp eyes. Penny might be correct about this play too—so far it was the one to beat, in my opinion.

A buzz reverberated around the house the minute the lights came up.

"I'll be back," Bill said and stood.

"That's what you said this morning," I reminded him.

"It's a long story, but I'll tell you the entire saga. Right now, I'm hungry. Didn't have a chance to eat all day," he complained.

"Where are you going?" I asked.

"The refreshment stand."

"What refreshment stand?"

"It's a theater. There're always refreshments. At least the ELT always has food in the lobby."

"Too late. You missed great hors d'oeuvres at the reception. Crabmeat, scallops in bacon, shrimp cocktail, prosciutto crostini..."

Bill groaned. "Stop. You're killing me."

"Hang on and we'll find something after the show." Bill was satisfied for the moment and hurried to the men's room.

I had a hunch about Jackson. He could ignore my texts knowing that I was gunning for him. However, if Lola contacted him to join her for a drink after the show, he might be more receptive. I switched on my cell. Lola had texted: *J will meet me at Bottom Feeder at ten...*

Yes! It worked.

Then she added: *Walter crazed Romeo complaining. Need that drink.*

Just an average, frenzied night for the ELT. I dropped my cell in my bag.

Bill plopped back into his seat. "Ran into Prince Charming in the men's room. Nice guy."

"Takes one to know one," I said sweetly.

This time when Bill reached for my hand as the curtain rose, I surrendered it willingly. I could play hard to get only so long. By now I was feeling sorry for him...poor guy had to run around between the state police and the car rental and had nothing to eat all day. The least I could do was offer him a little TLC.

The curtain ascended very fast, the batten to which it was attached smacking something in the ceiling resulting in a loud thud. We all sat motionless, feverish to know what had happened. A whispering campaign of speculation zoomed around the house like a swarm of insects. In blue light, Maddy marched onstage and gestured to someone in the fly space above the playing area. The curtain descended halfway, then zipped back up. The stage went black.

In the darkness, the Prelude to *The Sound of Music* trickled from the piano. The Von Trapp kids, nuns, and Maria harmonized beautifully. *The Sound of Music* was a sedative, playful and easy on the brain. Cotton candy had enveloped me. By the time we arrived at "So Long, Farewell," I was ready to snooze. It had been a long day. The audience erupted in applause, and a shout of "bravo" echoed off the walls. Now there were three genuine contenders.

People nattered on when the lights dimmed for *Arsenic and Old Lace.* I wished Lola and crew a silent "break a leg." Aside from the curtain mishap, the evening had gone smoothly. I prayed the ELT was not the first real disaster of the night. Abby and Edna were in full nutty-old-lady mode when the lights brightened and their postures as they swayed back and forth on the black boxes elicited giggles. Most likely Mildred, Carol, and the Banger sisters. No matter. Laughter is contagious and soon a rising tide of chuckles flowed toward the stage as they schooled their nephew Romeo on true empathy—dispatching lonely old men with poison! Romeo's sunburn—only slightly masked by his makeup—made him look boyish, as if he was blushing nonstop when he announced his intention to marry his love interest, Lola, who made her entrance and romanced him. Their scene was honest, even if Lola was robbing the cradle. Never mind, they breezed through the play calamity-free and earned a respectable, if subdued, ovation.

"Yay!" I clapped till my hands were red.

"Not bad," murmured Bill.

Whew. One down, two performances to go.

Closing the evening, *King Lear* was uneventful, his confrontation with the two ungrateful daughters appropriately tragic while his rejection of the one who truly loved him, sad. According to my high school English lit teacher: *There's trouble even in the best of families...*

We hung around the theater to congratulate the cast. Bill pecked Edna on the cheek—she was tickled by the kiss from her police chief boss—and I hugged Romeo, who usually got on my nerves. Tonight everyone deserved to celebrate.

Some folks ambled to the diner for food; Bill wanted to join them but I argued for drinks and he agreed to the Bottom Feeder. Walter was pouting because Lola didn't want to spend the rest of the evening with him so he marched off to the hotel. By ten thirty, Lola, Bill, Penny, Abby, and I were seated at a circular table facing a round of drinks. I had to think fast. I hadn't anticipated Penny and Abby; I'd intended to have Lola distract Bill while I lassoed Jackson, hopefully catching him off-guard with what I'd learned about Sam and Vinnie. At least that was my intention.

Food was ordered, a second round of drinks delivered, toasts on the success of the ELT proposed...and no Jackson. Outwardly, I hooted and chitchatted. Inwardly, I fumed. How like him to ditch Lola after agreeing to their meeting. She peeked at her watch, uncertain as she took a nip of her Creamsicle Crush. I'd gotten her hooked on them too.

"How can you drink those things?" asked Abby, who was sipping a second Scotch and water.

Thank goodness the cast had the day off tomorrow.

"They're delicious once you develop a taste for them." Lola hiccupped.

Bill snickered. He was pretty loose considering the day he'd had. "I told Dodie they sound like a kid's drink."

"I'm getting addicted," I said serenely. Where was Jackson?

Penny chortled. "I'm sticking with my martini."

"Somehow I never pegged you as a martini person," I said.

"O'Dell, you can tell a book by its cover, but you can't make it drink." The table was stunned into absolute silence. Then Abby guffawed, and Lola, Bill, and I joined in. Even Penny laughed at herself. A first. I was ready to throw in the towel and forget about Jackson, enjoy the rest of the evening, and live to pursue him another day, when Lola's eyes grew round. She cocked her head slightly in the direction of the bar—at my back—and put on a dazzling smile. Showtime!

"Whoa! It's a party." Jackson waggled a beer over his head. He inspected the occupants of the table, stopping in mid-waggle when he spotted Bill and me. His face fell.

"Pull up a chair," Bill said and scooted over, making room for Jackson beside me.

Jackson hesitated, getting a glimpse of Lola. "Nah. Don't like to be a gatecrasher."

As if.

"Nonsense," Lola said and motioned Abby and Penny to shift their locations.

Jackson had no choice. He took hold of a chair, wedged between Bill and me. Now if I could only keep him in place until I had a chance to grill him. We all took a drink.

"Jackson, I wish you had seen the show tonight. It went well, right?" Lola scanned the group for confirmation.

"Yep." Abby.

"Uh-huh." Bill.

"Really great." Me.

"All good. Except for that crash before the start of Act Two." Penny.

"What was that?" Me.

"The curtain went up to the ceiling." Penny.

"The stage crew could be more efficient." Abby.

Everyone agreed.

The lighthearted atmosphere had melted away. Was it Jackson's arrival or simply that people were getting tired as well as tipsy? I had to act fast. "I'm going to the bar. Anyone need anything?"

"I'll have another." Lola picked up on my subtext, she wasn't a diva for nothing—I needed an excuse to leave the table, with Jackson in tow.

"What the hay. I'm not driving. Make it another martini for me." Penny chewed her olive.

"Bill?" I asked.

"I'm fine."

"Jackson, can you give me a hand?" I asked sweetly.

"Well…I…uh…" Jackson hesitated.

"I'll come." Bill got to his feet.

"Jackson will help me." I waited for him to stand and move away from the table. Penny and Abby were oblivious, Lola knew what was happening. Bill gave me a strange look.

I gently nudged Jackson ahead of me. When we were two tables away from ours, I turned on him. "Where have you been? I've been texting you all day. And what were you doing in the arcade? I was intercepted by this brute of a guy I think they call Tiny. He works for Sam."

"Slow down. You were following me again?" Jackson exhaled. "You gotta let me go."

"I'd love to let you go, but now I'm trapped. I spoke with Maxine, Vinnie's girlfriend."

"What'd ya do that for?" Jackson frowned.

We reached the bar and I ordered the drinks. "Jackson, there're too many loose ends with Vinnie's death. For instance, Sam was your third silent partner on the *JV*," I said.

"No way. If it was Sam, he'd have told me when we talked about a job."

"Jackson, Sam was also Vinnie's partner on *The Bounty*. He must know something about Vinnie's murder." Did I believe that? It was the first time I'd allowed myself to say it out loud.

"Whoa. Now you're going too far. Vinnie's murder?" Jackson backed away from me.

"You can't go to work for him. He's too shady," I said urgently.

"Sam's a great guy," Jackson argued. "The theater festival and Sandy relief and all the people he helps down here."

Jackson had a point. So did I. "Why did you cut through the arcade today? And then escape out the back door? Were you hiding from someone?"

"Dodie, can't you let me alone?" he whined.

Suddenly I had an instinctive reaction. "If you're in trouble, we can help you."

"We?"

"Bill and I." Including Bill's name in this conversation was a mistake. He wanted no part of Jackson's antics. He'd made that clear.

"Yeah, right. Like, your new boyfriend is going to come to the aid of your old boyfriend."

I leaned into him. "Do you need someone to come to your aid?" I asked.

Jackson's eyes darted wildly. "No. I don't know."

"I'm sorry, but I accidentally found the money in your jacket pocket. And Vinnie's IOU."

"Now you're messing with my personal stuff? That's it. I'm collecting my things and cutting out." Jackson picked up two glasses.

"Where will you go?"

"Let's get the drinks back to the table," he said.

"If you need help—"

"Everything okay?" Bill put an arm around my waist.

"Here, man." Jackson handed Penny's martini and Lola's Creamsicle Crush to Bill. "Gotta hook up with some other dudes. Later, bro." He sauntered off as if he hadn't a care in the world.

"What was that about?" Bill asked.

"I'll tell you later, bro," I teased and walked back to the table.

11

By the time Bill and I reached our rental house, Jackson, true to his word, had packed up his belongings and hit the road. Bill gazed at Jackson's corner of the screened-in porch, his mouth ticking up on one end in his quirky grin. "Our guest has moved out. I don't suppose it had anything to do with that exchange between the two of you at the bar?"

I ignored Bill's implication that Jackson and I had had "words." "He said he had another place to stay." Sort of.

"Dodie, what are you not telling me?"

"Nothing." Why was I hesitant to share what I'd discovered about Sam Baldwin and my trip to the arcade with Bill? Because I knew he wouldn't approve of my digging into Sam's life and traipsing after Jackson. And bumping into Tiny. I was too tired to argue about my investigative instincts tonight. "Anyway, you ghosted me today."

"I wasn't avoiding you. Just...busy." Bill unlocked the front door and moved into the bungalow.

"Now who's hiding something?" I smiled.

"*Are* you hiding something?" he asked.

"Don't change the subject. It took you all day to sign a statement and get a rental car?"

"It got complicated. The Auto Unit had some intel on the car theft ring and I wanted to get an update. After I picked up the rental, I went to Philly." He busied himself locking the front door, switching off lights, filling a glass with water.

"You went to Philadelphia today?" I asked in disbelief.

"What? It's only an hour and a half from here. But traffic was bad coming back...sorry I missed lunch."

"And dinner." *Was* there something Bill wasn't telling me? It would have to wait until morning. I dragged my weary body to bed and was asleep in minutes.

* * * *

The Cinderella tiara fell off my head as I hopped over a series of black boxes. I stooped to pick it up, stumbling out of my glass slipper, which shattered into a hundred pieces. I hastily scraped up the shards of glass and deposited them into my traveling salesman suitcase while a dozen kids ran around singing "The hills are alive, the hills are alive, the hills are alive."

I jerked awake.

Bill sat up. "Wha...?"

"Sorry. Go back to sleep," I murmured.

He promptly did so, leaving me staring into the half-light of early dawn. I gathered the sheet under my chin. Whew. In my dream state I'd done a mash-up of the festival scenes becoming Cinderella with the Salesman's sample case surrounded by the kids from *The Sound of Music*. I shuddered. Talk about a nightmare.

It was barely 6 a.m., and the bed felt comfy; I should have snuggled next to Bill and gotten at least another hour or two of sleep. After all, this was our vacation. I hated to admit it, but this visit down the shore was becoming too much like Etonville: the theme food, the rehearsals, even the murder. After an hour of mind-racing activity, I submitted to the day and stole out of bed, careful to avoid waking Bill.

I took a cup of coffee to the porch and settled into the rocker. The town was snoozing, Atlantic Street undisturbed. Gunmetal-gray and white clouds occasionally gave way to patches of blue. Overcast. Not a great beach day. Never mind, the NJCTF was up and running, Grody's reception was a success, and my responsibilities as a best buddy were over. I could safely kick back and work on my tan after handling one niggling fragment of unfinished business. Jackson. The Candle Beach Police Department must have moved on from him since there were no more interviews—that I was aware of, or that Jackson was sharing—and Jackson was still roaming free and sleeping who-knew-where. Early this morning I had resolved that I would move on too. Let the authorities handle the loose ends, Vinnie's unscrupulous past, and Sam Baldwin's irons-in-some-suspicious-fires. Dodie O'Dell was on vacation.

I tucked my legs under me, sipped my coffee, and rocked back and forth. I would make the rest of this escape from Etonville an amazing time. We deserved it. Today Bill and I could take that drive to the lighthouse we'd talked about—

"Dodie?" Bill called out.

"On the porch. Hey, why don't we—"

"Have you seen my wallet? I thought I left it in my pants pocket last night."

"On the chest of drawers," I said. "Coffee's ready."

Bill appeared on the porch, his bedhead a tangle of sandy-colored spikes. He was dressed in a black T-shirt and jeans.

"Going somewhere, sailor?" I asked.

"Actually I am. Going somewhere," he said apologetically.

I stopped rocking. "Where? Let's get out of Candle Beach today and take a drive to the lighthouse. With that gloomy sky, the beach isn't such a great option."

"I'd like to see the lighthouse. Just not today," he said carefully.

I followed Bill to the kitchen. He poured half a cup of coffee, then downed most of it in a couple of swallows. "I got a text that the state police have a lead on my BMW. They'd like me to come by."

"That's great news, but couldn't they talk by phone?" I asked, a tad petulant.

"They want me to see some mug shots of perps recently arrested for car theft. See if anyone is familiar." He was in police chief mode.

"Give me a minute and I'll go with you." I bolted for the bedroom.

"Dodie! Wait. I'm a cop, remember? I've been through these sessions before. It's going to be tedious." He glanced at his watch. "It shouldn't take more than a few hours." He kissed the top of my head. "I'll text you later."

A few hours? I was disappointed to say the least. But I knew getting his beloved car back was a priority for Bill. Probably catching a car thief too. "No ghosting me today," I said firmly.

Bill raised his hands in defeat. "Got it." He snapped his NFL cap on his head and hurried out.

As long as I had the morning to myself, I would make the most of it. I had a leisurely breakfast of eggs and toast. I cleaned up the kitchen, tidied up the bedroom, and lingered in the shower, letting the warm water cascade over my head and shoulders. It would be cloudy but sticky today—my stretchy Bermuda shorts and a sleeveless tee would work. I could use a power walk along the shoreline, create a trail of footprints in the damp sand, drop into one of the shops on the boardwalk and buy souvenirs. I owed my nephew Cory something for his birthday next month. He was two going on three. Then I might pop into the Sandbar for a makeup lunch from yesterday. Bill could join me there.

I grabbed a visor, a bottle of sunscreen just in case, and my bag. I had barely locked the front door when my cell pinged. It was Lola: *What's up today? Lunch?* I hesitated. Bill and I needed some alone time. I texted back: *Not sure. Walk on beach? Meet me at tiki bar in ten?* Lola agreed and I set off. My cell rang. Could it be Bill already? I checked the caller ID. It was Jackson. *The Godfather* came to mind. *Just when I thought I was out he reeled me back in...*

"Hi." I was peeved.

"Dodie?" Jackson's voice quavered.

And exasperated. "Who else would be talking on my phone?"

"You gotta help me." A note of desperation had crept into his voice. "I think I'm toast."

"Where are you?"

Jackson spoke softly. "They, like, gave me one phone call. I'm—"

"Arrested?" My voice skated up the scale.

"No longer a person of interest." He tried to laugh. "Prime suspect. Call Sam."

"Sam Baldwin? What can he do?"

"Sam knows everybody. He can help," Jackson said.

I assessed the situation. "Hang tough for a bit. I'm on my way."

For the first time since Jackson returned to Candle Beach he sounded panicky. What had happened since yesterday? Did the police have new evidence? Where had they found him? All of my early morning resolve to back away and release my past melted with the knowledge of Jackson's catastrophe. As much as I wanted to power walk my way out of Jackson's life, I couldn't leave an old friend stranded. I called Lola and filled her in; she insisted on accompanying me to the police department. I didn't refuse her offer. I could call Bill, but what could he do? I ran to my MINI Cooper, jammed it into Drive and zoomed off to Lola's hotel.

Half an hour later, Lola and I were seated in the outer vestibule of the Candle Beach Police Department. Jackson was being kept in a holding pen awaiting a court appearance before a judge to set bail. We weren't permitted to see him. I asked to speak to the arresting officer and was told to wait here—I was dying to find out what the police knew. Lola twisted blond streaks of hair. I recognized the nervous gesture. I texted Bill to give him an update. No response so far.

"Want some coffee?" I asked, gesturing to a machine in the corner.

"I'll pass," said Lola. "What's keeping him?"

"No clue." I knew what could happen to a murder suspect when they lawyered up: The right attorney could get a person out on bail for any offense. But how would Jackson afford that kind of legal defense? His budget meant a public defender.

A receptionist motioned for me to approach her window. She slid it open. "The arresting officer is unable to meet with you at this time. You'll need to call later to make an appointment."

Behind the receptionist, the tall, thin cop who'd interviewed Jackson at my place swiveled his head and glared at me. Still no smile, still edgy, bouncing on his feet. He made my skin crawl.

I took a chance that this cop had been the arresting officer. "Are you sure? Because I think I see him right there—"

"You have a nice day." The receptionist snapped the sliding window shut in my face.

We needed to take Jackson's case to the next level.

* * * *

Lola and I drank coffee in the Candle Diner pondering my next move.

"What does Bill think?" Lola asked.

"I can't reach him." I doodled on a paper napkin, intending to create a to-do list. Unfortunately, the list was empty except for one word. *Sam.* Somehow Jackson thought Sam would help him get out of jail. Did they have that kind of relationship now? As far as I knew, Jackson had only met Sam this week in the course of applying for a job. He was totally in the dark as far as Sam being the silent third partner on the *JV* until I told him. However, considering there were no other options, it wouldn't hurt to try contacting him. "I'm going to see Sam Baldwin."

"The patron of the theater festival?" Lola asked. "What does he have to do with Jackson?"

I forgot that Lola was not privy to the Jackson-Vinnie-Sam triangle. "Jackson has been trying to get a job with his company and seems to think Sam might help him post bail."

Lola was skeptical. "Are they that close?"

"I don't know. I guess it's worth a shot," I said.

"I thought Jackson would be fun to know better..." Lola lamented.

Aka boyfriend material. "Sorry. For the present that would mean all dates behind bars," I said.

Lola drained her coffee cup and waved off the waitress's offer of a refill. "I'm meeting Walter to go over our *Arsenic* scenes. He thinks the pacing is off. We're not getting the reaction we should."

Good luck with that. "I'm going to the theater to see if Sam or Arlene is hanging around there," I said.

"And if not?" Lola asked.

"Baldwin General Contractors. The office is off of Route 195."

"Dodie, you're a terrific ex-girlfriend. I'm not sure I'd have done the same for Antonio, or Dale."

"Or Walter?" We both smiled.

"I'll meet with him while you visit the theater. Then let's hook up and if you decide to go to Baldwin's company, I'm in too," Lola said.

"Right." We split up and I headed down the boardwalk to the theater. I started to feel more confident about my agenda. After a visit to Baldwin General Contractors, lunch at the Sandbar was in order—with or without Bill. Grody had a contact in the county prosecutor's office who might know a thing or two about Vinnie's murder investigation.

The sky had been threatening rain all morning, a gale churning up the water. The beach was deserted except for the handful of resilient bathers who enjoyed the possibility of being pummeled by a potential downpour. Raindrops pinged off my head as I hurried into the lobby of the theater. All was dark and hushed. A huge change from last night, when the place was teeming with laughter and applause. As Penny would say, *that's show biz*—

"Can I help you?" A voice thundered out of nowhere.

I flinched. "Hello?" The place was empty.

"You want something?" The speaker was unseen, but there was no mistaking the voice.

"Hi, Maddy," I said. "Is Sam around?" I scanned the lobby. Aha…a surveillance camera and a loudspeaker were attached high on a far wall. Was there enough illicit activity in the Candle Beach Community Theater that warranted this kind of security?

"Who wants to know?" Maddy emitted aggravation.

Did she remember me? Probably not. "I'm Dodie O'Dell." I hesitated. Being an honorary member of the Etonville Little Theatre might carry no weight with the stage manager. I opted for another tactic. "I worked with the Sandbar and Sam to set up the reception for opening night."

"Wait a minute."

Within seconds Maddy materialized. "Sam's at work. Being the benefactor of the New Jersey Community Theater Festival isn't a full-time occupation, ya know," Maddy announced.

Her declarations were more and more like Penny's. "Right. By the way, you did a fantastic job stage managing the performances last night. I know it's hard work rounding up actors, dealing with their neuroses..."

"Like herding cats." Maddy regarded me with more civility. "Arlene's backstage if you want to see her."

I hadn't banked on approaching Sam's wife, but she was better than no one at this point. "I would. Thanks."

I trailed Maddy through the house and into a dressing room behind the stage, very much like the dressing rooms in the Etonville Little Theatre: parallel counters with chairs facing mirrors rimmed with light bulbs. Arlene was in dress-down mode—no wraparound skirts or linen ensembles in sight. She wore jeans and a button-down shirt several sizes too large. Her brown hair was swept up in a ponytail, her face devoid of makeup except for bright red lipstick. She concentrated on a ledger.

"Arlene? This is...?" Maddy gestured at me, her manner understated and respectful.

"Dodie," I said.

Arlene glanced up, took in both Maddy and me, and snapped the ledger closed. "I said I didn't want to be disturbed." Her tone was notably snippy.

"I'm sorry. I wanted to speak with Sam," I said apologetically.

"He's not here," Arlene said briskly. "Maddy can handle all theater issues." She rotated her body away from us.

"I'm not here about the theater festival. I'm here about Jackson Bennet."

Arlene's expression was a blank.

"He was a former partner of Vinnie Carcherelli. I understand Sam was also an associate of Vinnie's. That he was going to hire Jackson to run Vinnie's charter boat business." I mentally crossed my fingers that this white lie would elicit some interest from her. Given that she was also a co-owner of *The Bounty*.

"No idea who this Jackson is." Arlene Baldwin would never be Miss Congeniality. At least I had her attention now. "Why do you want to see Sam?"

"Jackson's in some trouble," I said.

"What kind of trouble?" she asked abruptly.

"I'm not at liberty to discuss the matter with anyone but Sam."

My explanation sounded silly to me. It apparently passed muster with Arlene. She whipped out her phone and tapped a message. "Sam's at the office." She scribbled an address—which I already had—on a paper towel and thrust it at me. "He's only there for the next hour."

"Thanks. I appreciate this."

"What's your name again?" Arlene asked.

* * * *

It wasn't an especially productive conversation with Arlene Baldwin. But I did learn that referring to Vinnie and the charter boat business earned me Sam's address. I swung by the Windward and texted Lola that I was outside, hoping to avoid bumping into any of the Etonville gang and having to invent a scenario for Lola and me. I needn't have worried. She was alone. I did a double-take. In the time I'd been at the theater, she'd huddled with Walter over the *Arsenic* script, and changed into a brown knit top, beige pencil skirt, and straw espadrilles. Designer sunglasses hung from a chain around her neck, and even though the day was cloudy, her blond hair was pulled back in a tight bun. She gave the impression of a runway model.

"Wow, you look…"

"Too much?" she asked. "I thought I'd dress for the occasion. You know, begging for money."

"I was going to say awesome." I paused. "If I get stuck pleading for Sam's support, I'll let you take over."

"Deal." She smiled serenely.

Baldwin General Contractors was a short trip from Candle Beach by way of Route 195. I used the GPS Genie on my cell phone to direct us, and in fifteen minutes we'd cruised down the highway and exited onto Mount Pleasant Avenue. A quarter of a mile down the road was a two-story, modern office building, with glass windows on all sides. A parking area bordered the entrance.

I switched off the engine. "Here goes nothing that I hope turns into something, for Jackson's sake."

We entered the vestibule and immediately stood in front of a woman sitting behind a desk. The lighting was muted, the carpeting a subdued gray and white pattern, the walls covered with photos of beautifully designed and executed construction projects.

"Can I help you?" the receptionist asked. She was middle-aged, kindly, and conservatively dressed in a black blouse and skirt.

"I'd like to speak with Sam. He's expecting me," I said with what I hoped was a dash of confidence.

The woman paged through an appointment calendar, frowned, and picked up the telephone. "You are?"

"Dodie O'Dell. From Candle Beach," I added as an afterthought. But I was pretty certain that Arlene had given Sam a heads-up and he'd know who I was.

The receptionist replaced the phone in its cradle. "Down that hallway. First door on the right."

Lola and I crept quickly down the hall, pausing to nod to each other before knocking on the door. I raised a fist but before I could land a blow, the door opened.

Sam smiled graciously at us. "Come on in."

"Thank you. We're sorry to disturb you, but Arlene—"

"Please. Sit down."

He gestured to beige leather seats facing a large, sleek desk. They were soft and cushy.

"What can I do for you? Arlene mentioned something about Vinnie's friend Jackson?" he asked.

I was shocked at his tone. Sam couldn't have been any nicer, any more accommodating. This was another side to him. "We met before. I helped with the theater reception, and this is Lola Tripper. An actress with the Etonville Little Theatre." Lola extended a hand, and Sam shook it warmly. *Yowza.* The two of them could have been playing a scene from one of Grace Kelly's sophisticated mystery movies. *To Catch a Thief* came to mind.

"Arlene may have told you that Jackson is a friend of mine. That's he's in trouble," I said.

"Oh?" he asked, noncommittal.

No point in beating around the bush. "He was arrested this morning for Vinnie's murder."

If my announcement came as a bombshell, Sam kept his reaction contained. He blinked once, then set his face in a mournful mask. "I'd heard something from a friend at the *Candle Beach Courier.*"

Geez. The news would ricochet around Candle Beach like a boomerang in the next hour. "When I spoke with Jackson this morning, he suggested I contact you. He had the idea you might possibly be willing to…" I hesitated. Both Lola and Sam waited expectantly for me to continue. How ridiculous was it that Jackson believed this well-to-do businessman would bail him out of jail for murder. I had difficulty even forming the words. There had to be another way.

"Willing to what?" Sam asked.

"Never mind." I stood. "I'm sorry to take up your time."

Lola gazed at me as if I'd lost my mind. We came here to get bail money, she seemed to be saying. "Mr. Baldwin…"

"Sam, please," he said, shifting his focus to Lola.

"Our friend Jackson is in deep trouble. He confided that he might be going to work for you," Lola chose her words carefully.

"We discussed options."

"He's in dire need. Without the means to…have himself released after his arraignment," Lola said sorrowfully.

"You're talking bail," he said.

"Yes. We wouldn't have come here if Jackson hadn't been an acquaintance of yours. Or if we had anywhere else to go." She rested her hands modestly in her lap.

Lola was first-rate! This was the best acting I'd seen her do in months.

Sam leaned back in his chair. "Sorry. I'm not in a position to take on this responsibility."

"Could *The Bounty* be put up as collateral in some way?" I blurted out. "You own part of it. As a partner you could choose to…"

As if in slow motion, Sam swung his head to face me. For a brief moment I saw a flicker of the cigar-chomping mob boss who'd threatened an employee on the phone outside the theater. "Not possible. Vinnie's estate is in probate. And I can't help your friend."

He ushered us out of his office, politely but firmly.

Lola and I sat in the MINI Cooper, both of us quiet. "Thanks for trying," I said.

"Well, it was always a long shot."

"True. Jackson had delusions of grandeur as far as Sam Baldwin was concerned. The guy may have offered to hire him. Bail him out of jail? No way." I turned the ignition key and flicked on the windshield wipers. A light drizzle had descended on the shore. "Lunch at the Sandbar? Let's get a table in the corner. Hidden out of the way when the news hits about Jackson's arrest."

12

Best laid plans. I scanned my lunch companions at the round table smack in the middle of the restaurant. We'd no sooner stepped foot inside the Sandbar when the Banger sisters cried, "Yoo-hoo!" Lola and I had no choice but to join Etonville for lunch. No being tucked out of the way for us. Of course, the *Candle Beach Courier* sat prominently among the fish sandwiches, clam chowder, shrimp salad, and lobster rolls. Me? I needed an aggressive approach to my afternoon, so I opted for red meat: a burger and fries.

"Poor Jackson," said Carol.

"Of course he's innocent," asserted Lola.

"Of course," Carol agreed.

"Dodie, what's going to happen to him?" asked Mildred.

I picked up the newspaper. The headline blared the obvious. FORMER PARTNER CHARGED WITH LOCAL MAN'S MURDER. No new information in the article, only that Jackson had been arrested and awaited his day in court. No specific mention of the evidence tying him to the murder. "I'm not sure."

"Does he have a lawyer? Now that he's a 10-15, Jackson's going to need to lawyer up," Edna said grimly. "He'll need bail too."

"He didn't do it, did he?" asked a Banger sister.

"I can't imagine that nice young man doing anything like this," said the other sister.

"Copy that. Jackson stepped up to the plate and filled in for Romeo during the dress rehearsal," Edna announced.

True.

"Abby said he served snacks for the cast at your house. That's an awfully generous thing to do," said Mildred.

Of course, it was my house and my snacks. Pauli eyed me and shrugged, his mouth full of fried clams.

"You can't spill your milk and not cry," Penny intoned wisely.

"What does that mean?" asked a Banger.

Penny shrugged. "What's done is done."

"You think he's guilty?" Mildred asked, her jaw dropping.

"We'll have to see if the handwriting's all over the wall," Penny added.

Everyone focused on me. Penny had a way of providing an inkling of truth in the midst of her mangled clichés. There must be some conclusive evidence. "I don't think he murdered anybody. I'd like to know what proof the police have."

The table was silent, all pondering Jackson's fate.

"Dodie, are you going to find out who did kill Vincent Carcherelli?" asked Mildred. "After all, you solved murders in Etonville."

"The shore's not Etonville," Vernon replied between bites of his lobster roll. "They don't do things the same way down here that we do up north."

Vernon was actually correct. Candle Beach was a sleepy town most of the year; in the summer its population swelled and its police force expanded. Not to mention it had the resources of the county prosecutor's office.

"If we were home in Etonville, we could hold a bake sale to raise bail money." A Banger sister.

"Or a jumble sale at the Episcopal Church." The other Banger sister.

"The chief could get him released," said Mildred. "As a professional courtesy?"

"For Pete's sake, Mildred, the man's in jail for murder," shouted Vernon. "The chief can't bust him out of the big house!"

Mildred tossed her head dismissively as if to say "we'll see."

I was glad Bill was out of range of this conversation. The Etonville crowd finished their lunch, provided more opinions on Jackson's future, and encouraged me to hang in there. Since a light mist continued to fall, some folks set off to join a bus tour of an historic village half an hour away. Lola gave my shoulders an encouraging squeeze and headed back to the hotel for a nap.

I was relieved to be alone, finally, and when the traffic in the restaurant slowed, I sat on a bar stool waiting for Grody to take a break.

"Thought that was you," said John Bannister at my back. He glanced at the newspaper spread out in front of me on the bar.

"Arlene said you stopped by the theater asking for Sam. Something about your friend?" he asked.

"Jackson was under the crazy impression Sam might be willing to put up his bail money," I said, almost embarrassed.

John was silent for a moment, leaning on his cane. "No luck there?"

"Nope."

"Maybe I could have a word with Sam," he said.

I stared at the kindly gentleman. "You'd do that?"

"Keep your chin up. Tell your friend to do the same." He nodded and walked away.

What a generous offer.

* * * *

"Pretty grim news, Red," Grody said. "Coffee?"

He filled a cup before I could say yes. Though Grody had lowered the acrylic sheets that served as temporary walls to retain some warmth, gusts of cool air found their way into the restaurant. The heat from the mug was welcome.

"Have you spoken to him?" Grody asked gently.

"I was his one phone call," I said. "He asked me to speak to Sam Baldwin about bail."

"He what?" Grody was as mystified as Lola and me about Jackson appealing to Sam.

"I know, right?" I said.

"So…?"

"I found him at his office. He was courteous, listened to our appeal." Or rather Lola's appeal.

Grody propped his elbows on the bar. "And?"

I ducked my head. "He politely rejected our request. Claimed he couldn't help Jackson." I wasn't banking on John Bannister having any better luck with Sam.

Grody frowned. "I know your intentions are noble, kiddo. For the record, I don't believe Jackson's guilty, but something bad is going on here. You should steer clear of this business and let the police handle the case."

"And if he doesn't get terrific representation and make bail, he'll sit in jail until his trial. That could be months." I sipped the coffee, allowing the heat to trickle down my throat and warm my belly.

Grody spread his arms in defeat. "What else to do?"

"If only I knew what evidence the cops have to charge him…" I permitted the thought to dangle.

"There's nothing in the *Courier*," Grody reminded me.

"You do know someone in the county prosecutor's office. Do you think you could—?"

"Whoa!" Grody backed off. "Wait a minute! Picking up a little gossip is one thing. Prying hush-hush information out of a county official is another."

"You're right," I said. "I hate to abandon Jackson, even if he is a pain in my butt. We have—"

"History. So you said before." Grody sighed. "It's not gonna be easy. I'll make a call and see if I can coax anything out of my contact."

"Thanks, Grody." I clasped his arms.

"No guarantees, but he owes me. I let him win at poker," he said.

"You're a nice guy," I said.

"Not really. He's my brother-in-law," Grody said wryly.

* * * *

Bill munched on fried clams as I steered my MINI Cooper onto Ocean Avenue, the wipers intermittently clearing the windshield.

"These are great. Tell Grody." He finished off the last of his lunch.

"I will. Sorry you missed the Etonville bunch."

"Me too." Bill chuckled, then turned sober. "Tell me about Jackson's arrest."

What to tell? I resisted sharing Grody's offer to dig around in the prosecutor's office. I knew what Bill's reaction would be to that, and I didn't have the stamina today to squabble over my efforts to free Jackson. "The newspaper article was noticeably vague. Just that the investigation had revealed evidence permitting the police to charge him."

"And Jackson? How's he doing?"

"He called. Had me reach out to Sam Baldwin about bail," I said.

"Who's that?" Bill asked.

Bill wasn't privy to my interactions with Sam during the past few days. "He's the patron of the community theater festival. Supposedly he's hiring Jackson for some job. He runs several companies."

"Are they good friends?" Bill asked. "Because if they are, why'd Jackson have to sleep on our front porch?"

"No clue," I said honestly. Since Jackson had removed his things last night, he'd likely seen the last of our bungalow.

"Well, the PD will get to the bottom of it. Hard to believe Jackson's the perp. 'Course we don't know what evidence the department has," Bill said hastily.

Not yet. "So, what held you up? Any of the mug shots familiar?" Although why criminals in the Candle Beach area would be recognizable was beyond me.

Bill shifted in the passenger seat and wiped his hands on a paper napkin. "Nope."

"You mentioned leads on the BMW," I reminded him.

"Nothing materialized."

Was it my imagination, or was Bill being deliberately evasive? I'd gotten this ambiguous treatment before...usually when he was on a case. The state car theft unit doubtless appreciated having one of their own on assignment with them. Still, it was our vacation.

"So...the lighthouse?" Bill said.

When Bill had arrived at the Sandbar as I was leaving, we made plans. While he ordered takeout, I Googled directions on my cell. With the on-and-off showers, we decided to take a day trip to the Barnegat lighthouse. It was an hour away, enough time for the clouds to clear a bit as per my weather app. By three o'clock the sun was struggling to peek out from behind a thick cloud cover. All traces of the morning's drizzle had faded.

"We have an hour and a half before it closes." I pulled into the parking lot adjacent to the park, whose website indicated that tourists were invited to partake of various activities: picnicking, fishing, birdwatching, hiking along its many nature trails, and climbing to the top of the catwalk on the lighthouse. All two hundred plus steps.

Bill craned his neck and shaded his eyes. "We're going all the way up there?" he asked skeptically.

"It'll be great. You'll see." Honestly, I had my own doubts about the trek to the top, but I'd gotten us here and we had an afternoon to kill. I needed something to take my mind off Jackson for a couple of hours until I heard something from Grody.

"Did you see the list of conditions that should keep people from attempting the climb?" Bill read the sign posted at the entrance to the lighthouse. "Heart trouble, back trouble, recent surgery, dizziness, fear of heights—"

"Come on, sailor. You'll be fine. The view's supposed to be spectacular."

"My back's been aching lately," he grumbled and followed me inside the lighthouse.

"Two hundred steps. Not even a tenth of a mile," I said brightly. Climbers were sparse today, three twenty-somethings ahead of us and a middle-aged man and woman a dozen paces behind. We set foot on the spiral staircase and began our ascent. I could swear Bill counted each step aloud, pausing periodically to take a break.

"Are we there yet?" he asked.

I'd given up conversation after the first twenty-five paces. The climb was more challenging than I'd expected. We reached the catwalk and burst out of the dimly lit stairwell to the bright light of day—while we were climbing, the sun made a bona fide entrance. "Yay!" I said as Bill huffed his way onto the catwalk and leaned into the guardrail. "We made it! Isn't this exhilarating?"

Bill wheezed. "Now I need to get my heart back inside my chest."

"What happened to that NFL body?" I put a hand on his arm. "Beautiful." From my vantage point you could see up and down the New Jersey shoreline for miles. The panorama was spectacular.

"This is nice," Bill said appreciatively. "Those houses are like playthings." He pointed to a nearby town whose rooftops formed a patchwork of squares. "This reminds me of Google Earth."

"Right!" I used Google Earth to sweep in on my parents' place in Naples. I got a kick out of seeing what they were up to.

We observed an ocean vessel—some distance off-shore—sail through the choppy water as it made its way south. I crossed to a plaque on the lighthouse wall and read. "In the past sailors needed this lighthouse to guide them through the shoals and swift currents." I gestured at the ship. "Wonder where it's going? Or coming from."

"Likely from the Port of New Jersey if it's hauling cargo. Could be going all the way to Africa." Bill stared at the ship. "According to the car theft unit, that's where most of the stolen vehicles are shipped."

The BMW was on Bill's mind. I took his hand and we retraced our way down the spiral staircase, emerging onto the pavement in no time from the rapid descent. Bill sneezed.

"Uh-oh," I said. "You okay?"

"Fine. Most likely an allergy." He sneezed again.

* * * *

Bill was silent on the ride back to Candle Beach. No other mention of the BMW, no warning me to stay out of Jackson's affairs, and when I asked what he was up for this evening—playing hard to get—he suggested

I go see the theater festival while he rested at the bungalow. Alone. I wasn't offended, only mystified. He claimed to be tired and achy. The sneezing seemed to be more than an allergy, he said. What was going on? He checked out. AWOL. According to Aunt Maureen *absence*—distance in this case—*did not make the heart grow fonder.* She believed in *out of sight, out of mind.* For the present, I was out of Bill's mind.

I offered to whip up something for dinner. Bill declined my offer, kissed me on the top of my head, and went to the bedroom to take a nap. I felt sticky from my hike up to the top of the lighthouse. I jumped in the shower, changed into a lightweight cotton skirt and blouse ensemble, and looked in on Bill. He was sleeping so I gave him a peck on the cheek.

"Huh...?" He rolled over without opening his eyes.

Possibly the bloom was off the romantic-vacation rose. I shook off my gloomy mood and decided that the theater festival had to be more entertaining than sitting in the house waiting for Bill to awaken from his nap. I had an hour to kill before the curtain went up on the NJCTF; Lola and company would be prepping for tonight's show; Grody would be over-the-top busy at this hour—and I wanted to give him time to communicate with his brother-in-law; that left a Creamsicle Crush at the tiki bar.

I settled onto a stool, and while I waited for my drink and appetizer, I checked email and clicked on my Facebook page. There were posts from ELT members about the theater festival and the other entrants, some pictures of the *Arsenic and Old Lace* cast, and a video of my brother Andy's son Cory in the wading pool. Andy loved to post videos of Cory running around in the backyard, eating pasta, and singing "The Wheels on the Bus." I smiled and reminded myself to buy and send my nephew's birthday present.

I scanned the national news and put my cell in my bag. A copy of today's *Candle Beach Courier* was folded in half, stuffed into the menu holder. Was that a comment on the local paper's quality? I reread the article on Jackson's arrest. The accompanying mug shot was unflattering, typical for this kind of photo. Dark circles rimmed his eyes, he sported several days' worth of beard, and his dark hair formed a curly halo around his face. I couldn't help myself. I felt sorry for my old boyfriend. And yet, he projected a hint of mischief. As though he thought this was all a game and any moment now he would be released to join his surfer buddies and thrill them with his escapade behind bars. Oh, Jackson...

"Like, hey." Pauli plopped down beside me.

"Pauli! Fancy meeting you here," I joked.

"I figured you'd be here if you weren't at the Sandbar."

"Nice detective work," I said. Pauli dipped his head and opened a folded paper napkin.

"What's that?" I asked.

"Like, I was at dinner with my mom," he said. "At the Sandbar. And like that guy you know…?"

"Grody," I said slowly.

"He gave me this. Told me if I saw you tonight…" He laid the napkin on the bar.

I picked up the paper and read: *Call after 8. I have news.* My pulse picked up.

Pauli studied me. "It's about the murder?"

Oh yeah. "I don't know. Why didn't he text me?" I said aloud.

"Said something about sticking his cell phone somewhere in the kitchen and I was handy."

Grody had seen Pauli with me earlier today at lunch. "Thanks. I appreciate you being the messenger," I said and sucked the rest of my Creamsicle Crush. "Want anything to drink?"

"Nah. Gotta bounce. Meeting up with some dudes at the arcade. So… if you need like any digital stuff…" he said eagerly.

"Got it." The kid was rarin' to go. An idea flashed on my inner mental screen. "Pauli, there's one more person I'd like you to do a deep search on. Jackson."

"The guy who got arrested, right?"

"Uh-huh. Jackson Bennet."

Pauli considered. "How far back should I go?"

"2012. Hurricane Sandy." I was privy to his life before that date.

* * * *

The second night of the theater festival was only slightly less festive than the opening. Though the wind off the ocean was nippy and threatened rain, the audience was large and enthusiastic, the house pulsating with energy. Once again, I had two tickets on the left aisle in the back of the house in case Bill had a miraculous recovery during his late afternoon nap and decided to join me. No real chance of that, I thought. Arlene Baldwin and John Bannister sat in the last row. No sign of Sam. Mildred, Vernon, and the Banger sisters planted themselves on the other side of the auditorium and waved. Vernon fiddled with his hearing aids, and Mildred gave me a thumbs-up. Which reminded me that I needed to vote for my favorite show before I left the theater. *Arsenic and Old Lace* was going to need all of the help it could get if it was going to have a fighting chance to win an award.

At a quarter to eight, spectators were getting restless, their pre-show murmur growing louder. Maddy left her place in the stage manager's box in the back of the theater and hurried backstage. Something must be amiss. Finally, the house lights dimmed and a hush descended on the audience. In the momentary blackness I sensed movement on my right. A body brushed my arm. Bill had come after all!

"Hi, sweetie," I whispered. "I'm so glad to see you."

"Me too, honey." The stage lights brightened. It was Jackson smirking.

"What are you doing here?" I choked out, clutching his arm.

"Ow!"

"Shh" came from someone in the row behind us. Cinderella sang. She couldn't wait to meet her Prince Charming. I couldn't wait until intermission.

I suffered through the rest of the fairy tale, then *The Mousetrap*, *Noises Off*, and *Death of a Salesman*, a knot in my stomach, my curiosity thrumming. I applauded mechanically, one eye on the stage and the other on Jackson. I resisted the urge to grasp his shirt and prevent his wandering off. The curtain had not completely fallen on Act One when I tugged on his arm. "Let's go."

"What? Where? I'd like to see the second half since I was actually a part of *Arsenic and Old Lace*. My fifteen minutes of fame." He chuckled.

"We need to duck out before anyone realizes who you are and waylays us." I jumped up and pushed Jackson into the aisle, through the lobby, and into the night. Heads twisted in our direction as we raced past, but nobody commented "there goes the murderer."

Once outside, away from the entrance to the theater, I confronted Jackson. "How did you get out? Who paid your bail? Did you hire a lawyer?"

He raised a hand to stifle the rush of questions. "Maxine."

"Maxine?" My mind did a backflip. I visualized her luxury home on the waterfront. She had the money. "She posted your bail?"

"And hired a lawyer. Big firm in New York. Works for her father," Jackson said.

"Why would Maxine do that?" Not that it wasn't a terribly generous act.

Jackson grinned. "For old times' sake." He became serious. "Because I was Vinnie's partner way back when. She knew Vinnie and I were tight." He crossed two fingers to demonstrate.

I was speechless. "Let's go somewhere we can talk."

"Okay. The Sandbar?"

"Too public." Though I did need to call Grody. "My place is not a possibility." Bill was there.

"How about *The Bounty*? I've been staying there."

"Vinnie's boat? That's where you've been crashing?" I asked.

"Vinnie invited me to stay there. Gave me a key. But then he died. It didn't feel right."

"Until you moved off our porch," I said.

I shadowed Jackson as we left the town park, walking in the direction of the marina where *The Bounty* was docked. I knew getting on the boat was borderline off-limits since it might be involved in Vinnie's murder investigation. But Vinnie had extended an invitation to Jackson, and by extension, to me. We hurried down the dock to the berth where the boat was moored, bobbing up and down in the choppy water.

"She's a beauty," Jackson said wistfully.

Selling farm equipment hadn't replaced his love of the ocean. *The Bounty* was indeed beautiful. I'd noticed its gleaming white fiberglass surface days ago, but I hadn't properly registered its modern, sleek design. There were poles and swiveling captain's chairs for eight fishermen in the aft. Below deck, Jackson unlocked a door that led into the cabin. He flicked on a light. "Watch your step."

I spun in a circle, taking in the luxury. The interior of the galley was all stainless steel appliances with cupboards, the living area an L-shaped sofa with a coffee table and flat screen television, and beyond it, a dining table with seating for eight. "This is amazing."

"Vinnie has expensive taste. Nothing like the *JV.*" He pointed toward the bow. "Two staterooms back there."

I slowly moved to the sofa and sank into its leather depths. "You could throw some kind of party down here."

"The dudes that came onboard *this* fishing charter expected to party. In style."

Jackson's personal belongings were piled on top of the dining table, marring the flawlessly decorated interior. "So you're bunking down here."

"On and off. Want a drink? I got white wine." He opened the refrigerator.

I needed to stay alert. "Is that a Keurig? I'll take coffee." Jackson banged around the galley, running water, opening and closing cupboards. "What evidence do they have against you?" I asked cautiously.

"The lawyer's working on it. Said it's circumstantial. He told me to go home and sleep…he'd be in touch. Believe that? The guy's super cool."

I hoped so for Jackson's sake. He handed me a mug of coffee and snapped open a beer can. I patted the seat next to me. "Let's get this all out into the open. You're going to have to come clean with your lawyer sooner rather than later, so practice with me. Tell me everything."

Jackson sat heavily and closed his eyes. "Vinnie was an awesome friend. I mean, he drank too much, liked to cut corners...but he was my best bud."

"I know."

"When he called me in Iowa about joining the new charter boat, I figured it would be like the old days."

"All play and little work?" I suggested.

"Whatever. When I got here, it was a different scene." He took a long drink of his beer. "Vinnie C was now Vincent Carcherelli."

That I knew.

"So we met up. That day after I crashed on your porch," he said. "The day you spied on me."

"I wasn't spying on you," I said indignantly.

"Whatever. At first it was like all sweetness and roses..."

Vinnie? Sweetness?

"My bro is wearing expensive duds, a S.W.A.T. watch, has this fantastic boat. So I figured it was the right time to hit him up for the money he owed me. We're talking, joking, about the old days and the *JV*, and then he does 360 degrees on me. Totally a different person. Says I'm ungrateful. He's 'giving me a piece of some action and all I'm thinking about is the past.'"

"What kind of action?"

"I dunno. He pissed me off and I kind of shoved him—"

"And he shoved you. Then what?"

"Then we came in here to cool down. He digs out a bag and gives me a wad of bills as a down payment. The money you found in my jacket pocket," he said. "A thousand bucks. Said he was cool for the rest and had a payday coming in this weekend," Jackson added. "Gave me an IOU."

"Like an informal promissory note between bros. What kind of payday? Like from a charter?" I asked.

"I dunno. All I know is that we parted on friendly terms. He was going to see about me joining him on the boat. He had to check with his partner."

"Sam Baldwin."

"Yeah."

"That was the last time you saw Vinnie?" I asked.

Jackson hesitated. "He called me at two a.m. Said he had to talk. To meet him here."

The little hairs were dancing on my neck "Did you?"

Jackson nodded. "Vinnie was drinking. Raving mad. Talking trash...
saying they couldn't take him for granted...he was getting revenge."
Jackson stopped to finish his beer.

"Who's 'they'?"

"He didn't say."

"Revenge? How was he going to do that?"

"I dunno! He was waving this black book around—"

"—black book? What black book?"

"A regular black book." He demonstrated with his hands. "About this big."
Three by five inches. A small notebook. "What was in it?"

"Beats me. Whatever it was, Vinnie was like bizzaro. Yelling 'it's all
in here' and shoving the book at me." Jackson stopped to take a breath.
Reliving that night was tough for him.

Where was the book now? "You know what this means?"

Jackson looked bleary-eyed. A night in jail and no sleep. He yawned.
"What?"

"If Vinnie had information that was damaging, someone might have
felt threatened enough to..."

A light bulb went on. "Whoa...murder him!" he said.

"Jackson," I said gently, "why didn't you tell me this before?"

"Vinnie said it was confidential. That I had to keep it to myself.
Besides...I wanted to straighten things out between Vinnie and me. Not
get anyone else involved," he said and hung his head.

"And Vinnie was alive when you left," I said.

"What d'ya think? He kind of passed out on the sofa and I figured, let
him sleep it off. I'd catch up with him the next day," Jackson said.

"But what about the arcade? Where were you going?"

My cell rang and I glanced at the caller ID. I'd gotten so focused on
Jackson's story that I'd forgotten to call Grody. I hit Answer. "Sorry! I
got distracted—"

"Where are you?" Grody asked abruptly.

"You're not going to believe this, but Jackson's out on bail—"

Grody lowered his voice. "Irish, he's in real trouble."

I eased into the dining area out of Jackson's hearing range. "I know."

"My brother-in-law came through with some info. He only shared it
because I told him whatever he knew would end up in the *Candle Beach
Courier* in the next day or so and that Jackson was a friend," he said.

"Thanks, Grody."

Jackson heated food in the microwave, oblivious.

"The police got an anonymous tip about a murder weapon, so they searched *The Bounty*. They found an ice pick in Jackson's backpack. The kind fishermen use to break up frozen bait."

The kind of instrument that could create a puncture wound like the one found on Vinnie's body. My pulse went wild.

I could hear Grody take in a deep breath. "It had traces of Vinnie's blood."

"Oh no."

Jackson walked toward me munching on the pasta in his frozen dinner. "What?"

"I owe you one," I said to Grody.

"Jackson's gonna need a powerhouse lawyer," Grody said.

"He's got one. I'll check back with you later."

Grody clicked off and I collapsed onto a chair at the dining table. I felt a tension headache coming on. "Jackson, did anyone from the police department or the prosecutor's office mention that they had searched *The Bounty*?"

Jackson swallowed a forkful of food. "Why?" he asked casually.

"Did they tell you what they found?" I shrieked, nearly hysterical. I counted to ten to calm down.

He tossed his dinner container in the trash. "My lawyer showed up right about then."

"They found the murder weapon—" I shouted.

"Here? On *The Bounty*? What was it?"

"An ice pick that—"

"Yo. Stabbed with an ice pick. Uh-huh." He bobbed his head emphatically. "Like I didn't think he drowned. I figured something happened to him before he landed in the ocean."

"The police figured that too—"

"So somebody with access to the boat murdered him. Who would that be?" he asked naively.

"You!" I screamed.

13

"He's being framed," I said softly to Bill. "This western omelet is delicious, by the way." I scarfed up another mouthful of Bill's savory egg concoction that he'd whipped up as a late-night dinner.

"It's the two cheeses. Gouda and Monterey Jack." He scrubbed the omelet pan. "You should slow down here. Accusing the authorities of false arrest is serious stuff."

Once I'd made it clear to Jackson that the ice pick was found among his belongings, I had absolutely no trouble convincing him to return to our rental to bunk for the night. I even tried to persuade him to sleep in the spare bedroom. He refused that offer and dropped his clothes in his accustomed corner of the porch. Now he was comfortably situated in his sleeping bag, exhausted.

"Jackson has no idea how that ice pick ended up in his backpack. He claims he hasn't owned one since he left Candle Beach."

Bill leaned over my shoulder. "That's what they expect him to say."

"You don't believe him?"

"I'm just saying…"

Bill was right. Jackson certainly had the opportunity and motive—if you assumed the money he was owed was an issue—and the ice pick gave him the means. I hadn't been a mystery and thriller reader all these years for nothing. Jackson had prime suspect written all over him.

"And the anonymous tip about the ice pick? Isn't that a little fishy?"

"Not necessarily. Someone could have heard or seen something the night of the murder and simply doesn't want to get involved. It happens all the time," Bill said. He dropped the dish towel in the drainer. "Dodie,

I can appreciate Grody wanting to help out by pumping his brother-in-law for information. But the two of you are flirting with disaster."

"You said you appreciated my investigative instincts."

"That's in Etonville, where I have control over the investigation. This is foreign territory. Anything you say or do may well be construed as obstruction," he said.

Bill was right…

"I know you have a past with Jackson, but he's got a lawyer now. From what you just told me, he sounds like a damn good one. You need to back off," he said quietly. "Because I might not be able to bail you out if you get caught digging into the facts of the case."

"What if the facts are wrong?"

"Let his lawyer sort it out." Bill sneezed, then yawned.

"All that sleep you got earlier tonight should have cured you," I teased.

"Sleep?"

"Right. When I left you were napping. That's why I went to the theater alone. So you could rest?"

"Oh. Sure. Guess I'm tired from that trek up to the top of the lighthouse," he said.

I followed Bill into the bedroom. "You need some special attention tonight." I kissed the top of his head as he took off his shoes.

"I'm going to crash." A quick kiss back and he was out like a light in minutes.

I sat on the patio in a chaise lounge mulling over recent events. I knew Bill was shaken by the theft of his BMW and was working with the state car theft unit to recover his automobile. But a gentle warning about "obstructing" the murder investigation was not like him. I expected a full-throated verbal trouncing for getting involved with Jackson's case. What was with him? He was carrying distraction to an extreme. We needed to have a heart-to-heart tomorrow morning.

My cell pinged, a text came in. It was Lola: *Did you see the disaster 2night? UGH. Meet up?* Uh-oh. Something must have happened in the second act. Lola needed some BFF time. It was ten thirty. Bill was asleep, Jackson was in for the night, and I was restless. I texted back: *come over here. out back on patio.* In twenty minutes Lola emerged around a corner of the house, her cell phone flashlight providing illumination.

"Whew. Dark out here. I parked in your driveway." Lola stepped into the arc of light thrown by a tiki torch. "Is that mound on your porch Jackson? How did he get out of jail?" she asked breathlessly.

I poured two glasses of iced tea and handed one to Lola. "You need to sit for this one." I shared Maxine's role in his release and Jackson's unbelievably great fortune in having a high-priced lawyer in his corner. I kept Grody's information about the murder weapon to myself.

"What a generous offer," Lola said. "Don't take this wrong. I think Maxine should be happy to see Vinnie's potential killer behind bars. Instead of posting his bail and providing legal help."

"It's strange." Paying her another visit was on my agenda in the morning. "According to Jackson, she did it as a nod to Vinnie and Jackson's past together."

"Hmm," Lola murmured.

"What was the catastrophe tonight?"

"When the front drape hit the ceiling last night I knew something was wrong with the curtain or the crew." She sipped her iced tea. "It was a little of both. It rose for the start of Act Two and suddenly stopped. Somebody on the crew yanked on the rope and the drape ripped, then fell to the floor, landing on black boxes. The cast of *Sound of Music* freaked out. The lights came up accidentally, and Maria von Trapp was standing stage center, her mouth in a huge O"—Lola imitated the terrorized actress—"her eyes bugging out of her head. She was so agitated she sang 'So Long, Farewell' while the pianist played 'My Favorite Things.' Maddy came onstage and called another intermission while they cleaned up and regrouped."

"Wow! Sorry I cut out after Act One."

"You didn't miss much. Our scenes were so-so, and King Lear went up on his lines. Altogether not the best night for the New Jersey Community Theater Festival." She exhaled. "One more night."

"I'm sure tomorrow will be smooth as anything," I said.

"Honestly, I'll be glad when the whole thing is over. It was nice to be included, but…"

I got it. Some things, or people, were not worth the effort. Was I thinking of Jackson? *Could he be guilty of murder?*

We finished our drinks, and I accompanied Lola to her Lexus. As she backed onto the road, I spied a white van parked a few houses down the street. I hadn't seen it before. I'd spent a fair amount of time on the porch this last week and was familiar with most of the vehicles on our block. Was it my imagination that made it appear ominous? I hurried onto the porch, locking the door. Not a peep emanated from Jackson's sleeping bag. I crept into the house and went to bed. Bill didn't move a muscle as I pulled the covers around my shoulders. His breathing was even and steady. Like him. I felt safe here.

* * * *

Light flooded into the bedroom. The hum of the air conditioner muted the clatter from outside the room, but something had awakened me and interrupted a delicious dream. Literally. I was at the Sandbar and Grody brought me a huge dish of steamed mussels. I gorged myself, becoming bigger and bigger until I was ready to burst. It didn't bother me; I ate away with a smile from ear to ear. I remembered the next bit of dream. I held an ice pick and suddenly popped like a balloon. *Geez.* My dreams, aka nightmares, were getting out of control. I reached for Bill's head on the pillow next to mine. It was empty. The alarm read 7 a.m.

"Bill?" I sang out in my early morning voice. He was probably in the shower. No answer. With all the sleep he got yesterday, it was no shocker that my guy was already up and going. I fantasized about breakfast. French toast, pancakes... The sun was out, so that meant beach time and the tiki bar. Bill was correct. With a high-priced lawyer on Jackson's case, there was little need for me to snoop around. Once I paid a final visit to Maxine to thank her and ask a question.

I slipped into my robe—I'd been there, done that with Jackson observing my nightwear—and opened the bedroom door. "You're up early—" The kitchen was quiet, no smells of impending breakfast. Not even coffee. I peeked out the door to the porch. Jackson's clothes were neatly piled, his sleeping bag rolled up, and all items pushed into the corner. What had I slept through?

Back in the kitchen I put on the coffee and spied a piece of paper with a scribbled message. *I HAD to go out. Business with my car. I will explain all. Call later. B.* As if I wouldn't know who it was from. It seemed to me that Bill had gotten himself too involved in the car theft. He should take his own advice: Let the professionals deal with it. Never mind, I didn't intend to let his agenda deter me from my agenda—enjoying the beach today. I planned to text Maxine and then Lola to see if she was up for sunbathing this afternoon. Last night it sounded as if she needed something to soothe frayed nerves before the last performance of *Arsenic and Old Lace.*

I lingered over breakfast, enjoying an extra cup of coffee while I skimmed through my email—lots of spam and a message from the Windjammer's previous sous chef, Wilson. He was back in Haiti visiting family and acting in a play at a local theater—the result of his involvement with the ELT's co-production of *Bye, Bye, Birdie.* Yay! My Facebook page boasted new pictures of my nephew Cory on a carousel at a carnival. I burst out laughing. Then I remembered... I'd asked Jackson about his escape from the Candle Beach arcade into the amusement park behind the building, but he never gave me a solid answer. I doodled on Bill's note, making a further list of the loose ends in the murder investigation. *Jackson and the arcade, the anonymous tip, the ice pick in Jackson's backpack, Sam Baldwin, Tiny, the black book...*

The black book. I dashed into the shower and speedily dressed in comfortable shorts and a sleeveless top. I slapped on my sandals and headed out the door, not before locking both the bungalow and the porch doors. If Jackson returned before I did, he'd need to text me about gaining access to his belongings.

I slid into the front seat of my MINI Cooper and switched on the ignition. Before I pulled out of the driveway, I quickly texted Lola about the beach and then Bill: *message received.* I hoped that wasn't snarky. Nothing left to say. We'd talk later. I put the car in Reverse and my cell rang. It was Pauli. I put the car in Park.

"Hey. What's up?" I asked.

"Like, I'm checking in," he said.

"If you have any info on the searches you're doing, let me know. See you at the beach later." I was about to click off.

"Like yeah, but wait."

Maxine had texted that she'd be available until eleven o'clock. It was a quarter to ten.

He took a bite of something. I could hear chewing as he talked. "I searched on Jackson like you asked."

A knot twisted in the pit of my stomach and I turned off the motor. "What did you find?"

"Pretty much nothing. He had like a minor run-in with the cops in Bannon, Iowa."

Where his brother lived.

I was curious. "What kind of run-in?"

"Like, some argument in a bar with these other guys and they sort of trashed the place."

"Was he charged?"

"Nah. They made the guys pay for damages."

Okay. Not too bad. Not a felony or a record. "Thanks, Pauli. If you find—"

"Yeah, and like one more thing." He took a drink of something. "Sorry. Breakfast. He got engaged."

"He what?"

"Like he's going to marry this woman. I saw their picture in the *Bannon Gazette*."

"Oh." Why was I surprised? We'd canceled our relationship years ago. I was in deep with Bill. "That's nice. What's her name? What's she look like?"

"Tammy Littleton. She's like awesome."

My heart plummeted. Jackson had never mentioned Tammy to me, while Bill and I had to put our relationship out in the open. It was irrational, I knew, but still...

"When's the wedding?" I asked brightly.

"Doesn't say."

"Thanks, Pauli." I ended the call with a promise to get back if I needed any other intel, and Pauli promised to keep digging.

I tore out of my driveway and cruised down Ocean Avenue toward Maxine's, irritated. Why didn't Jackson come clean about the engagement? And what impact did it have on his homecoming to Candle Beach? Did he intend to bring his bride here? And why was he openly flirting with Lola?

As I rehashed Jackson's love life, I noticed a white van a car length behind me. I turned off Ocean Avenue. The van turned off too. I continued down Land's End toward Maxine's yellow Victorian. I hit the brakes and the van slowed down as well. About twenty yards from Maxine's house, the vehicle suddenly spun right onto a narrow lane and disappeared. My hands were clammy as I gripped the steering wheel. *Someone was tailing me.* Odds were it was the same vehicle parked on my street last night.

I waited five minutes in my MC before I got out of the car in case the van showed up again. I knocked on her screen door, light winds swirling around the planters of flowers on the porch making them dip and bow. Reminded me of my aunt's flower beds at her home in Ocean Port. Soft rock music drifted outside from the interior of the house.

Maxine appeared at the door. In a white linen suit and stiletto heels, Vinnie's grief-stricken fiancée looked more composed, less fragile. "Hi."

"Hope I'm not holding you up?" I glanced at her outfit.

"No. I have an appointment with my financial advisor later this morning." About Jackson's bail? "Thanks for seeing me."

Maxine joined me on the porch, and we settled into the rockers as we had the last time we met. "You heard about the bail money?" she asked quietly, rocking, her hands resting in her lap.

"That's one reason I wanted to see you. To say thanks," I said.

She fluttered one hand dismissively. "I can afford it. Anyway, unless he skips town I'll see my investment returned." She smiled, Sphinx-like.

"Still, it was awfully generous of you. Considering Jackson is a suspect in Vinnie's…uh, Vincent's death."

"Call him Vinnie. That's what Jackson called him."

"At the memorial, right."

"Also when he came to see me here," she added.

Jackson was here?

Maxine shaded her eyes and peered at the ocean, where a cruise ship plowed through the waters. "I like Jackson. He told me stories about the *JV* and the fun they had together. How he and Vincent would take the boat out into the ocean and let it drift for hours. One time they fell asleep and got burned…"

I remembered that, the two of them red as lobsters.

"And the time they got stuck on a sandbar and had to wait for the tide to come in." She laughed like a little girl, then her eyes filled. "I miss Vincent." She faced me. "Do you think Jackson's guilty?"

I wanted to yell "yes!" He should have told me about Tammy. But I forced myself back to the conversation at hand. "Of course not. I doubt you'll ever see any reimbursement for the legal services, though," I said carefully.

"I can afford that too." She stopped rocking, her voice taking on a harder edge. "My father was glad to send his lawyer down here. In his mind, Jackson took care of a big problem. So why not help him out?" she said bitterly, then seemed to gather strength. "I would have hired a lawyer for Jackson even if my father disapproved."

Yikes…some really bad blood there. "I know Jackson appreciates your help."

"Sure." She scanned the shoreline once more as if searching for a particular sailing vessel. Maybe *The Bounty*.

"Jackson said Vincent told him I was the first person he really fell in love with," she said wistfully.

So Vinnie was actually ready to settle down…or else Jackson was providing some fabricated comfort to a grieving fiancée. Either way Maxine bought it. "Did Vinnie ever mention a black book?" I asked.

She gazed at me. "A black book?"

"Like a small pad." I indicated its size.

"No. Why?"

What to say? "He showed it to Jackson the night he died. Jackson thinks it might be important in the investigation."

"If it had anything to do with the charter boat, Vincent wouldn't have mentioned it. He never talked business when he was home."

"I thought maybe it would shed light on…things."

"I went through his clothes the other day..." She paused to collect herself. "Nothing in his pockets. That was strange." Maxine looked to me for confirmation.

I nodded agreement. It was kind of strange. My father continually left assorted items in his pockets that drove my mother nutty on laundry day.

"Except for a piece of paper with an address in a jacket pocket," Maxine added.

My little hairs twitched. "Oh? What was the address?" I asked nonchalantly.

"Some place in Walker." Maxine sprang out of her rocker and entered her house before I could comment.

Walker, New Jersey? New York? Pennsylvania? I'd never heard of it.

Maxine returned, holding the piece of paper in front of her. "Here."

I scanned the sheet, memorizing an address in Walker, NJ. 1410 Main Street. "I don't know that town. Do you?"

Maxine shook her head. "But Vincent had business stuff all over the place. Not only the charter boat. He'd call or leave messages from lots of towns."

"I suppose the police have his cell phone?" I asked.

"I wanted to keep it as a token. They said they'd return it eventually," she said wistfully.

After a beat, we exchanged pleasantries about the weather down the shore in summer and I offered my condolences again. Maxine invited me back anytime. As I walked away from her home, her eyes followed me, her loneliness palpable.

I drove back to my rental reflecting on the black book. Maxine didn't have it; odds were, the police didn't have it or Grody might have picked up some gossip about it. Where would Vinnie have stashed it? Perhaps the killer had taken it.

My mind whirled as I pulled into my driveway. I was musing on the mystery when I yanked open the door to the porch. Then I stopped. I was sure I'd locked it. "Hello? Anybody home?" I tiptoed down the porch to Jackson's pile. This morning he'd left everything in a neat mound in the corner. Clothes on top of the sleeping bag. Now the clothes—neatly folded—were set *next to* the sleeping bag. Someone had broken into the porch and rearranged Jackson's things.

I clutched the pepper spray dispenser that I kept on my key ring. I'd never had occasion to use it, but there was always a first time. My next thought was Jackson's money. I eased across the porch and rummaged around for his jacket. The wad of bills was still there. Whatever the motive for the breaking and entering, it was not Jackson's cash stash. I tried the handle of the door leading into the house. It was locked. I inserted my key and slowly squeezed the knob. "Hello?" Silence. The burglar was in all probability long gone. I shuddered.

I weighed calling the Candle Beach police department about the break-in but I could already hear the skepticism in the voice of the thin, edgy cop who'd interviewed Jackson: Are you sure the clothes were on top of the sleeping bag? Was anything missing? How did you know about the money in his pocket in the first place?

* * * *

On the beach, the sun rose higher in the brilliant blue sky, the temperature hitting eighty-five. Perfect weather. With heat beating on my head and baking my brain, I was content to let the incident on my porch melt away for a while. There was nothing I could do about it at the moment. Neither Bill nor Jackson were available.

"The sand is burning hot," said Carol, treading delicately around the multiple towels arranged in a square by the folks from Etonville, Pauli in tow.

I rolled onto my back and squinted through my sunglasses. "About time you showed up." Lola and I scooted our blanket to one side to make room.

Carol eyed Pauli, who was quiet and grumpy. He stripped off a shirt, dumped his flip-flops, and mumbled something before he raced down the beach to the ocean. I think it was "I'm going in the water."

"He's been upset for the past hour. Janice Instagrammed pictures from Boston. She's at a concert with some family friends," Carol said.

"Having fun," Lola murmured.

"One of the friends is a cute boy"—Carol raised an eyebrow—"teenage love."

We were all privy to Pauli's crush on Janice and the turmoil around them getting together while *Bye, Bye, Birdie* was in production. "Oops."

"I'm trying to distract him." Carol sighed, then perked up. "Walter's strolling on the boardwalk. Pale as a ghost. He said he's allergic to the sand."

"Also to hanging out with friends," Lola said wryly. "I tried to get him out here. No luck."

Vernon, Abby, and Mildred tiptoed through the hot sand, ice cream cones in hand.

"This chocolate chocolate chip is delicious," Mildred said between licks of her cone.

"I prefer plain vanilla. No chips, nuts, or swirls, for me," said Abby decisively.

"To each their own." Mildred settled herself on a towel next to Vernon, who munched on a waffle cone. "Dodie, want a taste?"

"No thanks. I'll get something later. You'd better eat up before it melts." Mildred swiped at a streak of chocolate that had dripped onto her beach coverup.

"Soak up the sun today," Vernon said ominously and gestured to his cell phone.

"Cloudy tomorrow?" asked Abby.

"Thunderstorm's coming in," he said.

"Didn't we have enough rain yesterday?" Mildred wiped her mouth with a napkin. "I think it brought bad luck to the show."

Penny, who'd been playing gin rummy with Edna, sat up. "No such thing as weather bringing bad luck to the theater. Whistling backstage, yes. A good dress rehearsal, yes. Saying *Macbeth*, yes. Weather, no."

"I think superstitions bring bad luck," Mildred asserted.

Abby scoffed. "I don't believe in superstitions. They're all silly. Finding horseshoes and four leaf clovers bringing you good luck? Phooey."

"Mrs. Parker called into the PD with a 10-60 one day. She was locked out. Claimed a black cat was responsible," Edna said knowingly.

"How is that even possible?" asked Carol, who snickered.

Penny cackled, shuffling the cards. "I walk under ladders all the time onstage. Friday the thirteenth might as well be the twelfth or fourteenth."

"I believe that if you sneeze someone is missing you," Mildred said firmly.

Vernon sneezed. All eyes shifted toward him, then Mildred giggled. "Oh, Vernon. I didn't know you cared!"

He manipulated his hearing aids. "What?"

Bill had been sneezing since yesterday...

Lola rubbed lotion onto her arms and shoulders. "Good luck or bad, I hope the curtain works tonight."

Heads bobbed in agreement.

"Tomorrow's storm is going to be fierce," said Edna, studying her cell phone. "Code N."

She glanced at the group. "Newsworthy event."

Sheesh. That was all the theater festival needed on its awards night.

"Lightning and thunder. It's the season," said Edna.

For summer storms yes, but not the kind of squall that became Hurricane Sandy.

Pauli dove in and out of waves, then shook off the water like a wet dog and trudged up the beach to the towels. "Hey. Water's awesome."

"This time of the year is the best," I said. "Warmer."

Penny headed to the hot dog stand, Vernon turned off his hearing aids, and everyone else decided to stick their toes in the ocean.

"Pauli, got a job for you." I did need some help, but I also figured it wouldn't hurt the kid to keep busy and keep his mind off Janice.

"Yeah?"

"Can you research an address for me? Find out what it is?" I asked.

"Easy peasy."

I handed him a piece of paper. "Maybe we can connect later tonight at the show. That'll give you some time with your laptop and websites. It's in a town I can't identify."

"Cool."

I flashed on our view from the catwalk on the Barnegat lighthouse... how Bill and I could see up and down the coastline and the layout of the town below us. That gave me an idea. "Pauli, how about checking Google Earth? See if the address is a residence or some kind of company. What kinds of other buildings surround it."

"Google Earth. Awesome," Pauli said. He brushed the damp hair off his forehead, whipped out his cell phone, eyed the Main Street address, and tapped on his phone. Up popped an aerial photo. Pauli zeroed in on the location.

I'd used Google Earth before—besides checking out my parents' home in Naples, I'd spied on Bill's house early in our relationship. "Let's see that," I said and Pauli handed me his phone. "It's a large building. Obviously more than a residence." Pauli peered over my shoulder. The picture was a miniature, but the gradations in tones from white to gray to black indicated clearly enough that the structure was substantial in size.

"A warehouse," he said.

"Maybe." According to Maxine, Vinnie "had business stuff all over the place." What significance would this location have for Vinnie that he'd kept the address in his pocket?

"Like an Amazon warehouse," Pauli added.

I agreed. "Where they store and ship packages."

We both stared at the photo. "Looks like it's in the middle of nowhere. No houses or other buildings close to it. That empty space could be fields or parking lots."

Pauli went back to work on his phone. "Like, from here the location is only thirty minutes away."

"What kind of town is Walker, New Jersey? What's the building used for? Could you—"

"Already on it." Pauli's eyes sparkled.

"Text me later? Not sure where I'll be," I said.

The rest of the Etonville crowd traipsed up the beach and packed up their beach gear. It was approaching five o'clock. Lola, Abby, Edna, Penny, and Carol decided to eat a light snack and shower before going to the theater. Mildred and Vernon were joining the Banger sisters at the Candle Diner later. Vernon had had enough of Cinderella and Prince Charming, the singing kids from *The Sound of Music*, and Shakespeare. Instead, he planned to attend a concert on the beach—it was oldies night and cover bands were playing sixties music. I was in perfect agreement with him. I intended to "second act" the theater festival myself, arrive during intermission in time to see *Arsenic and Old Lace*, applaud enthusiastically, and submit my vote for best show. Meanwhile, I'd have time to change and visit the Sandbar. I pulled on a pair of shorts, ran my fingers through my wavy mane, transformed into a halo of curls a lighter shade of auburn thanks to the sun, salt water, and humidity, and folded my beach blanket.

"Any word on Jackson?" Lola whispered as we headed to the boardwalk.

I shared my visit with Maxine, her comments on Jackson, and the address she'd found in Vinnie's coat pocket.

"Walker, New Jersey?" she asked. "I've never heard of it."

"Me neither."

Mildred caught up with us. "I don't care what Penny says. I think fate will smile on the ELT tonight. This gorgeous weather makes everyone feel better." She patted Lola's arm.

I waved good-bye to my friends. I wasn't certain the ELT had a chance to win the theater festival, but making an impressive showing was important. After all, as Lola said, the ELT had its reputation to maintain, whatever that reputation was.

14

I was on my second Creamsicle Crush when Grody planted himself on a bar stool next to me.

"How about an appetizer to go along with those? I got some fresh scallops. Tonight I'm featuring a grilled scallop cilantro. Fresh lime juice and red chili flakes give it a zing—"

"Oooh, yummy. But I think I'll pass. I don't have much of an appetite."

Grody gave me the eyeball. "What's the matter? Besides the fact that your current boyfriend has been pulling a disappearing act and your ex is out on bail for murder?"

"When you put it that way…" We exchanged grins.

"Irish, you've been a good friend to Jackson. Now that he's got a lawyer, you need to let him take over."

"That's what Bill said."

Grody hesitated. "The evidence is a problem."

"Circumstantial, according to Jackson's lawyer." I sucked up the last of my drink.

"The ice pick was in his backpack."

"Which anyone could have placed there," I argued. Plus Jackson's fight with Vinnie the night he died and the matter of the IOU. The evidence, circumstantial or not, *was* a problem.

"Have you ever heard of Walker? It's a town about thirty minutes inland," I asked.

Grody frowned. "Don't think so. Why?"

Better not to reveal the address at this point. Grody had done enough digging around for Jackson. "A friend from Etonville has relatives there,"

I improvised, changing the subject. "Since it's close to Candle Beach, I thought maybe we'd visit and—"

"Wait a minute." Grody snapped his fingers. "One of my customers mentioned Walker a few weeks ago. Showed me an article in the *Candle Beach Courier* last month."

"True?" What a coincidence! I tried not to come across as too interested. "What did it say?"

Grody poured himself an iced tea. "The article? There's ghost towns in the Pine Barrens. Abandoned communities people left. Just walked away from businesses and homes. Mostly in the 1800s. Early 1900s."

The Pine Barrens was a rural, heavily forested coastal plain that sprawled across more than seven New Jersey counties. "Walker is a ghost town?" I asked. "From the early 1900s?"

"Not really. Walker got included in the story because it was deserted a few decades ago. My customer and her husband got lost driving around in the area. The only thing they saw was an old factory. Nothing else. I guess the rest of the town died. Hey, kiddo, no way your friend has relatives living there."

"I must have misunderstood," I said lamely.

He gestured to one of his servers. "I'll be back."

Vinnie had saved the address of an abandoned factory. Why on earth would that be of interest? And did it have any connection to the charter boat business or, more importantly, his death?

It was six thirty. The show started in an hour. I still had time to kill. I weighed my options. I could hang around the Sandbar and wait for Bill, who might or might not show up, or I could hang out at home—which I was not eager to do given the recent visitor who'd rummaged through Jackson's things. Speaking of the devil, I could drop by *The Bounty* and see if that's where he'd stashed himself. Or…I could take a quick drive to Walker, New Jersey, and visit the abandoned factory.

I left a twenty-dollar bill under my drink glass and swung my bag over my shoulder. Across the restaurant, Grody was acting captivated by two patrons who bent his ear. I diagnosed the body language—been there, done that.

On the boardwalk, evening was fast approaching—the sun inching toward the horizon, the light wind picking up, the aromas of food wafting forth from eateries up and down the walkway. My stomach rumbled. I'd eat after the show. I hurried to the marina where *The Bounty* was docked. Boats bobbed in the water, a fishing vessel backed into its berth, a bell clanged. Two men in deep conversation passed me on the pier, nodding as they went by. I approached *The Bounty* cautiously and stepped onto the deck. No one paid me any attention, and I peered down the stairs to the cabin. No lights were on, and the door was locked. No sign of Tiny or Sam or Jackson, for that matter.

I opted for Plan B. I'd pick up my MINI Cooper and trek to Walker. It was a nice night for a sunset drive. I covered the few blocks to my bungalow, hoping to see Bill's rental car in the driveway. No luck. He apparently wasn't at home, not that I expected him to be. I'd been keeping my focus on Jackson in part to take it off Bill. I worried about him, about us really. My instincts told me he was keeping something from me... I shrugged off my uneasiness and cranked the engine, backing onto the street. I hoped my GPS would be able to locate Walker. I had only gone a block when my cell rang. My heart soared. Bill! I pulled to the curb. It was Pauli.

"Hey," I said, disappointed.

"Hey. So like I found out about that place in Walker."

"Let me guess...an abandoned factory?"

"Walker Machine Tool. Went out of business in 1984. Walker's, like, a ghost town. Nobody lives there anymore. That's why it's, like, in the middle of nowhere."

"Can you find out who owns it now?" I asked.

"No problemo."

"Nice work."

Pauli mumbled his thanks.

"You going to the theater tonight?"

"Dunno," he said.

"If you do, tell Lola I'll see her afterward, okay? I've got an errand to run." I figured Pauli knew my destination.

"Totally." He clicked off.

I was now running off schedule and needed to pick up my pace if I was going to make it back for the second act of the festival. I zoomed out of Candle Beach onto Highway 195 heading west for ten minutes, then my Genie led me off the highway onto a state route through a number of small towns for ten miles. So far, so good. This part of the state was largely unpopulated compared to the rest of Jersey. I passed dilapidated barns, forests, a lake, fields of wildflowers and tall grasses. Fifteen minutes later I was a mile from the address, according to my GPS, in the middle of what looked like a swamp.

My cell pinged. I steered my MC to the side of the road, onto a gravelly lane that sloped downward. It was Lola confirming that we'd connect after the performance. I sent a best of luck emoji and dropped the phone into my bag.

I glanced in my rearview mirror to check the road before backing onto it. *A white van whizzed by going well beyond the speed limit.* My little hairs stood at attention. A white van on my street; a white van stalking me to Maxine's. Bill would tell me it was all in my head. My instincts told me this was no coincidence. Someone who had been keeping an eye on me was now in an isolated area of the state, possibly heading to the same location as I was. Nothing else in Walker, right? The van's speed and deep shadows slanting across the highway had probably prevented the occupant from detecting my MC.

I put my car in gear and slowly crept forward. The road was bordered by a tangle of trees and wild grasses. Off to my left was a pond with a skim of algae on top. The sun was nearly down. When it set, the road would be completely dark. Night noises emerged, an owl hooting, crickets chirping. I was too far committed to give up and go home though I had a weird feeling. Besides, my curiosity was crushing me. Whenever I questioned my habit of delving into the unknown as a kid, my aunt Maureen informed me that *millions saw the apple fall...only Newton asked why.* Asking why had become routine for me.

I came to a dead end and turned left. Out of the night a series of shapes materialized on both sides of the roadway. Shells of former houses, a general store in ruin, several shop fronts wrecked with roofs and windows missing. A sign indicated this was Main Street in Walker, New Jersey.

Another quarter of a mile and Main Street narrowed to a lane, pitted with potholes, covered with scattered stones, and marked with stubbles of grass growing between cracks in the cement. I bounced along. Ahead of me, a chain-link fence appeared, and I tapped the brakes. A rusty gate with a "No Trespassing" sign hung off its hinges. Beyond it, I could see the hulking silhouette of the two-story building. Either the windows were blacked out or the place was empty. No light was visible. Where had the white van gone? Driving five miles per hour, I eased my car to the right and decided to track the fence and stay on the road that circled the building.

The factory was enormous. No openings in the chain links on this side. I reached the far end of the structure, about to ease around the corner, when I spotted a pinpoint of light in the distance. I flicked off my headlights and pulled to the edge of the lane behind a stand of large trees. My heart throbbed. I'd been in some frightening scrapes before, but being alone in this New Jersey wilderness sent my dread-o-meter into overdrive. I instinctively scooted down in my seat. Which I knew was ridiculous; it was my MC that was in danger of being spotted. Not me.

I squinted into the dark. Up ahead was an open, wide concrete surface. The space that Pauli and I had spotted on Google Earth. A parking lot! Of course. In its heyday the factory probably employed hundreds of workers. I opened the driver's side door, grateful I'd worn black capris. I grabbed a dark jacket from the back seat and zipped it up to my chin. I checked my cell phone battery—50 percent. It would have to do. I whispered a silent prayer to the snoop gods and set off, creeping a dozen yards to the chain-link fence. I had no intention of going inside the fence, but from out here I might see something that—

"Yo," a voice yelled.

In the still of the clear night, sound carried well.

"Gimme a hand, Tiny."

I froze. How many Tinys were there in this part of the state?

A man appeared out of the shadows. The sudden creaking and scraping of metal on metal meant he'd raised the door of the old factory. A swath of light escaped and illuminated an opening in the fence. Also a parked white van and its bulky driver. My pulse, already pounding, skyrocketed into panic territory. It *was* my Tiny. He joined the man who'd entered the building.

I rubbed my sweaty palms on the legs of my pants. I knew I should run for it, but what was the point of coming out here if I never found out what was going on in the old structure? And what importance it held for Vinnie. I counted to five and sneaked to the angle in the fence. I told myself one peek into the building and then I was gone. Voices rose and fell as though Tiny and his accomplice were arguing vehemently. I was too far away to make out much of what they were saying except for the occasional swear word and "the hell with them."

I crouched down and duckwalked twenty feet or so until I was almost opposite the entrance to the factory. I darted into the cover of the trees bordering the road and craned my neck to peek into the opening. It was a deserted machine tool company, right? Probably all I'd see was a dirty, junk-laden factory floor. Scraps of metal, machine parts. Just a little farther, I told myself. I counted five steps. Then I stood and stared into the light.

I gasped. No dirt, no messy floor, no rusted tools. Inside the abandoned factory were at least a dozen gleaming, beautiful luxury automobiles. The one closest to the entrance was a gold BMW. Bill's car! What had I stumbled on? My hands trembled as I dug my cell phone out of my bag. I couldn't imagine what this place meant to Vinnie, but I needed to contact the police. I tapped on the keypad and hit 911. Nothing happened. A cold sweat ran down the back of my blouse. No cell service out here. Walker was in the middle of nowhere, as Pauli had pointed out.

Tiny walked out of the building and headed to his white van.

I darted backward too quickly and, in the dark, tripped over a pipe only half-buried in the ground. "Damn!" I said aloud before thinking.

"Who's there?" Tiny whipped toward me.

Running away was not an option. I stopped breathing, fell to my knees, and tucked into a fetal position. Tiny flicked on a flashlight, sweeping it back and forth, cutting an arc through the trees, the fence, and the road. I clenched my mouth shut to keep my teeth from chattering. I grasped my pepper spray.

"I'm gonna find you. So give it up." He paused, stared into the dark directly at me. I shut my eyes, desperate to believe that if I couldn't see Tiny, then Tiny couldn't see me.

He lifted his flashlight and aimed it at my car twenty yards away, mostly hidden by the tree line. "What the…?"

Tiny took two strides toward me, and I made up my mind. I *had* to run. I tensed my muscles, forming fists, ready to leap forward.

Without warning, a spotlight shot directly into the front of the building. The hollow, distorted squawk of a megaphone blared out of the night. "This is the state of New Jersey Auto Theft Unit. We have you surrounded. You are under arrest."

Tiny stopped dead, whirled to his right, then back toward me, as if he couldn't make up his mind. His hesitation spelled his doom. A SWAT team, heavily armed, wearing night goggles, flew out of the forest on the opposite side of the building. Some cops swarmed into the factory with others securing the perimeter. Two spotted Tiny, who remained glued to the earth, and swiftly cuffed him. As they led him away, he rotated his head toward me. I gulped the night air to calm down.

Police officers gathered near the entrance. I was relieved but shaken. I had no interest in explaining what I was doing here. It was enough that I'd seen Bill's car. *Wait until he found out.* He would be so happy!

"Bill, take a look at this." One of the officers motioned to a guy whose shape I knew intimately. I'd recognize that spikey hair and NFL physique anywhere.

My mind spun. Bill's behavior since the theft of his car was beginning to make sense. Somehow he'd gotten himself involved with the state unit investigating car thieves. I was totally flabbergasted, excited for Bill, but annoyed that he'd kept his participation a secret. Was this where he'd been for the last few days? Now I really had to scram. I couldn't imagine what he'd say if he found me crawling through the underbrush at this crime scene. I half ran, half race-walked to my MC. Inside, I switched on the ignition and held my breath as I slowly rolled out from between the trees and onto the lane. The commotion at the factory served as an excellent diversion. Only Tiny might have figured out that I was eavesdropping, but I doubted that he'd be talking.

* * * *

I jammed my foot on the gas pedal and tore down the road away from the old machine tool building, retracing my route to Candle Beach. I didn't slow down until I was on the outskirts of town and could attempt to sort through all I'd witnessed tonight. Probable facts: Tiny was involved in the car theft ring; Vinnie was aware of the operation; the organization was on hold for the moment. Was Sam onboard somehow? Why did Vinnie die? His planned "revenge" must have had something to do with the little black book.

I phoned Jackson and left a message: "Things have taken a strange twist. We have to talk tonight. I'll be at the theater. Meet me there." The message was terse but clear. Things were at a crisis point. I was glad I had promised Lola I'd be at the performance tonight. I needed some amusement to cool down.

Since I was running late, I drove directly to the theater and parked on a side street. It was eight forty-five. The gazebo and park were empty, signaling that patrons had returned to their seats for the start of the second act. I opened the door to the lobby and moved swiftly past the curtain barrier. It was standing room only! I motioned to an usher that I would stand in a far aisle of the house, out of the way in case an emergency should arise.

The cast of *The Sound of Music* was onstage giving the audience the whole enchilada. Dancing and frolicking and mugging to the patrons, who loved the musical theater assault. Apparently, the community theater from Cape May decided to pull out all the stops tonight in an effort to win spectators' approval and the grand prize. They'd saved the best for last. All of a sudden, the cast marched off the stage and into the house!

Even from where I stood, I could hear a hubbub emanating from the stage manager's booth. Maddy was no doubt going berserk. As they sang "So Long, Farewell," the Von Trapp Family, led by Maria and the captain, hiked up one aisle and down the other, shaking hands and waving. The light crew scrambled to keep the actors visible with an improvised spotlight that swept from house left to house right, making the theater look like the subject of a grand opening. There had to be mass confusion in the lighting booth as first the house lights rose, then dipped down, then rose.

There would be some noses out of joint before this night was over. Not content with keeping the actors in the light, Maddy erupted from her stage manager's box, gesturing frantically to the cast. "Get back onstage!" she seemed to be saying. Everyone ignored her and Maria proceeded to pull a spectator to his feet, encouraging him to sing along. Amazingly, he obliged. People guffawed and cheered and applauded the effort. I had to laugh too. The New Jersey Community Theater Festival had been reduced to bedlam. However, there was no denying it: The audience loved the improvised performance. Arlene Baldwin strode purposefully to Maddy's booth while John Bannister stood and joined in the applause.

The Von Trapps trooped back onstage, hit their final notes, and bowed to the standing ovation. Poor Lola and the ELT. No way *Arsenic* could top this. Everyone sat, settled down, a ripple of amusement reverberating around the auditorium. Folks were certainly alive with the sound of music!

"Yo." Jackson appeared at my side.

"I've been trying to reach you," I said. "Where have you been?"

"Got your message to meet here. Wassup?"

I edged closer to him. "Plenty. Someone rifled through your clothes, Tiny's arrested for car theft, and we have to find that black book."

Jackson regarded me blankly. "Huh?"

"Never mind. When the show's over, I have a plan," I said.

"Cool. I'm going to get a drink. I'll see you after."

I grasped the back of his shirt. "Oh no, you don't. I'm not letting you out of my sight. You're staying here until I leave," I said grimly.

Jackson leaned against the wall. "Yes, Mother." The house lights dimmed.

"By the way, why didn't you tell me about Tammy?" I whispered.

In the dark it was difficult to read Jackson's expression, but his vocal smirk was unmistakable. "Jealous?"

"No," I hissed and crossed my arms.

The blue light rose, the black boxes rearranged to accommodate the home of the batty old Brewster sisters who poisoned old men. For some reason I was nervous. I knew the scene forward and backward by now. I also knew Abby and Edna had a competitive streak a mile long. How would they react to the shenanigans of *The Sound of Music*? I soon had my answer.

"Hey, O'Dell," Penny muttered and squeezed in between Jackson and me. "Had to see this from the house," she said smugly.

Uh-oh. "Walter's restaged scenes?" I mumbled.

"Nah. Edna and Abby hatched this one on their own."

I'll bet. Abby and Edna entered and sat. The stage went black. When the lights came up, the two elderly characters were no longer sitting on their black boxes. Instead, the Brewster sisters, arms hooked, each held a bottle of elderberry wine with one hand, smiling wickedly, and had hiked up their skirts with the other. Edna did a tap step, Abby followed suit. The two of them posed together. Then Abby and Edna leapt into a tap routine to "Puttin' on the Ritz," singing, acapella, a parody about bumping off old gentlemen and burying them in the basement. OMG. I couldn't believe my eyes. I recognized the number. A year ago Abby and Edna had created the musical spoof of *Arsenic and Old Lace* for the ELT end-of-the-year awards banquet. In their minds this must have seemed like the perfect occasion to resurrect it.

A titter was launched from the left side of the house—Mildred and the Banger sisters. Maddy ripped off her headset and threw it on the floor. The NJCTF had gone rogue. Meanwhile, the audience, warmed up by the cast of *The Sound of Music*, went wild, cheering and clapping as Abby and Edna executed their final steps, shuffled back to the black boxes, and took their seats.

"Yo. They killed it!" Jackson whistled through his fingers.

I had to admit, it was a fun, *kind of* appropriate way to begin their scene. If *Arsenic* had been a musical.

"This'll put the ELT on the map," Penny said, shooting a glance at Maddy in the stage manager's booth.

Romeo dashed onto the stage, ripped off the opening dialogue to get the scene rolling. The laughs continued to build, peaking with Lola's entrance. Spectators couldn't get enough of the kooky Brewster family. And then it was over. The stage went black, lights rose on the cast taking a sedate bow. The applause reached a crescendo as Abby and Edna stepped forward, then back, allowing Lola and Romeo to get their moment in the sun. Not too shabby. I had no desire to hang around and see if *King Lear* would attempt to outdo the two previous shows.

I tugged on Jackson's arm. "Come on."

He knew better than to resist at this point, and we sneaked out of the theater before the lights rose on Shakespeare.

"Where are we going?" he asked.

"To the boardwalk." I strode swiftly, pausing only when we reached the marina. "I went to a warehouse tonight where I saw Tiny, who works for Sam, arrested for his part in a car theft ring. Luxury automobiles all stored—"

"No way." He sat on a bench.

"Yes. And Sam might be a part of it," I added, sitting beside him.

"Sam's an all-right guy. He got me a job. No way is he a car thief. Anyway, the guy's loaded. He doesn't need to steal anything."

Sam Baldwin certainly seemed to be loaded. Never mind his bankruptcy. I was curious. "What kind of job?"

Jackson looked chagrined. "Basic construction. Helping hang Sheetrock. Cleaning up the site. Assisting wherever. It's temporary until something happens with the charter business."

"Sam didn't mind that you're out on bail?"

Jackson shrugged. "I report to the foreman."

So that's where he'd disappeared to this morning. "Let's forget about Sam. It's Vinnie we need to focus on." I explained about the address Maxine found in Vinnie's pocket, that it belonged to a warehouse in Walker, New Jersey, and that I, coincidentally, had arrived on the scene minutes before the state descended with a SWAT team. The missing link was the black book.

Jackson whistled. "Nancy Drew. Girl detective."

He could be so maddening...

"Do you want to spend time in prison?" I asked.

"Sorry. I gotta thank you for what you're doing, but I don't see what Vinnie's book has to do with the car thing," Jackson said.

"I'm not sure either," I admitted.

"Or his murder. And what's this about my clothes?"

"I think someone rifled through your things. The door to the porch was jimmied, and your pile of stuff was...rearranged."

"You noticed that?" Jackson tensed.

"I'm pretty sure. It's like someone was hunting for something..."

"Money?" he asked, suddenly alert.

"The money's still there."

Jackson exhaled. "Whew. Then what? I don't own anything else anybody would want."

True. "I'm thinking the black book. If Vinnie was threatening someone with it, they could have become desperate and murdered him for it."

"Then whoever killed him would have it, right?"

"Not necessarily. They might think you have it. That's why they went through your stuff." I paused. "I'd like to search for the book."

"Where?" he asked.

"*The Bounty.* It's the most logical place."

Jackson was skeptical. "I hate to throw shade on your thinking, but don't you figure the murderer would have, you know, scoured the boat?"

"That's where you come in. You knew Vinnie. The two of you used to be thick as thieves. Sorry about the reference…"

"Yeah," Jackson said without a trace of irony.

"If you were thinking like Vinnie, where would you hide something important?"

Jackson studied me. "Not a clue."

"Come on," I said and coaxed him to his feet.

"Why can't my lawyer handle all of this?"

Good question.

* * * *

Half an hour later we plopped onto the beautiful leather couch. Frustrated. In the galley we'd examined the inside and outside of all the spotless appliances as well as the cupboards. We found a case of cold champagne, jars of caviar, and a stack of frozen dinners. There were dishes, pots and pans, and silverware but no black book. Obviously Jackson had not been cooking much on the boat. Next we tackled the bathroom and staterooms, checking the toilet and shower, under the mattresses, and inside a closet. Vinnie had a minimum of clothes on *The Bounty*—a suit, sport shirts, pairs of cargo shorts, and underwear. He must have kept most of his personal possessions at Maxine's. Standing at one end of the closet was a surfboard, two feet by six feet, that looked brand new.

"Was Vinnie still surfing?" I asked.

"I guess," he said.

A small nightstand, situated between two beds, had three drawers that were empty except for a DVD of Super Bowl XLII when the New York Giants defeated the New England Patriots, old copies of *Sports Illustrated*, and a tube of lipstick. The last item the only hint that Maxine had visited the boat at some point. In the dining area we examined the table, television, sofa, and coffee table.

"Let's forget about the book. It's not in here," said Jackson.

I agreed with him, but my stubborn streak wouldn't let me give up. "Come on, Jackson, think. Where would Vinnie—"

"I don't know!" Jackson pouted. "I used to hate it when you got like this."

"Like what?" I asked, perplexed.

"Like you knew best and no one else could have any opinion."

Jackson's words brought me up short. I was like that? "I was never like that when we were together," I insisted vehemently.

"Uh-huh. Yeah, you were. Remember the time I wanted to take the *JV* out for a midnight run, just the two of us, and you said you wouldn't go because it wasn't safe?"

"You mean that first summer? I remember that night. It was cold, gusty, you hadn't operated the *JV* all that long... It was ridiculous to go out."

"See what I mean?" he said.

Jackson might have a point. "That was the past. I've changed. You can ask Bill."

"Like I'm gonna ask him about the two of you now." Jackson slumped down on his spine. At times like this he reminded me of a teenager Pauli's age... Without Pauli's common sense.

"Jackson, let's focus on the present and—"

"Vinnie's book. Yeah, yeah." He closed his eyes. "Dodie, I don't think it's here. I need to get some food, chill, and hit the sack. I have to be up early."

"Did Vinnie mention Sam the night of your argument?"

"Mention how?"

"Sam was his partner. Was he angry at him? Could Sam have been the person who was 'taking him for granted'?" I suggested.

Jackson glanced at me. "He never said. Sam was his friend."

I wasn't so sure about that. "Someone made Vinnie furious that night, according to you. Who could it have been...?"

"Dude, I don't know, and thinking about it is making my brain hurt." He held his head in his hands.

"Okay. So, it isn't here." I picked up my bag and followed Jackson up the stairs to the main deck. We were about to get off the boat when it occurred to me. "We didn't examine the rear of *The Bounty*. The captains' chairs and fishing rods."

Jackson groaned. "*You* search the aft. *I'm* going to the head. I'll be back."

He unlocked the cabin door and returned to the lower deck. The light flicked on in the bathroom. I walked carefully to the aft of the boat, stepping over a coil of rope. Vinnie, or someone else, had left *The Bounty* in shipshape condition. Nothing out of place. In the security lights from the marina, I could see the outlines of the chairs and vertical lines of the fishing rods beside them. I felt my way around the seats, starting at the bottom and running my hands around the base on the deck, then the seat cushion, and finally the seat back. Nothing. I moved on methodically from one chair to the next. I didn't expect to find anything. Who would hide a valuable item like the black book out here where it was subject to the elements? Such as wind, water, beer…

"Let's go." Jackson waved at me from the top of the stairs.

"Take it easy. Only one more."

Jackson grumbled and joined me, collapsing into a seat, swiveling from side to side while I bent down and felt around the base of a chair. Nothing.

A voice floated down the pier. "Hi, Bob. How's the fishing today? The fluke running?" The speaker stopped his progress down the dock as there was a faint response to his greeting. A conversation ensued. Goose bumps emerged on my shoulders and arms.

Jackson sat up straighter and bobbed his head. "That's Sam."

"Shh!" I pushed him into the chair and scooted into the one next to him. "Be quiet."

"What are you doing? I'd like to say hi. Thank him for the job." Jackson tried to stand, I grabbed his arm.

"What if he asks what we're doing here?" I whispered.

"I'm allowed to be here. Vinnie invited me to stay."

I'd heard that explanation before. "I want to see what he's up to."

"Dodie, it's Sam. He's not up to anything—" Jackson protested.

"Shush. Keep your head down." The captains' chairs had tall seat backs and if we hunched down we wouldn't be visible from the lower deck. If that was where Sam was headed. "Humor me," I muttered, folding my legs under me.

"Whatever." I could hear Jackson's cynicism.

"Have a good night," Sam called out, his footsteps louder on the wooden slats of the dock.

He moved onto the deck of *The Bounty*. Silence for a moment, then the thud of his footsteps descending the stairs, the door unlocked, the lights switched on. I was dying to sneak a peek below deck but we couldn't risk being discovered. I had absolutely no reasonable explanation for my presence. And Sam and I weren't exactly bosom buddies.

"How long are we gonna stay out here?" Jackson whined.

"Sh. Until he goes." I plastered my finger on my lips.

Muffled echoes from below suggested Sam was moving around. Hunting for something? Light poured out of the cabin, sending shadows skittering across the deck. I scrunched down as far as I could and motioned for Jackson to do the same.

What seemed like hours was only minutes, I realized. I felt calmer. We could get out of this scrape without having to confront Sam Baldwin. The cabin lights flicked off, footsteps grew louder. He was on deck. A match scraped against a striking surface, a flame flared. The smoke of his cigar wafted our way. Was he staring in our direction? A clomp behind us meant he had stepped closer. I tensed my body.

Then footsteps receded as Sam walked away from us, moved onto the dock, and disappeared. I waited a couple of minutes in case he changed his mind and reappeared. Jackson had closed his eyes, his breathing even. He was falling asleep. I nudged him gently.

"Wha—?" He sat up.

"The coast is clear."

He yawned. "That was fun."

Seriously? "We can go now."

"Great. 'Cause I'm starved. Nothing but frozen dinners here." Jackson hauled himself out of the captain's chair and stretched. "Vinnie kept the bar stocked. Food? Not so much."

I shuddered, a tingling running down my arms. It wasn't the cool night air. "Vinnie didn't cook, did he?"

"Nah. In the old days, when we were out on the *JV* between charters, if I didn't fix something for us, we'd go hungry. Once he didn't eat for twenty-four hours because—"

I yanked on Jackson's arm. "I think I know where Vinnie stashed the book."

"What? Where?"

"Let's go." I darted to the door of the lower deck. I was operating on instincts that had proven fairly reliable in previous investigations.

"We searched all over down there. You said it yourself. The book is *not* in the cabin," he complained.

"Come on, Jackson. Man up," I said.

He reluctantly unlocked the door. I hurried down the stairs and tripped on the bottom step. "Oof," I said as I fell forward.

Jackson caught me from behind.

"If Vinnie didn't cook—"

"Never," Jackson said firmly.

"Then why does he have a set of cookbooks stashed in the cupboard?" I asked.

"What cookbooks?"

"You looked in the appliances and cupboards on the right side. I took the left," I explained.

Jackson flipped on the light in the galley.

"I didn't think anything of it. Lots of people have cookbooks they never use, so I didn't open them. But if Vinnie never used the books, one might make a great hiding place."

"How? I don't get it?" Jackson scratched his head. "I'm sooo over this book thing."

I walked to the cabinets I'd examined earlier. The last one on the left had a lower shelf of mixers and bottles of booze. The shelf on top had a collection of gourmet cookbooks. I knew them, all written by a French chef. I planned to buy a set for the Windjammer, but Henry would not be thrilled: too chichi for him. I dragged a chair from the dining table and clambered up. There were six books. I opened the first and fanned the pages. Nothing. The second and third were equally empty. Maybe my bright idea was just that. Then I removed book number four from the shelf. It was heavier than the others. My pulse zipped from zero to sixty. I opened it slowly, hesitant. There it was. A small black book embedded in pages that had been cut out to accommodate Vinnie's prized possession. "Aha!" I crowed triumphantly.

Jackson's mouth dropped open. "Yo, Dodie. You *are* good."

I replaced the cookbook and climbed off the chair.

"So what's in the book?" Jackson asked impatiently, hanging over my shoulder.

The cover was blank, the first page had nothing but dates: April 1– September 1. "That was the week before Vinnie died," I said. I turned the first page. It was a list of names. I flipped through the pages. More names. And addresses.

"Who are they?" asked Jackson.

"I don't know. They were important to Vinnie." The list stopped halfway through the book—I estimated a hundred names. "Let's get out of here before Sam comes back." I stuffed the black book into my bag.

"What're you going to do with it?" Jackson flicked off lights and locked the door.

"Figure out what they all have in common."

"How will you do that?" Jackson asked, baffled.

"I have a secret weapon."

15

As we raced down the dock, I formulated my plan. Both Jackson and I needed to eat, so a quick stop at the Sandbar for takeout would work. Then home to study the black book and contact Pauli. He would no doubt have some theories on how to translate Vinnie's list into usable intel. At least I hoped so. I hadn't heard from Bill, though I knew he was busy rescuing his beloved BMW. I wanted to share my findings with him...Vinnie's address, my trip to the warehouse, the black book...but I knew he'd insist I speak with the Candle Beach police. I wasn't ready to surrender to them yet.

We were about to enter the restaurant when my cell pinged. Lola: *where are u? come to hotel ...cast pool party...drinks and food...whole Etonville gang here. some night!* I wasn't up for an ELT cast party, especially one that featured folks in bathing suits. Yet, the whole Etonville gang meant that Pauli would be present and we needed to talk. In person was even better than by phone.

"I'm in," Jackson said when he heard the invitation.

"Don't you have to get up early?" I asked.

"Sounds like a good party."

Jackson hated to miss a good party. While we discussed his social life, my cell rang. "Dodie?"

"Bill! Where have you been?" I asked, feigning ignorance. "I've been worried sick."

"You would not believe this. I have my car back." He was so excited it was touching.

"You what?" I played along.

"It's a long story and I want to tell you everything. Where are you?" he asked.

"On the boardwalk. I'll be home in ten."

"No, I'll come to you," he said.

Ever the good sport, and being in a terrific mood, he agreed to join the festivities at the Windward Hotel. I offered to skip the cast party. Bill insisted we attend. I'd have to find a moment to pull Pauli aside...

* * * *

"Whoa!" Jackson ducked as a tsunami of water splashed out of the pool and onto the table and chairs where he, Lola, Carol, Edna, Penny, and I were sitting. "Crazy, dude," he said to Romeo who surfaced, grinning, after his cannonball dive. The hotel management had graciously set up a banquet table for pizza and a portable bar, making the atmosphere decidedly convivial.

"Behave yourself or I'm going to issue you a 10-7," Edna yelled to Romeo, teasing.

Lola sipped her wine. "What's that?"

"Out of Service." Edna gathered stray, wet hairs and jammed them back into her bun.

"Some performance tonight," I said to her and raised my wineglass in a salute.

Lola, Carol, Jackson, and Penny joined me.

"Walter loved the audience response," Lola said.

I glanced at Edna, who winked and grinned.

"But you know Walter. He's one part overconfident and two parts anxious."

"There's a rumor that Maddy wanted to disqualify *Sound of Music* for that stunt," Penny said.

"Well, it *was* over the top," Carol giggled. "I've heard of audience participation but..."

"You see that guy in the house who tried to sing along with them?" Penny cackled. "Talk about NT." She bit into a slice of pizza. "No talent."

"If they disqualify *Sound of Music*, they might also have to eliminate *Arsenic*," I said.

"Dodie has a point," Carol agreed.

"No way. The ELT never left the stage. As long as you're onstage it's legit," Penny asserted.

I wondered...

The Banger sisters and Mildred glided past on inflatable rafts, holding hands to form a single float, oblivious to Romeo's antics. "Whee!" one sister cried, as the group float twirled in a circle. They reminded me of synchronized swimmers in an Esther Williams movie I watched with my mom one rainy day.

We applauded their efforts. Vernon, beer in hand, had dumped his hearing aids and opted for an inflatable recliner. Very high tech! He paddled by. "Going to rain tomorrow," he warned us.

It was nice to see everyone so relaxed, enjoying themselves. It had been a stressful week. Tonight's pizza-beer-wine banquet was just what the thespian doctor ordered. As a bonus, they didn't have to be concerned about performing tomorrow night. Only waiting backstage to see if their number was called when the awards were announced. "Where's Walter?" I took a bite from my slice of pepperoni pizza.

"He and Abby left to get something to eat on the boardwalk. They'll be here later," Lola said.

Jackson rose to get a refill on his drink, Carol went into her hotel room to detach Pauli from his computer, and Edna scooted to the edge of the pool to dangle her legs in the water.

Lola leaned toward me. "Jackson's not too upset about the arrest."

"I think he's confident now that he has this high-end lawyer. Still, they found the murder weapon in his backpack."

"Oh no! They did?" Lola choked on her wine.

Oops. I let that cat out of the bag. "That's between us," I said in a hurry.

"Got it." Lola hesitated. "What was it?"

"An ice pick. Vinnie had a punctured aorta."

"Dodie, that's awful." Lola was genuinely concerned.

"I know. But there's more…"

Across the patio, Jackson waggled his beer at us—really at Lola—offering to get more drinks. I shook my head. She raised her glass in thanks. I noticed the interaction and made an executive decision.

"Lola, hate to break the news, but I discovered that Jackson's spoken for."

"He's what?" Lola cried.

"Pauli found the engagement photo in an Iowa newspaper," I said gently. Lola moaned. "All this time he seemed so…"

"Available?"

Lola narrowed her eyes. "That's it. I'm swearing off men."

I'd believe it when I see it. "Tammy Littleton."

"What's she look like?" Lola asked tentatively.

"According to Pauli, awesome," I said.

Lola pulled her hair into a topknot, slipped off her beach cover-up, and sashayed to the pool to drown her disappointment. Forty-five minutes since I spoke with Bill. What was—

"Bill!" Lola gestured to him from the diving board where she was testing its springiness.

He stood on the walkway leading to the patio and opened the gate. Bill looked sexy at any time of the day with his former-football-player physique—flat belly and pumped-up pecs.

But now, tanned and tranquil, his upper arms testing the limits of his tight white T-shirt, his hair neatly combed... *Yowza.* He waved to Lola, and to the pool folks in general, accepted a beer from Jackson, and cut across the patio to my table.

I pulled out a chair. "Hey, stranger."

He put his hands on my shoulders and squeezed, then sat down beside me and took a long pull on his beer. "I missed you today."

My heart did a flip-flop. "Me, too. Can't believe you got your BMW back. Thought by now it would be chopped into individual parts."

"I was lucky."

"I'll say." I smiled at him. "So...the state theft unit rescued your baby?"

"Something like that." His eyes glittered.

Geez. He was enjoying this moment. "In good condition?"

"Yep. A number of small scratches. Nothing like the last time you drove it," he added wryly.

During the run of *Bye, Bye, Birdie.* I decided to ignore his dig. "So no chop shop."

"Luxury autos are warehoused and shipped out. Africa is a popular destination," he said.

"Warehoused?" How much longer could I play this game? "In Philadelphia?"

"Nope. Right here in Jersey."

"No!"

"Yes!"

"So the state cops found your car in a warehouse? And you drove it away?" I said.

"Not quite that uncomplicated. Actually there was a raid and I—"

"Dodie, come on in!" Edna yelled from the opposite side of the pool. "The water's warm."

"I think I'll pass," I said.

Bill whipped off his T-shirt, exposing his pecs, lats, and biceps. I normally took his torso for granted but it had been a long day. Smokin' hot. Eyes surveyed his dive off the side of the pool and underwater swim to the diving board, where he surfaced and chatted with Lola.

"The dude's happy," Jackson said and deposited himself in a chair.

"He has his car back."

"Nice." Jackson yawned. "I need to get some sleep."

I lowered my voice. "The car was in the warehouse where Tiny was arrested. The address of the warehouse was in Vinnie's pocket, remember?" I said pointedly.

Jackson stared at me. "You think Vinnie was in on the car thing?"

"I don't know. Why did he have the address?" I asked bluntly.

The question registered with Jackson. "Whoa."

"Keep this to yourself. The black book too until I can figure it out."

"Aye-aye, cap'n." Jackson saluted. "Got to hand it to you."

"Thanks. Now we need to clear you of the murder charge."

Jackson clinked his beer bottle with my wineglass. "That's what my lawyer's for."

I took a last drink. I needed to chat with Pauli and coax Bill out of the pool and into another venue...

Bill and Romeo crept up behind me, lifted me out of my chair. "What are you doing? Hey! Stop!"

They unceremoniously threw me into the pool, accompanied by the loud whoops and cheers of Etonville's citizens. I went underwater, gasping, my clothes clinging to my body, my hair covering my eyes. I bobbed up, spitting water and spitting mad. Whose idea was this? Bill grasped me, coughing, hauling me to the shallow end of the pool, laughing all the while.

I sputtered. "My watch!"

"Waterproof," Bill said.

I scanned the onlookers. It was impossible to stay annoyed when everyone was thoroughly enjoying themselves, even if it was at my expense. I splashed water at Bill, then muttered, "Just wait..."

Penny threw me a towel. "O'Dell, anybody ever tell you you're all wet?"

"Ha-ha."

* * * *

I changed out of my wet clothes and tugged on a dry pair of shorts and shirt, courtesy of Lola's wardrobe, brushing my snarled locks into a ponytail. I should have brought a bathing suit to the party. I borrowed her eyeliner and mascara and checked my reflection in the mirror. Thanks to my Irish ancestors on both sides of the genetic spectrum, green eyes gazed back at me. The sun had sprinkled additional freckles on the bridge of my nose. Bill said they were "cute."

I opened the door of Lola's room, stepped across the hallway, and knocked on the door of Carol's room. She had tried, unsuccessfully, to pry Pauli away from his laptop. He was posting things on Instagram for Janice's benefit. "Pauli? It's me," I said hoarsely.

After a few seconds, he unlocked the door. "Hey," he said.

The sun had done a number on him today—face and arms were bright red. "You need to put something on that burn."

"Mom gave me a hard time for falling asleep on the beach." He stretched and winced.

Oooh. I remembered those days down the shore as a kid. *Trying* to burn... Now it was all about avoidance and protection. "I need your help."

My request must have been enticing. Pauli lit up. "Sure." He swung the door fully open and stepped aside.

I glanced into the hall to confirm that no one was approaching. I could hear another round of cheers from the pool. *Who got tossed in this time?* I entered the room. "This is strictly hush-hush."

Pauli nodded solemnly. I didn't need to remind him. "Whadya got?" He was all business.

I withdrew the black book from my bag. "This could tell us who murdered Vinnie," I said. We stared at it for a moment.

Pauli took it out of my hands and flipped through the pages as Jackson and I had done earlier. "Got it. Who are they?"

"Here's where your skill comes in," I said. "I have no idea what this list means. Who these guys are. Why did Vinnie keep track of a bunch of names and addresses?" I didn't need to mention that the murder victim also threatened to use the book for revenge.

Pauli frowned. The wheels already turning.

"Do you have a software program like you used in the past to find patterns in lists? I'd like to know what they have in common."

Pauli touched each page individually as if he was absorbing the names.

"I have this feeling that these people are the key to Vinnie's death. Find out who they are and we find out why someone wanted him dead," I murmured.

Pauli placed the book in his backpack. "I'm on it," he said confidently.

"I know you are." I resisted the urge to hug him or kiss him or even ruffle his hair. That would not be cool. "Text me as soon as you find something out. Anything," I added with a trace of desperation. "We're about out of time."

Pauli jiggled his head and a hank of hair flopped over his forehead.

* * * *

The night was silent except for the creak of the rocking chair on our screened-in porch as I tipped it up and down. The mood was mellow—swimming, alcohol, and the recovery of one's car made for a relaxing trifecta. Bill and Jackson were definitely chill; I was fidgety, my mind on Vinnie's black book.

"Hey, bro, super cool about your wheels," Jackson said from his spot in the corner where he lounged on his sleeping bag.

"Thanks. I'm really relieved," Bill said.

I was curious about Tiny's involvement in the car theft ring, but I knew I had to tread carefully without giving away my knowledge of his involvement. "I guess you caught the car thieves?"

"Oh yeah. According to the state unit, the crew they caught in Walker…" Bill shifted his position on the chaise lounge to face me. "Ever hear of Walker? It's a small town about thirty minutes from here."

"Walker…?" I hinted at complete ignorance.

"I'd never heard of it either. It's where the thieves stashed the cars in a deserted warehouse. Used to be a machine tool company. Anyway the theft unit thinks it's the tip of the iceberg," he said.

"There's more warehouses with stolen cars?" I asked.

"Probably. They could be part of a major trafficking ring."

"They?"

"This crew apparently targeted cars up and down the East Coast. In fact, one of the guys was connected to Candle Beach."

"No kidding?" I was skating on a razor-thin edge and hoping Jackson had remembered my warning to keep quiet about Tiny, Sam, *The Bounty*, the black book, and anything else related to Vinnie and the murder. For the time being.

"His name is Robert Stenowski. Big guy so they call him Tiny. He's a street thug with a rap sheet. Theft, burglary, assault, mainly in the shore area."

My heart thumped.

"He's being tight-lipped. Not saying much. Protecting the higher-ups in the outfit."

Jackson cleared his throat. "So…"

Please, Jackson, no mention of—

"How do they do it? Steal the cars and stash them away?" he asked.

Relief flooded my body. I could have kissed Jackson for steering the conversation away from Tiny. Almost.

"Why? You thinking of getting into the business?" Bill teased.

"I'm in enough of a mess," Jackson said.

"Sorry," Bill added hastily. "It's pretty straightforward. There's a market overseas for luxury cars. Mercedes Benz, Porsches, Land Rovers, Jaguars. And BMWs."

"You said they ship them to Africa?" I asked.

"Africa, the Middle East, Eastern Europe," Bill said. "Places where there's a demand for the cars and no manufacturing of these models."

"Whoa. It's big business?" Jackson looked at Bill wide-eyed.

"Huge profit. Hundreds of cars stolen and millions to be made. Street crews handle the thefts and carjackings. They're paid to steal. Then they deliver the cars to the warehouses. Middlemen create new VIN numbers, fake titles, and a shipping manifest. The paperwork looks legitimate."

Who was the middleman in Tiny's operation? And the boss? I was banking on Sam's participation. "Sounds well organized."

"Then the automobiles are placed in cargo containers and transported to ports. Port of Newark in this case. Next stop is somewhere overseas." Bill sat up on the chaise lounge. "It's sophisticated. Not only have they figured out how to steal cars with key fobs and remote starters, they're smart. The vehicles are dumped in safe parking lots like hospitals or kept in the warehouses for a day or two to make sure the hot car isn't equipped with an anti-theft device."

My used MINI Cooper would never make it on the most wanted list. "If you hadn't raided the warehouse in Walker, would the ring have been caught?"

Bill shook his head. "Who knows? Customs agents at the port do targeted searches of cargo containers based on suspicious shipping companies, manifests, or destinations. It's a guessing game."

"Talk about luck," I said. "That they found your BMW before it got carted to Newark."

"Also lucky that the state theft ring had their eye on this warehouse for a while now," he added.

Something was bothering me...

"The ironic thing is that there's been a decrease in overall car theft but a rise in the robbery rate of luxury cars."

"Hey, man, glad I sold my Beemer," Jackson said.

"Since when did you have a BMW?" I asked.

"Just kidding, dude."

"Jackson, I hear you have a whip-smart lawyer," Bill said carefully.

"Yeah, like my guardian angel came through." He laughed.

"Talk about irony. Vinnie's fiancée paid for the lawyer," I added.

Bill became more alert. His background in law enforcement kicked in—unusual phenomena triggered his interest. "I didn't know that. Very generous."

"Maxine's a real cool lady," Jackson said.

Bill approached the door of the porch and studied the sky. "Thinking about tonight's sunset. Red sky at night—"

"Sailor's delight," Jackson finished.

I knew the rest of the proverb suggested the possibility of danger with a fiery sunrise—red sky in the morning, sailor's warning. "How are those constellations coming?" I asked, joking with Bill.

"Too cloudy. The weather app says we could be in for trouble tomorrow." He turned to me. "Hope that doesn't interfere with the theater festival. Tonight could be the calm before the storm."

Prophetic words as far as the New Jersey Community Theater Festival was concerned. Every night had had its own tempest. Hopefully the awards ceremony tomorrow would be smooth, without turmoil. Everyone—actors, crew, even Maddy and Arlene—deserved an easy night.

A gust of wind blew the screen door open another few inches. Bill ducked inside, then locked up. I shivered. Something felt ominous besides the weather...

16

A branch blew into the bedroom window, rat-tat-tatting on the pane. A tempest whirled around the house, growing louder and stronger until it reverberated like a buzz saw that would rip the house in two. I stood in the yard outside and gazed upward, a downpour drenching me, blasts of icy air sending me into spasms of shaking. A gale force knocked me off my feet. I continued to stare up at the elm tree in the yard next door. Something came crashing down on top of me and the roof of my house.

I awoke in a cold sweat, my body damp, my breathing ragged. I closed my eyes again and reentered the nightmare. It was Hurricane Sandy, and I felt as vulnerable now as I had that October night in 2012. I was disoriented for a minute. I inhaled deeply, exhaled slowly to calm the thudding in my chest.

We knew the hurricane was coming back then, had been warned to buy gas and stock up on food. The lines at service stations were long, occupied by impatient drivers. The shelves at the local grocery store emptied. Still, people hadn't panicked during the weekend before the storm.

I'd been through hurricanes before, but nothing prepared me for Sandy. Or to spend the twenty-four most terrifying hours of my life alone. After Grody closed the restaurant on the Sunday before, he begged me to go home with him. Jackson texted me that he'd be back in plenty of time before the worst of the storm hit Candle Beach. Famous last words.

I hunkered down at home, but when the power went out, the wind howled, water flooded my basement, I felt trapped and helpless in the cold and dark, that my house would blow over. My neighbor's elm tree landing partially on my roof was the last straw. By the time Jackson returned to Candle Beach forty-eight hours after the hurricane hit, I'd hung a flashlight from a chandelier for light, been charging my cell in my trusty Chevy Metro, and had wrapped myself in layers of long underwear and a sweat suit to stay warm. I was angrier with Jackson than I'd ever been during the five years we'd been together. He'd abandoned me. He claimed he left the Jersey Shore for a new business venture with his brother in Iowa. Maybe it was my anger that drove him off.

Next to me, Bill was asleep. Oblivious. I marveled that he never awoke when I had these middle-of-the-night hallucinations. The alarm read 3 a.m. I tossed from side to side, practiced breathing exercises I'd seen Walter conduct with actors to bring them into the present. Usually it sent them into sleep or boredom or fits of giggling. I'd never tell him that I found them useful. We didn't have much of a relationship these last couple of years since I was instrumental in closing a murder investigation that pegged him as a person of interest. Even though he was exonerated, he never got over it.

Something besides memories of the hurricane kept me awake. It was what Bill said, or didn't say. He gave Jackson and me a detailed description of the car theft process. Yet he neglected to mention how the thieves knew his car was available. How were they able to steal it so easily. Did they wander the streets digging around for potential targets? That seemed terribly inefficient to me. I would confront him first thing in the morning. I drifted off, no more dreams of wind, rain, and crashing trees.

Awakening in the middle of the night took its toll. My body refused to acknowledge the alarm clock the next morning.

"Wake up, sleepyhead," Bill said and planted a kiss on my cheek. "You're missing another of Jackson's 'specialties.'" Bill made air quotes. He smelled of caffeine and sugar.

The room was gray. "What time is it?" I asked.

"Nine thirty. You better get out there before he eats the rest of the pancakes. Golden brown. Covered in powdered sugar and blueberry syrup. Yummm..." Bill stepped into the shower.

My mouth watered. "I'm up." I swung my legs out of bed and wrapped my robe around me. "Did you hear the wind last night?" I knew most of the weather elements I experienced were due to my Hurricane Sandy nightmare. In spite of that, I was sure Candle Beach had had its own tempest.

"No, though lots of branches were thrown around. Some lawn furniture from next door wound up in our backyard. In fact I think we're due for a mini-nor'easter. It's already raining. No beach today," Bill said.

My nightmare was a premonition. "Where are you off to?" I asked.

"Returning my rental car and picking up my BMW."

"Need company?" I asked and ran a brush through my hair.

"I'm good. I'll get a ride to the impound area in Trenton."

"That's efficient service from the state police. Your car is recovered one day, picked up the next."

Bill switched off the water and toweled himself dry. "I got some expedited service for helping out."

"What kind of helping out?" I asked.

His face went blank. I'd seen this police-chief-facial-armor before whenever I'd asked questions about an official investigation. "The usual. Filling out paperwork, computer research."

That didn't make sense. The state of New Jersey had a special unit of officers dedicated to car theft. Why did they need Bill to fill out paperwork? "Is there something you're not telling me?" I asked. *Besides the fact that I saw him at the raid on the warehouse.*

"What do you mean?" Bill avoided my gaze and tugged on jeans and a long-sleeved knit shirt.

"Yo, Dodie!" Jackson yelled from the kitchen. "You got thirty seconds until these hotcakes are history."

Bill gave me a quick hug. "I'll be back for lunch. See you at Grody's?"

"Sure," I said to his back as it moved out the door.

I didn't have the energy to pursue him to his rental car; I needed calories and coffee in order to do that.

"Here you go. A short stack for short stuff." Jackson gave me a lazy grin, reverting to an affectionate nickname he'd used in the old days—I wasn't short, unless I stood next to him—and set a plate of pancakes in front of me. They oozed fat and sugar, dripping blueberry glaze and melted butter. He set a mug of coffee on the table.

"What happened to work this morning?"

"Work's canceled. The weather," he said.

I inhaled the aromas of breakfast. My mouth watered. "Where did you learn to cook anyway? You were MIA in the kitchen when you left the shore after the hurricane." I dove into the pancakes. Utterly scrumptious.

Jackson dismissed my question with a gesture. "I got schooled."

It occurred to me that Tammy, the bride-to-be, was no doubt his teacher. "She did a first-class number with you."

Jackson studied me, sipping his coffee. "We called the engagement off right before I came back to Candle Beach."

I set my fork on the edge of my plate. "Sorry to hear that."

"Tammy's idea. She said I wasn't motivated enough to get married. That I didn't have any ambition." He avoided my eyes. "You think that's true?"

I flashed on Jackson and Vinnie fooling around on the *JV*, surfing, playing beach volleyball at sunset, drinking on the beach after dark. "Well, you and

Vinnie…weren't exactly the most serious guys. At least you had memorable times together."

"We did. We were tight." Jackson stared off into space as though focusing on the past.

"It was a good thing you took off for Iowa. If you'd stayed, you might have gotten roped into Vinnie's shady deals," I said.

"What shady deals? You don't know that he was involved with anything…"

"Illegal? Jackson. Think about it," I urged.

He hung his head. "I kept hoping it was a simple drowning, you know, he got lit and fell overboard."

"That would have been less messy."

"Vinnie and I were opposites. He had to constantly play angles. Me? I went along to get along."

"Is that why you tried to ditch me in the arcade last week?"

"What are you talking about? I didn't ditch you," he said firmly.

"I followed you through the arcade—"

"Like, what was that about? Tailing me?" he asked.

"—and I got intercepted by Tiny. Tiny! Who's now arrested for his involvement in car thefts? He distracted me until you ran out the back door," I finished.

"I didn't run out. I had a meeting with Sam to talk about some work and I got a call from Arlene. She said to go through the arcade and come out the back door. That Baldwin Contractors was doing some cement repair in the parking lot behind the games."

Legit enough, but why did Tiny waylay me long enough for Jackson to escape?

"You talked to Arlene in the parking lot?"

"Nah. She got a last-minute conflict. Instead a guy who worked for Sam picked me up and he drove to a construction site." He frowned. "What're you getting at? First you have Sam mixed up in Vinnie's murder and now you think Arlene is guilty of…what?"

I didn't know.

"Any ideas on the black book?" he asked. "Got an appointment with my lawyer this afternoon."

"I'm working on it. Let's keep it between us for now. Plenty of time to fill him in later." I pushed back from the kitchen table. "Thanks for breakfast. Tammy did a good job with you."

Jackson finished his coffee. "Ha. My luck to hook up with two can-do women."

"Did you ever think it was our luck to fall in with a surfer boy?" I said lightly.

"Huh." He cleared my dishes. "I'll see you tonight at the theater."

My cell pinged. Lola: *some weather...hanging out until tonight...lunch?* I replied: *maybe. talk later.* I helped Jackson clean up. By the time I was dressed in jeans, sneakers, and a hoodie, he'd left and the bungalow was quiet. I was eager to hear from Pauli but resisted texting him. I knew he'd be in contact when he had something to report. I drummed my fingers on the table, glanced at the wall clock—11 a.m.—and debated another cup of coffee. I was already jittery from a combination of caffeine and adrenaline. No sense in making things worse.

Something nipped at the back of my brain. Did it have to do with Arlene? Jackson said Arlene called him to meet behind the arcade, but I distinctly remembered her saying that she "didn't know who this Jackson is" when I went to the theater searching for Sam hoping he'd post Jackson's bail. Was I wrong? No, I knew I was right. Why would Arlene lie? My cell pinged. I was hoping for Bill. Pauli was the next best thing: *got some stuff. talk?* Yes! I tapped his number.

"Like, hey," he said. Then his voice was muffled, but louder. "On the phone," he shouted. "Okay. See you later." After a beat, he returned.

"Your mom?"

"She's going to the boardwalk. Shopping and stuff," he said.

"What did you find?" I asked hurriedly

He cleared his throat. "So like you got ninety-seven names on the list in the book."

"Right."

"And like I did this new thing." He became animated. "Like I ran this software from my last digital forensics class where we took a bunch of data and figured out commonalities using—"

"An algorithm?"

"If the math is right—"

"Pauli," I asked gently, "what did you find?"

"Okay, so I started with where they're from," he said.

"That makes sense."

"Mostly East Coast. Jersey, Pennsylvania, Delaware. Five guys from New York. One from California." He paused. "Kind of funny that a guy would come all the way from San Diego to the Jersey Shore."

I'd been to San Diego many times when my brother Andy lived there. It *was* kind of odd...

"Vinnie had the names so they're probably connected to his boat," I mused. "Customers?"

"I'm checking out stuff like what kind of jobs they have."

"That's a great idea."

"And since this is, like, a *murder*...I'm looking at criminal records," he added solemnly.

I was thunderstruck. The kid was a genius. "Pauli, that's fantastic!" Could one or more of these men be guilty of colluding in the car theft ring? If so the state unit would need these names. Not, however, until I knew exactly what they meant to Vinnie.

Pauli assured me that he would keep digging and text later. I leaned back in my chair. It wasn't much to go on.... Still, I had faith in my Internet guru. He'd never let me down yet. And, frankly, I was at my wits' end. If nothing materialized as a result of Pauli's high-tech mining, the investigation was in the hands of the county prosecutor. Even if Jackson's lawyer was able to get him acquitted, would they ever find out who killed Vinnie? Would his former partner's death hang over his head indefinitely?

I needed to move. I jammed my arms into a slicker, grabbed my bag, and walked outside. A blast of wind hit me, the rain coming down at an angle pricking my face like pins and needles. *The Jersey Shore was in for a drubbing.* I hopped in my MC and drove to the boardwalk. I assumed on a day like this with sunbathers scared off, parking spaces might be plentiful. I was right and found a spot close to the Sandbar.

Grody had battened down the restaurant—removing the tables and chairs from the sand and lowering the plastic, see-through shades that ran around the perimeter of the restaurant.

"You're expecting the worst?" I asked after settling into a table by the bar.

He studied the gray sky, the relentless rain. "The weather report's not so hot."

I shuddered. The wind whipped debris off the boardwalk, sent the warning red flags on the beach flapping: *Danger. No Swimming.*

"We could get fifty-mile-an-hour gusts tonight. Three or four inches of water." He nodded grimly. "A good evening to stay in."

I speculated about the theater festival. What kind of crowd could they get for the awards event tonight? At least the Etonville group would be here to applaud, especially if *Arsenic and Old Lace* won something for their efforts. Though I had my doubts after Abby's and Edna's tap routine. With few customers, Grody tried to keep himself occupied, wiping clean tables and studying inventory sheets. He joined me.

"Were you ever on Vinnie's charter boat?" I asked.

"*The Bounty*? No. I've been on other luxury charters, though."

"What are they like?"

"What you'd expect. A bunch of guys drinking and fishing for hours on end."

"I was aboard *The Bounty...*"

Grody cocked an eyebrow.

"Don't ask. The cabin was gorgeous. A beautiful galley with stainless steel appliances, a plush salon with a huge flat screen TV, dining room seating for eight. Two luxury staterooms. It didn't seem like the kind of place for a beer and burgers gang," I observed.

"It wasn't. A full day of fishing can run a couple thousand. You add up six to eight guys, and Vinnie was pulling in big bucks."

Vinnie and his partners, Sam and Arlene. "What about the food and drink?"

"Mostly catered. I did a few charters earlier this summer. No-expense-spared seafood buffets. And the liquor? Top-shelf booze and champagne," he said.

I marveled again how Vinnie's fortunes had changed since his days with Jackson. These fishing excursions were not for the average visit-the-shore-for-a-day-of-fishing Joe. No wonder Sam got involved. A lot of money to be made. "And the clients?"

Grody rubbed a thumb and index finger together. "Loaded. Some trips are corporate events. Getaway days as rewards for work well done. I even catered a bachelor party. That was interesting." He grinned.

Rich clients that Vinnie kept track of in a black book.

"...for Bill?" Grody asked.

I'd lost the thread of the conversation. "Sorry?"

"I said are you eating or waiting for Bill?" Grody went behind the bar and drew a seltzer for me. "I have blackened grouper we're featuring for lunch." He cast a glance out the front of the restaurant, where the boardwalk was empty, the rain falling, though with less force than earlier. The wind still blustered.

"I'm not sure." I hesitated. Bill had been so unreliable these past few days. Now that his BMW was recovered, we could get back to our vacation. His response to my text wasn't encouraging: *on my way but start without me.* Judging from his recent efforts to meet up, "on his way" could mean anywhere from fifteen minutes to two hours. I texted Lola: *join me at the Sandbar?*

* * * *

Thirty minutes later, Lola blew in, huddled in her Eddie Bauer trench coat, blond hair in a tight chignon. As usual, she could have strolled off a runway instead of the boardwalk. "Whew. If this keeps up, we'll have to swim to the theater tonight." She plopped down beside me. "Do you think it's too early for wine?"

I chortled. Something hot was more my speed at the moment. On days like this I used to love to eat hot chowder or lobster bisque while watching fishermen bring in their catch. "Everyone hopeful for the awards ceremony?"

Lola removed her raincoat. "I spent the morning coaxing Walter to calm down. He's certain we have a chance, which I doubt, but if we do win something, he might need to make an acceptance speech." She exhaled loudly. "Dealing with his anxiety is a full-time occupation."

"Walter likes making curtain speeches. Why is this any different? I realize it's not about someone's death. He'd still be the focus of attention."

"I think it's about getting up in front of his peers. He has a streak of insecurity," she said knowingly.

A server brought chowder for me, a chardonnay for Lola. She took a big gulp. Then leaned across the table. "What's happening with Jackson? Any news on the investigation front?"

I filled her in on the car theft raid, including the arrest of Tiny, who was known to Vinnie and Sam Baldwin, and she sat there stunned. "At least Bill recovered his car. But what does it mean about Vinnie?"

"Not a clue." I kept the black book to myself. The fewer who knew about its existence at this point, the better. "I suppose if the cops get Tiny to talk there could be hell to pay for his accomplices."

"Umm." Lola rested her chin on her palm. "It's so strange. Sam's the patron of a theater festival and potentially a criminal. Stealing cars...he doesn't seem the type. Of course, my judgment of men hasn't been so hot lately."

"Looks are deceiving. Take Jackson..."

Lola grinned. "I'd like to!"

Geez. "Years ago, he couldn't feed himself, never mind feed anyone else. Now he's a gourmet chef!"

"I hope his lawyer is on the ball," Lola said, serious.

"He's certainly got some terrific credentials."

A blast of air whooshed into the restaurant, sending menus and napkins flying. "Praying we get an audience tonight," Lola said.

We ate our blackened grouper on freshly baked rolls. They were delicious, we told Grody, who looked lost at the absence of customers. I knew how he felt; I'd been there in my early days at the Windjammer restaurant. Lola and I finished our lunch and, since Bill hadn't shown up, I elected to head back to the bungalow and take a nap until showtime. Or until Pauli called with more information. I dropped Lola off at the Windward, telling her to break a leg, and drove to my house, plowing through puddles. Some streets had flooded, and I zigzagged to avoid standing water in the roadway. I pulled into our driveway and ran to the porch to get out of the weather.

I inserted my key into the lock on the house door. Without turning the key, the door opened. I stiffened. "Hello? Bill? Jackson?" The house was dark. Empty. Shivers ran down my spine. I crept inside, and from where I stood, I could see that the living room had been tossed: furniture rearranged, sofa cushions dumped on the floor. Whoever had broken in this time had not bothered to cover their tracks by neatly placing objects in their rightful locations as they'd done with Jackson's clothing. I hated to think what else had been disturbed.

I fumbled through my bag for my cell phone. This warranted 911. My hand wobbled as I tapped on the numbers and relayed the information and my address. I was told the police would respond shortly. I stuck my head in the kitchen. Cupboard doors were open, contents of some shelves thrown on the counter.

I heard, but couldn't see, the screen door open. My chest tightened. I reached in my bag for my key ring container of pepper spray with one hand and clutched a skillet off the stove with the other. I was ready.

Footsteps thumped on the porch and moved into the house. My hands were damp. I raised the skillet and pepper spray and held them in front of me. Someone was feet away.

"Arrgh!" I yelled and swung the skillet.

"Dodie!" An arm shot out and grabbed mine. "What's going on!" Bill yelled.

Reinforcements had arrived. I collapsed on the floor, smashing my pan against the tile. "It's about time," I said. "Where have you been? Someone broke in and trashed the living room—"

"—I can see that." He put an arm around me.

"—I can't imagine what they did to the bedroom."

"Stay here." He hurried down the hall, then came back quickly. "Some cleaning up to do in there," he said grimly.

Flashing blue and red lights caught his attention. "You called 911? Good. Someone was hunting for something. Any idea what?" he asked as the officers entered the house.

* * * *

Twenty minutes later, the two Candle Beach cops who'd interrogated Jackson only days ago stood in the living room wrapping up the interview.

"We'll have a crew dust for fingerprints, but these types are careful and use gloves," said the tall, wiry cop. He made no reference to Jackson or my visit to the CBPD after Jackson's arrest.

"We've had some other break-ins in Candle Beach this summer," said the younger, friendly one. He made no reference to our conversation on the boardwalk.

"I assume the perp was searching for something." Bill looked at me.

"It's summer. Tourists. People get careless and leave money and valuables lying around," the older officer said. "Keep your door locked. Put valuables out of sight."

I wanted to scream. The doors were locked and there was nothing of value to steal except for Jackson's thousand dollars and the perp had already bypassed that. My instincts told me someone thought I had the black book and was desperate to find it. Pauli! He was in danger as long as the book was in his possession.

Bill walked the cops to the door and thanked them for coming. They assured him a CSI unit would be on the premises within the hour and asked that we not disturb anything. The front door closed.

"What's going on?" Bill asked me.

"What do you mean?"

"What are you not telling me? If I know you, and I think I do, this has something to do with Jackson's arrest," he said.

Why was I so hesitant to come clean? Because the moment I did, the black book and any hope of finding Vinnie's murderer would vanish. The state was bent on convicting Jackson; Jackson's lawyer was bent on getting him acquitted. Who cared about Vinnie?

"What are you not telling *me*?" I asked. With Bill, a good offense was the best defense.

He regarded me warily. "You have something you want to ask me?"

"Where have you been?"

"I got to the Sandbar after you left. There's flooding on Route 195. I had to take the long way back here—"

"I don't mean today. I mean all week. You've been pulling a disappearing act ever since the BMW was stolen. I know you were helping out the state unit and wanted to be in on the raid, but why did they target your car? How did they get it so easily? I can see how if a driver left keys in the ignition..."

Bill was silent. My neck hairs stood ramrod straight.

"Did you...leave the keys in your car purposefully?" My voice flew up an octave. "Were you a part of a sting to capture the thieves?"

"I intended to tell you the whole story once the assignment was over. I should have known you'd work it out," he said ruefully.

"Assignment?" *Whoa!*

"I have a buddy on the state task force investigating these car theft rings. Especially in the shore area. So when he heard I drove a BMW and was going to be down here..." Bill sat next to me. "I agreed to install a GPS tracking device so when or if the BMW was lifted, there would be a trail. Dodie, it was a crap shoot. A number of other luxury cars were used as bait too. My luck the Candle Beach crew fell in love with a gold BMW."

I was gobsmacked. Bill was playing cop while also playing the aggrieved car owner. "You're a pretty talented actor," I said crisply. I wanted to be justifiably annoyed at being left in the dark. I couldn't, considering what I hadn't told him about my snooping around: the warehouse, the black book, Tiny, *The Bounty*, the ice pick—

"Sorry. I hate to keep things from you," he said. "The task force kept everything under wraps. No leaks."

Now I felt guilty. I had to get out of this conversation. "No problem. Do you mind hanging around for the CSI techs? They'd rather talk with you anyway." I smiled sweetly.

"Where are you going in this weather?"

"I told Lola I'd pick her up at the hotel and we'd go to the theater together." Did that make sense?

"It's not even four o'clock. The show's at what...seven thirty?"

"She wants to talk about the ELT season for next year." I found my bag on the kitchen floor. "I'll see you tonight?"

"I didn't plan on going to the theater tonight. We can hunker down with dinner and wine and Netflix. And then see what happens..." He put his arms around me and laid a big one on my lips.

Talk about feeling torn. "I'll leave as soon as I can. Meet you back here," I said.

"This is no night to be out wandering around—"

I waved good-bye and darted out of the house.

"Dodie?"

I had to find Pauli.

17

The wind died down, and the rain eased up during the hour I was in the bungalow with Bill and the Candle Beach police officers. I sent a prayer of thanks to the weather gods—the theater festival might be able to forge ahead with the awards as planned. Regardless of tonight's entertainment, I had to find a safe haven for Pauli for the next few hours. Or until something broke with his algorithm. I couldn't take the chance that the same person who'd assumed I had the black book had been keeping tabs on me and somehow found out that it was now with Pauli. There was one place that served my purposes. The theater. But how to get Pauli to stay there without freaking him out by warning him about the possible danger?

I guided my MINI Cooper through the run-off on the streets to the Windward. I parked and hurried to Lola's room. I heard a babble of voices on the other side of the door. Then a loud cheer. I knocked. The door swung open and everyone greeted me.

"Dodie, you're dripping wet." Lola.

"Come on in!" Carol.

"Get in the game." Mildred.

"I'm winning!" Edna.

"O'Dell, got any money?" Penny.

Apparently, I'd created monsters in the spring when I undertook teaching this crew poker. A table and chairs had been set up in the center of Lola's room and the five of them were having a high old time. Stacks of poker chips were piled in front of each player, a dish of coins off to the side. Penny shuffled the cards.

"A high-stakes game," I said.

Mildred giggled. "Nickels and dimes."

"The way I'm winning, there'll be some 10-67s before dinner," Edna said.

"What's that?" Lola asked.

"People needing help," Edna answered with a cackle.

"Dodie, you want to play?" asked Lola.

"No thanks. Actually, I want to see Pauli."

Carol stacked her chips. "Why? He's in our room."

My brain tap-danced. "I need to...talk about the Windjammer's website," I finished lamely. My go-to excuse whenever I had to confer with her son.

Penny dealt the cards. "Ante up."

Carol placed a chip in the center of the table. "He's probably Instagramming or texting or whatever. He misses Janice. I'm glad he has that laptop with him. He'd be lost without it."

If she only knew. Jackson and I would be lost too.

"Seven-card stud, aces wild, low diamond in the hole splits the pot," Penny announced.

"Be right back," I said. No one noticed.

Across the hall I paused before tapping on Pauli's door. I took a breath to settle myself. I didn't want to alarm him unnecessarily. Pauli opened the door. "Hey." He looked over my shoulder. "Mom's with Lola. Playing poker."

I slipped into the room and closed the door. "Any more luck with the black book?"

"Like, I'm running an algorithm. But ten of the guys have records."

"They do?" We were getting somewhere.

"Mostly parking tickets, moving violations, and like one breaking and entering. His own home." Pauli snickered.

Maybe not... Trying to find information that connected these names was like searching for the proverbial needle in a haystack. "Keep at it."

Pauli nodded.

I stalled. "Are you thinking of coming to the theater tonight?"

"Nah. Seen it all a bunch of times. You think the ELT has any chance of winning?" He looked doubtful.

"I don't really think so. Unless the Etonville crowd stuffed the ballot box."

Pauli guffawed. "Right."

"How's Janice?" I asked.

His face brightened. "Like good. She gets back Labor Day."

"Guess you've missed her," I said.

He blushed. "Guess so."

Young love...nice that Pauli and Janice found each other. When all of my friends in the sixth grade were "in love," and I wasn't, Mom assured me that love wasn't something you found. It was something that found you. Is that what happened to Bill and me?

The door opened. Carol and Lola bounded in. "Edna called a Code 7—"

"Meal break," said Lola.

Five o'clock. I had to think of something fast. I caught Lola's eye and motioned to the hallway. She signaled she understood.

"I'll grab my purse and meet you in the lobby," she said to Carol.

Carol counted her change, thrilled about her poker winnings. "Okey-doke."

Lola followed me into the hallway.

"I need a favor."

"Sure. What's up?" she asked.

"Pauli should come to the theater festival tonight to take photos," I said.

"He doesn't need to. We've got plenty from rehearsals and performances—"

"Lola, I can't tell you everything…"

She stared at me.

"I'd like Pauli to stay in the theater tonight. With the rest of the Etonville crowd."

Lola gasped. "Oh, something's happening?" She knew enough not to ask more questions than necessary when I'd gotten myself involved in murder investigations.

"I don't know. Until I do, the theater is the safest place for him," I assured her.

Lola's expression transitioned from surprise to worry and ended with determination. "I'll get him there. Never fear."

"Thanks, Lola and—"

"I know. Mum's the word," she said, pleased to be an asset.

* * * *

The ELT dressed in rain gear and headed off to the boardwalk for dinner, Pauli in tow. Lola had convinced him that pictures of the award winners—whether or not *Arsenic and Old Lace* was among them—would be great publicity for the Etonville Little Theatre. The kid was puzzled and grimaced, as if to ask "Really? After all I snapped for the last five days?" Nevertheless, he was a good sport, shrugged off his doubts, and picked up his digital camera. I suggested he take his laptop and work on the "Windjammer website" before the evening's events began. Pauli winked and jammed the computer into his backpack.

I declined to join the group, claiming that I needed to speak with Bill, which earned me a few giggles. Etonville never tired of commenting on my love life. Once on their way, I was free to jump in my car and drive the short distance to the theater. I had an impulse that demanded attention and not a lot of time to tend to it.

The parking lot was mostly empty; it was at least an hour before the companies would check-in with stage manager Maddy. I opened the front door of the theater and was hit with a dank, musty odor. The wooden structure had absorbed more than its share of moisture this week. All was quiet. I wanted one last chance—because I knew by morning I would have to surrender my evidence to the police—to confront Sam Baldwin. To ask him point blank about Vinnie and his partnership. About Tiny and the stolen cars in the warehouse. About framing Jackson with the ice pick. It was a bold, hazardous move, but I was tired of pussyfooting around. I wanted answers and Sam was the only one who could provide them. I trusted my instincts. If he lied to me, it was straight to the PD in the morning. With or without Pauli's findings on the black book. Sam had to be here…it was the final night of the festival he sponsored.

I stepped into the house. An eerie silence permeated the dark, unoccupied theater. Only a security light onstage provided limited illumination.

"You looking for someone?" Maddy, emerging from the shadows, asked in her characteristic curt manner. She defined prickly.

"Hi, Maddy. How's things?"

She stared at me.

Trivial talk had no impact on the stage manager. "Is Sam around?"

"Who wants to know?" She put her hands on her hips.

Who? Really, Maddy? After all of our interactions, she still had no clue who I was? "Dodie O'Dell? Sandbar catering? I need to see Sam about the bill," I said firmly.

She looked unconvinced. "He's not here."

"Is he due in soon? I can just wait around," I said helpfully.

Maddy grunted. "He's not been around today. Don't know if he's coming tonight." She sounded forlorn, as though she missed Sam.

I knew there was a possibility he wouldn't have arrived yet. I assumed he'd have to show up eventually. "He isn't giving out the theater awards?"

"Don't know," she said.

"Dodie!" a booming voice interrupted us.

John Bannister walked off the stage and up the aisle.

"Hey there. Haven't seen you around Candle Beach recently. Keeping busy with the festival?" I asked.

"This and that. You're a little early for the festivities. The ceremony doesn't begin 'til seven thirty."

"Right. I wanted to speak with Sam. Have you seen him?"

John frowned. "Not this afternoon. Is there something I can help you with?" he asked courteously.

"Catering bill for the opening night reception," Maddy offered.

"Ah, yes. That was quite a seafood feast. Very clever hors d'oeuvres. Were you responsible?"

I glanced from Maddy to John. How much could I get away with? "I assisted Grody Van Houten from the Sandbar."

"Do you have the bill with you?" he asked.

*Yikes...*now what? I rummaged around in my bag as though it was in there somewhere. "Uh..."

"Never mind. Email it to Baldwin General Contractors. I'm sure his secretary can take care of it," he said.

"Great. Thanks, John."

Maddy tapped her clipboard impatiently. I knew the gesture. I'd seen it often enough with Penny: Let's get on with this.

"Is there anything else?" John asked, then checked his watch.

"No. That's it." This visit had been a bust. No Sam, no confirmation that he'd be in the theater anytime in the next hour or so, no asking about Tiny, Vinnie, framing Jackson—

"Would you like to get a drink sometime?" John asked, his brown eyes twinkling.

"A drink?" I stammered. Was this kindly older guy hitting on me?

John laughed. "Didn't mean to startle you. I think you're a rather interesting person that I'd like to get to know better."

I was? I could hear Maddy rolling her eyes.

"Well...um...sure. Of course, I'm only here into next week," I said.

"Fine. Can I have your cell phone? I'll put my number in your contacts," he said.

I tapped in my password and handed my cell to John whose thumbs manipulated my phone as fast as Pauli's did. Wow...pretty awesome. My parents couldn't begin to maneuver their cells like this.

"When the festival is officially over tonight my appointment as greeter will be completed." He returned my cell. "By the way, you're connected to the Etonville Little Theatre? I've seen you with them."

"Yes. Very observant," I said archly. I was flirting with a senior citizen!

He leaned in conspiratorially. "I think they have a good chance to win something."

"You do?" Was he kidding?

Maddy harrumphed. "John, you're not supposed to—"

He raised a hand to silence her. "As good a chance as all of the other theaters." Then he winked at me.

Yowza! If he was twenty years younger and I wasn't practically engaged to Bill—did I say that?—I might be tempted to—

"John?" Arlene called from the stage. "Can I see you?"

She was dressed for the night in a sleeveless crew neck maxi dress. Tie-dyed pale pink and white with toeless spiked heels. Doubtless genuine Jimmy Choo. Not the knockoffs that I wore. Her ensemble reeked of expensive. I felt dowdy in my hoodie and rain slicker.

"I'll be in touch," John said, patted my arm lightly, and walked back to the stage.

"Whoa," I said aloud without realizing it.

"A real ladies' man. Been divorced twice." Maddy stuck her clipboard under her arm. "And, uh, you can ignore that stuff about Etonville winning something. The envelopes are sealed," she said decisively.

Maddy stomped off. I was at loose ends; at least half an hour before actors would arrive, another hour before audience members would drift in. I debated. Hang around the theater hoping Sam showed up? Or run to the boardwalk in the soggy, chilly night and grab something to eat? If Sam arrived on the scene in the next hour it might be a challenge to buttonhole him for a down-and-dirty chat with Maddy hovering in the background. Still, I intended to give it a try. I was sure I could wheedle information out of him. Maybe incriminating.

I opted to brave the elements and jog to the Candle Diner for a quick takeout dinner. Coffee and a sandwich would be fine. Then I would jog back and wait for Sam. In the lobby I inhaled sharply. Walking rapidly to the entrance, bent head covered by a hooded sweatshirt, was Tiny. I hadn't counted on Sam's fixer showing up. Tiny must be out on bail too, probably paid by Sam. My feet were glued to the floor. I had to do something and fast. Tiny would recognize me from the arcade and maybe the warehouse. I had no intention of confronting him.

I darted back into the theater and scanned the space. Maddy was gone and the stage was empty. Where to go? I sprinted through the house to a middle row of seats and ended up near the far aisle. I crouched down. I would only be discovered if Tiny chose to do a broad sweep of the house. What were the odds of that? I counted to ten.

The door into the theater nearest to me rustled, followed by his voice on a cell phone. Damn. Couldn't he have come in the other door? This aisle would bring him close to my hiding place.

"...see me tonight," Tiny muttered as he stopped a couple of rows away. "I'll see what I can do."

Who was he meeting? I didn't dare pop my head up in case he was still in the house. Hungry and frustrated, I resigned myself to hunkering down in this awkward position until people arrived. The minutes ticked by slowly. I adjusted my legs, then my backside. I checked my email. My eyes shut. I might have dozed off.

"Excuse me. Is this seat taken?" a voice asked, then cackled.

I sat up and blinked. "Hi, Penny." The ELT cast had gathered behind her, gawking at me on the floor.

"Dodie?" Lola said, alarmed. "What are you doing down there?"

"It's a long story." I stood and brushed myself off. "I'll save it for later."

"O'Dell, you sure know how to have a good time," Penny laughed.

"Funny. Where are Carol and Pauli?" I asked, alert.

"They'll be here," Lola said pointedly. "Carol wanted to buy souvenirs."

The company trooped backstage to hang out. I casually glided into a theater seat as though I was one more patron anxious to witness the last night of the New Jersey Community Theater Festival. Other casts trickled in, whooping it up, enjoying the final hurrah. Lights flicked on in the theater. I texted Bill to say I'd be back as soon as the award winners were announced. He sent a smiley face emoji. He was, no doubt, in a fantastic mood.

While I had been in a semiconscious state hiding on the floor, a notion had emerged. What kind of booking information did a charter company request from its guests to register for a day at sea? Credit card info, phone numbers, addresses. Pauli had worked on those for the men on the list. What else?

I mentally slapped my forehead! Vinnie must have advertised his business, had a website. I'd gotten so caught up reading about Vinnie's partner that I neglected to click on his website link. Maybe there was useful information there. I Googled Vinnie's name with boat businesses and sure enough there it was—Carcherelli Charters. The website was slick and classy with a home page that featured a photo of *The Bounty* and a beaming Vinnie on its deck. Other pages outlined charter trips and rates for daily expeditions, corporate events, and parties; a fishing report for the Jersey Shore; a photo gallery of satisfied customers displaying their catches; and an online registration form. A half page was devoted to the charter's valet service: pull up to the dock and your car was parked for you. That had to be a nice perk. Grody was right—these fishing excursions were pricey events. If Vinnie's customers filled out the registration form they'd supply name, address, phone, email, and intended dates. Nothing unusual there. No information that might provide Vinnie with blackmail fodder, if that was how he intended to get revenge. I was stumped.

"Hey."

A spray of raindrops peppered me as Pauli removed his jacket and slumped into a seat.

"Taking more photos tonight?"

"Like I took about a thousand already."

"Lola wants to spotlight the ELT if it wins something." I remembered John Bannister's words.

Pauli fidgeted with his camera.

"Between shots you can work on the list."

"Got it. I'm gonna bounce soon as I can and go back to the hotel," he said.

I had a sudden flash. "Do you have the names from the book in your computer?" I asked.

"Uh-huh."

"Then I'd better take the book for safekeeping," I said softly.

Pauli regarded me wisely. "Cuz like, if somebody found out I had it..." He finished the thought to himself. "Awesome."

He was enjoying the detective stuff too much. I soft-pedaled my concerns. "I don't want us to lose it," I said casually.

Pauli scanned the house, opened his backpack, and attempted a clandestine move, passing me the book. I placed it in my bag.

"Brrr. It's getting downright cold out there." Carol whipped off a rain cap. "The drizzle is turning into another downpour. Pauli, are you staying for the whole show?"

"Nah. I'm taking some shots at the beginning and cutting out."

"Stay until the winners are announced. You never know...!" She bobbed her salt-and-pepper curly head and walked off.

Hope sprang eternal in Etonville.

The house was filling nicely, despite the rising wind and steady deluge. People took off slickers and jackets and settled into their seats. I found mine on the opposite side of the theater and joined Mildred, Vernon, and the Banger sisters.

"My, the weather is simply atrocious," said a Banger sister.

"I like this kind of weather. Puts me in a pleasant mood," said Vernon.

"Storms like this remind me of Hurricane Sandy," said Mildred. "I remember the gale force wind and the water everywhere. Dodie, I know you remember it," she said sympathetically.

All four of my friends looked at me. I had nightmares, like last night, whenever the weather forecast hinted at a possible hurricane. "I do."

The house lights dimmed, people shushed each other, and excitement rippled through the theater. Arlene appeared in a spotlight center stage, fabulous in her maxi dress and sporting a queenly smile. I spotted John down front in the first row, but no Sam. Arlene thanked everyone for coming out in this "dreadful weather" and introduced Graham from the Westfield community theater. The genial gentleman gave a brief summary of the festival's highlights—opening night reception, wonderful attendance, and brilliant performances. A blast of wind shook the theater. People murmured but Graham soldiered on announcing the night's entertainment—a medley of songs about theater sung by the casts of *Cinderella* and *The Sound of Music*.

"Give My Regards to Broadway," a couple from *Cabaret* and *Chorus Line*, and "There's No Business Like Show Business." When the actors from *Cinderella* began to sing "Don't Rain on My Parade" from *Funny Girl*, they earned generous laughs from the crowd as intermittent gusts beat down on the building. The songs came to an end—to a well-deserved round of applause—and Graham took the stage to present the seven community theaters who had been finalists. One by one, the companies hustled onto the stage, took a bow, and received a certificate of commendation from Graham.

When it was the ELT's moment, Walter stood prominently center stage flanked by a dignified Lola and a smirking Romeo. Abby seemed unimpressed, but Edna had enough enthusiasm for all—she waved to her supporters in the crowd and Etonville cheered loudly. Pauli snapped away.

"Yay!" Mildred yelled. "Oh, I hope we win," she said to me.

I gave her an optimistic thumbs-up.

The stage lights blipped off and then back on immediately, the electricity under duress. Patrons shared concerns with each other. Graham sensed he might soon be losing his viewers and hurried through the final presentation of actors: *King Lear*, whose title character did a Shakespearean bow with bended knee. And finally, after days of rehearsal and performances, the winners of the NJCTF were about to be announced. Mildred clutched my hand on one side, a Banger sister on the other. We were in solidarity.

"Third place in the New Jersey Community Theater Festival goes to…" Graham opened an envelope with a flourish. Took a second to register its contents and then intoned, "*Death of a Salesman.*"

Shouts erupted in the house as the company ran onstage and accepted its bronze trophy graciously. If they were disappointed to place third, they didn't show it.

When the audience grew quiet, Graham announced the second-place winner: "*Cinderella.*"

Never mind the bulky glass slipper or petulant lead actor, the show had hit its mark and earned the cast a silver award. The tension in the theater grew. Two of the strongest shows had already won. Who was left? Did *Arsenic* actually have a chance?

Graham waited until he had the entire house in the palm of his hand. He gestured with the last envelope. "And now ladies and gentlemen, the first-place award goes to…"

A crash from outside startled everyone. The theater went dark.

18

Everything happened simultaneously. Screams from the audience, Graham attempting to maintain order by begging everyone to stay calm, shouting from the stage as the crew struggled to figure out what went wrong. Cell phone flashlights created a hundred pinpoints of light. I reassured Mildred and the Banger sisters that the theater must have a back-up generator. After all, this was run by Sam Baldwin who did seminars on surviving the aftereffects of Hurricane Sandy.

In the hubbub, Pauli leaned over the seat behind me. "Gotta bounce."

"Be careful out there," I said.

He gave me a thumbs-up.

"Text me if you find anything. On the list, on the warehouse, on Vinnie. Anything."

He nodded, jerked on his rain jacket, flipped up the hood, and took off. There was nothing to do in the theater until the lights came back on so we—

My cell binged. A text from Jackson. Great. Hadn't seen him all day and I wanted to catch up. *Dudette*... He hadn't called me that since the day he first showed up on our porch. *...found some evidence on the Bounty. meet me there at nine.* Something to clear him of the murder charge? It was eight forty-five. I had just enough time to scoot out of here and dash to the dock. I said good-bye to the town and guaranteed that the show would go on—once another source of electricity was hooked up—and promised to see everyone tomorrow before they left Candle Beach.

I pulled on my slicker and by the light of my flashlight rushed out of the lobby and into the night. I stashed my cell inside my hoodie to keep it dry. An overhead street lamp swung violently sending an arc of light back and forth. I raced through the town park, pelted by rain, to the deserted boardwalk where businesses had closed down. A lone man trotted to the safety of the Candle Diner. Security lights atop poles that lined the boardwalk gave off a fuzzy glow, their rays diffused by the torrent of water. My sneakers were completely soaked, and water had wormed its way past the snaps on my slicker. I ducked my head deeper into the hood of my raincoat.

The blustery weather was getting worse. My cell buzzed. No way I was stopping to check out messages until I reached *The Bounty*. A garbage can blew over, its contents strewn on the ground and swept into the air. A swirl of paper napkins and plates from a nearby pizza stand blew into me. Another blast of wind at my back thrust me forward. I treaded carefully onto the pier where Vinnie's boat was docked, working to maintain my footing on the wet boards. My shoes sloshed with rainwater. Bells on several boats rang wildly as they bounced up and down in the choppy water. I approached *The Bounty*. It was dark. Where was Jackson? I climbed onboard, scanned the deck, fore and aft, and took hold of the handrail by the stairs leading to the cabin below.

"Jackson?" I said. The hairs on my neck quivered, my radar warning me that something wasn't right. The door into the cabin was unlocked. I turned the handle and entered, flicking the light switch. Nothing happened. The power was off in the boat too? That didn't make sense. *The Bounty* would have its own generator. The boat tipped sideways, the sudden motion making me dizzy. Of course, I hadn't eaten since lunch, so it might be a lack of food that—

Strong arms grasped me from behind. "Who—? Wha—? Jackson?" A hand jammed against my mouth. I was half-dragged, half-carried—kicking and yelling—into one of the staterooms and unceremoniously tossed on the bed by someone who smelled of cigarette smoke.

"You!" I said.

"I know you too," he said, his voice like gravel in the dark. He slapped a piece of duct tape over my mouth.

"Tiny!" I managed to spit out as the tape struck my face.

I struggled, but Tiny was too powerful. He had my hands and feet immobilized before I had a chance to fight him off.

"I told 'em you were gonna be trouble. Sticking your nose into Vinnie's business." He grunted as he wound the last of the duct tape around my ankles. "This'll fix you, sister." The door to the stateroom slammed shut.

Tiny spoke like a gangster from a 1940s classic on the movie channel. If my mouth wasn't taped shut, or my life threatened, I would have laughed at his clichéd speech. Where was Jackson? Had he met the same fate as me? Soft groaning from my left startled me—someone else in the room with me. I groaned back, running my voice up and down the scales as quietly as I could. Who knew where Tiny was lurking? I twisted back and forth on the bed, my arms pinned beneath me in an awkward, painful position. Tiny had run a length of tape from my hands to my feet in case I got frisky and tried to travel off the bed. Too bad for Tiny because I had no intention of surrendering. I needed to find Jackson. I rolled onto my side and returned to my back, repeated it several times to gain momentum and, suddenly carried away, I made a complete 360-degree rotation, flew off the bed and onto a body that broke my fall.

"Oommmph," I grunted, my face smashed into a stubbly one.

"Oommmph," a deeper voice grunted.

Even in the darkness, I could make out the halo of curly hair. Jackson.

Obviously, he was as incapacitated as me. Our compromising position meant that faces, chests, and torsos were locked as one in an embarrassing *pas de deux*. It had been four years since Jackson and I found ourselves this close. The two beds in the stateroom were only a few feet apart. Easily enough room for two people, if one was stacked on top of the other. A buzzing from the inside of my hoodie made us both freeze. Jackson's eyes bugged out of his head.

I tried to say "cell." I'd put my phone inside my bra for safe-keeping when I ran from the theater. "Cuh...cuh." It had to be either Bill or Pauli texting me.

Jackson shook his head, confused. I gave up.

"Geh, geh," he said and pointed his head to my right. Go! He wanted me to shift spots so that we were both on the floor. More comfortable, less humiliating.

We wiggled our way until I slid off his body and we lay parallel to each other on our sides, panting, inhaling through our noses, pausing in the dark to listen for Tiny. Jackson scooted down toward the foot of the bed. I couldn't see him very well, but I could hear him scrape against the carpet. Suddenly he was still, then the scraping sound was replaced with a soft scratching. I propped myself up on one elbow. Jackson inched his way to the bottom of the bed frame, swaying back and forth. I scooted down to help.

I could see him rubbing the tape on his wrists into the metal corner of the frame. There was a stabbing pop, then a slight ripping noise. Jackson yanked his arms free. He tore the duct tape off his mouth, then off mine. Ouch! I gulped air.

"Th-thanks," I stuttered, wiping my mouth on the sleeve of my hoodie.

He took the tape off my hands. "Sh!" He cocked his head to listen. The cabin outside the stateroom was quiet. "Tiny's probably still out there," he muttered.

I dug my cell phone out of my chest and hit Messages.

"That was the buzzing? Thought I was having a heart attack," he joked quietly.

I checked the text. Pauli: *gotta hit. ten guys on list filed police reports last three months. car theft.* My stomach churned.

"Good thing you have your cell," Jackson murmured. He tackled the tape on his ankles. "Tiny took mine. They made me text you. Hey, how'd you like 'dudette'? That was a signal that something was up. I knew you hated me calling you that so I figured if you read a text from me and I said 'dudette' you'd know to call somebody."

Vinnie's black book had a long list of customers. Most were probably wealthy clients. With luxury automobiles. A number of whom had their cars stolen…Tiny is arrested at the warehouse where stolen cars are stockpiled. I gasped.

"Did you?" Jackson asked quietly.

"Huh?"

"Call somebody? To get us out of this?" Jackson tore at the tape binding his legs.

"Jackson, do charter fishing boats normally offer valet service?" I whispered, my voice unsteady.

"Valet service? What are you talking about? We gotta get out of here." Jackson unwound the tape on my ankles.

"Do they?"

"Not for the kind of charter Vinnie and I ran."

Maybe for Vinnie's new charter business. I didn't know how the crew had done it, but I was willing to bet the valet service gave the car theft ring access to victims. What came first? The plan for the high-end charter or the plan for stealing cars? Vinnie must have threatened to pull the plug on the operation with his black book and it got him killed—

"Gimme that," Jackson rasped and snatched my phone.

"Stop! I'll call," I said and reached for it.

He bobbled my cell and it slid out of his hands. "Where is it?" he muttered.

"I don't know. Why'd you take it from me?" I asked, irritated and scared.

We felt around on the floor, Jackson running his hand under the bed, while I covered a swath of carpet near me. "I figured out why Vinnie was murdered. And who probably did it."

"If we don't find your cell, somebody's gonna have to figure out who wasted *us*."

Jackson was right. We crawled in different directions until we'd separated to opposite sides of the room. My phone hadn't skated *that* far away from us. I sat back on my heels. "Forget the phone. We got to find some kind of a weapon to get us out of here!"

From a few feet away, Jackson snorted softly. "Weapon? In a bedroom? Like what, pillows?"

"Check the closet. Maybe there's a—"

My phone pinged again. We stopped moving.

"Under this bed," Jackson said and dove for it.

I knew better. The pinging was on my side of the room. I swept my arm back and forth, finally smacking the errant cell. It had landed near the head board. I retrieved it, my hands shaking.

Footsteps clomped on the deck of *The Bounty* and down the stairs to the cabin. A door slammed outside the stateroom. Tiny? Sam? My heart jumped. Jackson eased his way to me and grabbed my hand. "Can't call 911. They might hear us. I'll text Bill," I whispered.

Jackson nodded. My fingers were clumsy: *sos. on vinnie's boat at pier. captive. help.*

I read the second text from Pauli: *warehouse owned by a. bannister baldwin*. Wait, what? *Arlene Bannister Baldwin*? Arlene was related to John?

"Turn off the phone! They'll hear texts coming in," Jackson murmured.

"I'll put it on vibrate—"

"Off!" Jackson bit the words tensely.

They knew we were in here but hopefully presumed we were still taped up.

Voices rose and fell from somewhere in the living room. One heavy, one lighter.

I shut off my phone. We sat immobile waiting for the next move. I stuffed my cell back into my bra. Seconds ticked away. I couldn't sit still any longer. Pauli's texts proved how dangerous—and probably desperate—Vinnie's killers were. I crawled past Jackson to the only closet in the room. When Jackson and I had searched *The Bounty*, there were few articles of clothing hanging in there. There had to be something else that would save us when they barged in here. Anything that might hold them off until Bill arrived with reinforcements.

"What are you doing?"

"Shush." I opened the closet door. I felt around for something, anything… then I patted it. I pulled the surfboard out of the closet.

"What didya find?" he asked.

I shuffled toward Jackson. He reached out. "Dude, a board?" Jackson whispered skeptically.

The voices grew louder. No mistaking them—a male and a female.

"You have a better idea?" I handed Jackson the surfboard. "Get behind the door. I'll stand between the beds and distract whoever comes in. A bait and tackle to buy time."

We positioned ourselves. I inhaled slowly to steady my nerves. *Bill... come on!*

A minute later, someone walked to the stateroom. "...tied up. We gotta dump 'em and clear out," Tiny said and jerked the door open.

The room was flooded with light, blinding me momentarily. I blinked furiously.

"What the...?" Tiny eyes darted around the room, then he lunged at me. I backed up, forcing him to come after me, stepping further away from the door. I extended an arm to defend myself as Jackson lifted the surfboard and brought it down on Tiny's back. The big guy howled, more in anger than pain I imagined. Jackson's blow hit a sweet spot compelling Tiny to turn away from me. I threw everything I could get my hands on: an alarm clock, a table lamp on the dresser, even pillows. Tiny fought off my barrage as Jackson pushed the board into him, the two of them doing a tug-of-war. Tiny had size, but Jackson was more agile.

Tiny swore a blue streak, while Jackson grunted. The two of them landed on the floor. I hopped on Tiny and threw the comforter over his head.

"What the hell's going on in here?" Arlene stood in the doorway, the gun in her hand pointed directly at my head. "Tiny? Get up!" Her tie-dyed maxi dress and Jimmy Choo heels were replaced with a heavy jacket, jeans and boots. *Dressed for traveling.*

Tiny threw Jackson off him and untangled himself from the bed cover. Both Jackson and the surfboard bounced off the closet door.

No surprise here. Arlene was a business partner with Sam. It made sense that she was in on the car theft ring. Besides, she owned the warehouse in Walker. Sam would make his presence known any minute now.

Bill had better make his known too.

I needed to stall. "The theater festival and Baldwin Contractors weren't enough to keep you busy?"

Arlene barely batted an eye. "Tie them up." She tossed Tiny a coil of nylon docking rope. "And this time do it right."

Tiny had fire in his eyes. He gripped Jackson roughly and bound his hands behind his back, running a line from his wrists to his feet. "Try 'n get out of that." He pushed Jackson onto the bed.

"The car theft was your idea, right? Vinnie was just a pawn. Paying off gambling debts," I said.

Jackson looked puzzled. I read his expression. *What are you doing?* He had the good sense to remain silent and let me do the talking.

"Told you she'd figure it out," Tiny said triumphantly to Arlene. His face darkened. "Shoulda let me get rid of her after the warehouse."

So he did see me there…

"Shut up and take care of her." Arlene waggled her weapon at me.

Tiny yanked my arms behind me and wrapped the cord around my wrists, already sore from the duct tape.

There was no more time. "Too bad you never found Vinnie's black book. He wanted revenge, right? Were you too greedy? Cheating him out of his share of the money?"

Tiny stopped tying, Arlene confronted me. "You should have minded your own business."

"You can have it now. It's in my bag. It won't help you though." Let them rummage through my stuff and eat up more time. "The authorities have a copy of the list." Partly true. Pauli *was* an authority when it came to digital forensics. I was swinging for the fence. "You shouldn't have set up Vinnie's clients with the valet service."

"Too damn smart for your own good." Tiny jerked the rope and wound it around my ankles. He shoved me onto the bed next to Jackson.

A rumbling from the deck was like a loud explosion. The engine… someone was piloting the boat. Sam. *The Bounty* pitched and rolled as it backed out of its berth. My stomach plunged down to my toes, bile rose in my throat. I shot a look of desperation to Jackson, who struggled with his ties.

"Go ahead," Tiny snarled. "This time you ain't goin' nowhere. Until we toss you overboard."

Overboard? I gulped. The plan was to dispose of us in the ocean? The boat glided through the choppy water.

Arlene repositioned herself away from the door. "Get them on top."

"I g-guess Sam's doing the driving?" I said as Tiny lifted me off the bed.

"Sam?" Arlene threw back her head and roared. "That's a good one."

Footsteps bumped down the stairs to the cabin.

"Hello, Dodie." John Bannister stood behind Arlene, dark raincoat and marine boots creating an altogether different image of the kindly gentleman. No cane was visible.

"John?" I said, flabbergasted.

"Had you fooled, didn't I?" He smiled sympathetically. "Sorry we won't have that date this week. You see, you have a different kind of date." He nodded at Tiny. "This time the two of you…" he pointed at Jackson, "… will *actually* drown."

Unlike Vinnie who actually had a punctured aorta. "You won't get away with killing us," I said with as much bravado as I could muster.

"On the contrary. By the time your bodies are discovered, if they are ever discovered, we'll be far away." John poked Tiny. "Let's go. We don't have much time," he said.

Tiny and John lugged me to the deck, securing me in one of the captain's chairs. The boat cut through the black water, bouncing me up and down. The wind whipped at my slicker, the driving rain pelting my face, strands of my hair smeared into my eyes. I could hardly catch my breath.

"Let her go. She can't go anywhere," yelled John above the roar of the engine, his words scarcely reaching Tiny who steadied himself with the aid of the railing. "…get him."

I was alone for a moment before they reappeared. I started to cry. I stared into the inky night. It wasn't in my DNA to surrender but even I had to admit, as Aunt Maureen would say, *the jig is up.*

Jackson was thrown into a chair next to me, his brown locks plastered against his scalp.

"Now?" Tiny asked John.

"Not yet. Another mile out to sea. I'm going below. Stay here." John handed Tiny the gun and dashed below. Tiny, not happy at having to stand guard in this weather, withdrew to the cover of the stairway leading down to the cabin, well within reach of us.

Jackson leaned into me. "Can you swim?"

I rotated in my chair. "You can joke at a time like this?"

"What else can we do? I haven't seen weather like this since—"

"Hurricane Sandy. The night you and Vinnie left me alone so you could scuttle the *JV*," I yelled in his ear.

"What?"

"I heard about it. The insurance scam Vinnie wanted to run."

"Vinnie, sure. I said no. We parked the *JV* in the marina at Ocean Port. It was no use. The storm beat her up." Jackson rubbed his face on the sleeve of his jacket.

Even in the midst of my terror, I was happy to hear that Jackson wanted no part of Vinnie's insurance rip-off. I bumped into his shoulder. "I'm still mad you left me to go through the hurricane alone!" I shouted.

Jackson gawked at the angry, roiling waves. "I'm here now!" he shouted back.

Yes, he was. The shore receded into the background as the remaining lights of Candle Beach vanished. John joined Tiny on the deck and the two of them struggled to gain their footing. Roaring wind blasted our bodies as the boat lifted and dropped. John motioned to the pilot house, *The Bounty* reduced to idle speed.

"Get him first," John ordered Tiny who released Jackson from the chair, pushing him into the railing.

"No!" I fought my ropes. "At least untie us. If they find us like this, they'll know it was murder," I screamed into the wind.

Tiny grunted, struggling with Jackson. "Ha. The fish'll get you first."

Sharks. All at once Jackson bit Tiny's hand, the fixer howled into the night, I threw myself on John as the boat tilted sideways, dislodging his gun, and a brilliant light exploded from a Coast Guard cutter that sped into place alongside *The Bounty*.

"Cut the engine!" boomed a voice from a loudspeaker.

* * * *

I huddled under a blanket in the galley of *The Bounty*, my teeth chattering, sipping hot coffee. I was soaked to the bone. No slicker could provide protection against such a violent storm. Jackson sat opposite me, equally wet, cold, and exhausted. On deck, lights and voices blared, the thunder of feet thumping as officers transferred John, Arlene, Tiny, and the pilot to the cutter to be transported to the Candle Beach PD for immediate processing, before being handed over to the state police to answer to murder and kidnapping charges, as well as their part in the auto theft ring.

Bill emerged from the activity up top. "How you two doing?" he asked, all sympathy.

"F-fine," I said, wrapping my hands around the hot mug.

"Think you can steer this bucket home?" Bill asked Jackson.

Jackson threw off his blanket and pulled on his slicker. "I'm down for it." He stuck out his hand. "Thanks, dude."

Bill took it, they did their bro handshake.

Geez. Jackson climbed the steps to the deck and Bill settled in beside me. "Have to hand it to you," he said.

"You do?" I asked warily.

"You outdid yourself this time."

I winced. "I did?" I was afraid of what he was suggesting.

"Tying Vinnie's murder to the car theft ring. And getting Jackson off," Bill said.

"I suppose so…" My radar was on high alert. Who was this understanding guy and what had he done with my boyfriend? After all, there was a lot I kept from Bill. Of course, there was a lot he kept from me—

"Kind of nifty pursuing the address in Walker. Finding the warehouse full of stolen vehicles. And the black book? That was outstanding work," he said with a smidgen of admiration.

"What's up? How did you find out about the address and the book?"

Beneath us the engine of *The Bounty* rumbled to life as Jackson slowly directed the boat toward its berth in Candle Beach. Bill pulled me to my feet and enfolded me in his arms, blanket and all. He kissed my neck, then my cheek, and finally my lips. "I have my ways."

He planted a solid kiss on me and my knees, already wobbly, went weak. My pulse raced. I was not going to be distracted. "C'mon. Give."

Bill hugged me tighter, the warmth of his muscular body penetrating my damp clothes. I relaxed into his embrace. *Oh well, he can keep his secrets. This is all that matters.*

His lips toyed with mine. "Pauli should really consider a career in law enforcement."

I leaned away from him. "P-Pauli? You know about Pauli?" My magic bullet. "How?"

"You're not the only one with detective skills." He grinned and headed for my lips again.

I held him off. "But…"

"He phoned me after you didn't respond to his texts. The kid was afraid for you."

Pauli…

"Nice to have a good friend," Bill said.

Yes, it was. Especially nice to have a *really, really* good friend. I wrapped my arms around his neck, the blanket fell from my shoulders, and he smiled a second time before covering my lips with his.

Yowza!

19

Labor Day. A day of rest after last night's escapade. Our summer vacation was coming to an end in three days. I dug my toes deeper into the sandy beach outside Grody's restaurant as early evening shadows deepened along the shoreline. I knew summer was over when I received an email from Henry asking about next week's food inventory. Etonville seemed like a million miles away at the moment…a distance I intended to maintain for the next seventy-two hours. The ocean was calm, the surf gently rolling onto the shore, a slight breeze lifting the hair off the nape of my neck. The nasty, schoolyard bully of a storm was becoming a dim memory—both the weather and our brush with death.

My cell phone pinged. I checked my texts. "It's the video from the theater," I said to Bill who was semi-dozing in the setting sun. He was also enjoying his last days of freedom before heading home to police chief responsibilities in Etonville without having to worry about his BMW. When I'd seen the ELT crew off this morning after minimal sleep, they promised to send the video Vernon had taken on his cell phone as the New Jersey Community Theater Festival announced its first-place winner. A tie between *The Sound of Music* and *Arsenic and Old Lace*! I was dumbfounded—as were the ELT members. Not that I wasn't over-the-moon happy for my theater friends. It must have been Abby and Edna "Puttin' on the Ritz."

I tapped on the video and witnessed emcee Graham apologize for the delay as the audience waited for the backup generator to kick in. Then he, once again, opened the envelope with great anticipation and grinned broadly before he announced the winners. "It's a tie! *The Sound of Music* and *Arsenic and Old Lace*!" This year's entrants "demonstrated extraordinary talent," Graham gushed.

The Sound of Music was ready for their award and glided onstage, Maria, the kids, and the nuns, and basked in the glow of their accomplishment. The *Arsenic and Old Lace* company was totally discombobulated. Walter ran out, stopped, stared into the dark house like a deer caught in headlights, gestured wildly to the cast offstage who bumbled on: Lola, ever the diva, graceful once in the light; Romeo swaggering, hands in his pockets; Abby, eyes like saucers, couldn't believe it; and Edna beaming, hands clasped above her head in a victory salute. The audience went wild! I supposed going off-script on the closing night's performance didn't hurt either winner, probably much to Maddy's chagrin.

As the ceremony ended, no one seemed to notice the sponsors were missing. Arlene, John, and Sam had bigger fish to fry. Arlene and John were already on their way to dispose of Jackson and me, and Sam, who had begun to realize something was up with Tiny's warehouse arrest, had offered to give a deposition to the Candle Beach police. Regarding Arlene and Tiny, Sam added two and two and came up with five. Rumors circulated this morning that Sam and Arlene were effective business partners when it came to Baldwin General Contractors, but lousy marital partners. Arlene was happier with her brother John.

Early this morning I met the ELT folks in the parking lot behind the theater where they loaded out their costumes and props. They'd been partying late into the night but were none the worse for their extended celebration.

"Oh Dodie, I'm so glad you're safe. You and Jackson both." Lola flicked her blond hair over one shoulder. "Speaking of Jackson…"

I put an arm around Lola. "He's off to Iowa to mend fences with Tammy. Said he's had enough of the ocean for a while."

Lola sighed. "All for the best. I'm going back on the Internet and do a bit of browsing."

"You go girl," I said and hugged her. "Don't give up."

"Never!" Lola said grimly. "I'm a woman on a mission."

Edna stacked prop boxes in the back of the van. "Hey, that must have been some kind of wild night for you and Jackson. A 10-29F which could have been a 10-32. Luckily no 11-42 or 11-80. Still a 207 is nothing to sneeze at."

"Copy that," I said, stifling a grin.

"Let's go. Into the van." Penny corralled Walter and the actors.

"Hooray for you, Dodie. Solving the crime, getting Jackson off, catching the real murderers." Edna winked. "I think the Chief should get you an office in the Municipal Building."

"10-4." As if. Bill and I had yet to talk through the entire Vinnie-murder-car-theft-ring caper...

Penny checked her clipboard, jammed her pencil behind one ear, and pushed her glasses a notch up her nose. "O'Dell, some people don't go looking for trouble, it finds them," she said.

"Okay."

"So, if you're on a bridge over troubled water, remember, there are no accidents and either you sink or swim."

Yikes. "Got it." I waved as Walter drove the van out of the parking lot. The theater was becoming my second home, third really after the Windjammer. Acting fascinated me from the day I first stepped foot in the Etonville Little Theatre, watching Lola and other cast members get onstage and pretend to be someone else. Convincingly. It was something I could never do. Pretend to be someone I was not. Yet, I'd seen plenty of acting this past week that had nothing to do with the ELT. Arlene acting like she was only a community theater director when she was the maven of a multimillion-dollar stolen car ring, keeping track of Vinnie's customers and their rides with her underling Tiny, whose bail she posted. She'd cunningly schemed to partner with Vinnie on *The Bounty*, convincing Sam that it would be an excellent investment, conveniently hiding the car theft plot.

John? Pretending to be a regular gent, even flirting with me, when he knew I was such a threat to his criminal venture that he had to bump me off. As he did Vinnie when the former dude got greedy and threatened to inform Sam about the car theft business. John Bannister had half a dozen aliases in as many states.

Simply based on appearances, I would have pegged Sam for a Jersey crime boss or a money-launderer. When in fact he was a genuinely decent guy. An honest, true friend of Vinnie's who, at Vinnie's request, agreed to keep his partnership of the *JV* silent and a secret from Jackson, even as Sam helped to pay off some of his partner's debts.

Vinnie was the most convincing player of all—acting as though he was Jackson's friend when he was willing to ensnare his "friend" in an illegal racket to settle his gambling habit.

And then there's Jackson, continuing to act the part of the-ex-boyfriend-surfer-dude who left me stranded during Hurricane Sandy when he arrived in Candle Beach, only to have that façade torn away in time to recognize who his true friends were. Bill, Maxine, Tammy...and me. I had come to appreciate Jackson during these last days. I remembered what had bugged me about him; now I also remembered why we'd been a couple. Our past was about fun and living in the moment, beach days and boardwalk nights.

And the occasional outing on the *JV.* Jackson was a sweet, laid-back aspect of my pre-Sandy life. I wished him the best.

Which left Bill. So credible as the victim of a stolen automobile that I was totally stunned when he showed up during the raid on the warehouse. I never presumed that he'd rigged his BMW to help trap the bad guys.

I'd left him snoring at the bungalow when I came to say good-bye to the theater folks. I needed coffee, food, a shower, and sleep, not necessarily in that order. I had one more errand to run before I returned to him. I'd spent the past days avoiding the obvious—my former residence in Candle Beach. Until this morning I couldn't bring myself to visit the scene of that horror four years ago. Now having gone through yesterday's traumatic ordeal, I was ready to see the place and let go of my Hurricane Sandy past. I cruised down Ocean Avenue and cut over Atlantic to Elm Street. I slowed as I neared number 114, steered my MINI Cooper next to the curb, and clicked off the motor. There it was. The roof had been repaired where the elm tree had smashed it, the old paint replaced with green siding, and new young trees planted in the front yard—peaceful, cozy, a warm and inviting home. A woman in her bathrobe opened the door and walked onto her porch. She picked up the morning paper and looked at me. She smiled and waved. I waved back.

I wasn't immune to the acting bug that had hit Candle Beach this summer. Though I acted as if I was the same person who'd left Etonville ten days ago, I knew *that* Dodie had bitten the dust. In confronting my superstorm past, I released the terror and anger that had weighed on me these last years. I was Sandy-free.

* * * *

"Hey, Irish, how about another round for you and the cop?" asked Grody later that night. He grinned, holding a tray with two drinks, a gin and tonic and a Creamsicle Crush, and a plate of fried oysters. He hadn't waited for us to signal the waiter.

The last bit of sunlight slipped below the horizon, the light of the tiki torches muted and romantic.

"Thanks." Bill took the tray.

"Nice work, Surfer G," I teased.

"You two deserve some R&R…hope the next couple of days are completely boring. No cops, no crime, no boats…"

"No theater," I said.

"Especially no theater," said Bill. "I think we had enough performances to last a while."

Grody laughed. "Enjoy this show." He pointed down the beach to where a fireworks display began. "Serving shrimp boil tonight. I'll send a waiter." He walked back to the bar.

Explosions of color erupted into the night—red, blue, green, and white pinwheels and stars burst in the sky. The pyrotechnics were astounding. "Wow! I haven't seen fireworks like this in a long time."

"Me neither. Unless I count most days around you," Bill said dryly.

"Meaning?"

"Life's always exciting with you."

"Then it's lucky you get a break from me sometimes." I sipped my drink.

"I've been thinking about that," he said.

"Oh?" I was about to make a smart remark on the benefits of living alone when Bill sat up and dug something out of his beach jacket. It was small, lost in his hand.

Those hairs on my neck were bopping. What was going on? He flipped open the lid of a jewelry box. My pulse went nuts. I blinked to make sure I wasn't seeing things.

"How'd you like to—"

"Yes!" I took the ring out of its setting, the diamond brilliant in the light of the flaming fireworks, and eased it onto my finger. Bill kissed me sweetly.

Double OMG!

Printed in the United States
by Baker & Taylor Publisher Services